T0367860

Man
under the
Mountain

Man
under the
Mountain

A West Virginia Homecoming

LESLIE DALTON, JR.

Archway Publishing books may be ordered
through booksellers or by contacting:

Archway Publishing
1663 Liberty Drive
Bloomington, IN 47403
www.archwaypublishing.com
1 (888) 242-5904

Because of the dynamic nature of the Internet, any web
addresses or links contained in this book may have changed
since publication and may no longer be valid. The views
expressed in this work are solely those of the author and do
not necessarily reflect the views of the publisher, and the
publisher hereby disclaims any responsibility for them.

Any people depicted in stock imagery provided by Getty Images are
models, and such images are being used for illustrative purposes only.
Certain stock imagery © Getty Images.

ISBN: 978-1-4808-6863-2 (sc)
ISBN: 978-1-4808-6862-5 (e)

Library of Congress Control Number: 2018911185

Print information available on the last page.

Archway Publishing rev. date: 10/11/2018

Prologue

No story about the southern Appalachians can leave out the Twin Cities of Bluefield, West Virginia/Virginia that served as the marketplace for the coalfields and historically serves as a barometer of the downfall of King Coal in the fifties' and sixties'.

The Associated Press (December 1, 2015) suggests that "Even coal is barely surviving in coal country — and coal is about the only thing that Central Appalachia has."

Mechanization has reduced the number of human workers to mine that coal. In the 1940's West Virginia coal employed some 130,000 miners; that number in 2015 was about 20,000. It doesn't take a Ph.D. Economists to calculate the spending loss of 120,000 workers and their families. The once thriving wholesale business in Bluefield is gone; the Four movie houses are gone or closed. One hospital has been torn down, and another is a nursing home. The West Virginian (hotel) is a retirement home, and the other downtown hotel demolished. Most of the numerous stores are closed or turned into parks or parking lots. The once active railroad switching yards, bursting at the seams with filled coal gondolas, is now empty.

This is the West Virginia that David Cabot, MD—formally of the United States Army Medical Corp and fresh out of a MASH Hospital in Korea—entered when he began his medical practice in 'Almost Heaven' in May 1953. The 'Heavenly' component was a lovely nurse that met him at the now-defunct Piedmont Airlines gate of the Mercer County Airport. She was to be the glue that held him through the pathos of Black Lung Disease, cultural inertia and singular dependence on coal.

One

David Cabot, a superbly qualified physician, as well as an accomplished surgeon, was discontentedly serving his time as a draftee in the Army Medical Corp. He and several other draftee doctors were responsible for still another set of draftees, the front-line soldiers. The assemblage of doctors, nurses, corpsman, cooks, ambulance drivers, helicopter pilots and others worked within in a new concept, a Military Advanced Surgical Hospital (MASH), in U.S. Army acronym lingo. In previous wars minimally, trained fellow draftees were assigned the task of providing enough first aid—medic or corpsman—to get the wounded troops out of combat to a secondary patch-up facility and then, if they survived, to a hospital where treatment could finally begin.

The Korean Conflict brought the MASH unit to the front lines so that the wounded could receive the finest immediate-care available and even provided the impetus for future trauma centers in hospitals. The presence of MASH facilities reduced the time lost in the initial delivery of

superior medical care of the wounded by being next to the
action.

Dr. Cabot was one of the MASH surgeons whose skilled
hands had saved many who would not have survived the
1918 'War to end all wars' and the one that followed some
18 years later. How many of the 521,715 deaths in those two
wars could have been saved by the existence of MASH? No
one knows, but such questions plagued Dr. Cabot and fed
his reluctance of being a party to another war. His angst at
being in Korea was palpable, but his love for his profession
and his concerns for the many young men of many nations
for whom he cared was limitless. He was a physician with
a heart.

Now the war was winding down. Daily rumors from
the peace talks were rampant causing a constant state of
anxiety. Finally, the end came: July 27, 1953. On the same
day, a miracle occurred. Dr. Cabot received an unbelievable
opportunistic letter from his father.

THE LETTER

July 15, 1953

My Dear David:

*Your mother and I are thrilled with the prospects
of your returning to the sensible use of your
medical talents and training. That war in Korea
has driven a wedge into the fabric of our country.
Many of us were conservatively opposed to*

entering into another war at a time when we were beginning the healing process from the greatest of all wars. We had thought when our boys returned from around the world in 1945 that we were through with war. Well, on to the more cheerful news. In our last correspondence, you stated that you were uncertain as to what you would like to do once you returned stateside. You could, of course, begin the slow process of building a practice of your own or joining me. There is another opportunity that has presented itself to allow you to make up the three years spent in the army. A very dear friend and classmate of mine passed away last week. His death leaves behind a successful and satisfying solo practice that requires only a physician to continue. I understand that until they find a replacement a very competent RN is holding the practice together. Stan was one year behind me at Harvard Medical. Our paths crossed several times as we rotated through the program. I assure you that you will find his practice in more than a satisfactory array, reflective of conscience, a physician who cares about his patients. While in Boston

Capt. Cabot peeled the first page of the two pages contained in the envelope, slid the first page under the second, and continued to read:

he developed a very loyal and generous following where finances have never been a concern.

I have checked with my lawyer, and he will gladly look into the estate and arrange for purchase if you are interested in taking over Stan's practice. Let me know your wishes.

The weather here has been typical Boston with the feeling of fall in the air. I hope the weather there is a bit more tolerable now that you have moved out of those horrible MASH tents that you have called home for the past two years. We look forward to your arrival home and Godspeed.

Affectionately,
Father

Two short pages presenting such an extraordinary opportunity! He would be a fool not to accept. He wasted no time over-thinking the possibilities and rushed to the Orderly Room to arrange for a telegram. It read: PLEASE PROCEED WITH PURCHASE OF MEDICAL PRACTICE RE DR. FIELDS BOSTON POST HASTE STOP I WILL HANDLE DETAILS UPON MY ARRIVAL HOME STOP.

Chapter

Two

Boston, Massachusetts two weeks earlier:

Dr. Alexander Cabot slowly eased the phone back into its cradle. He had just recently learned of the death of his longtime friend and medical school classmate, Stanford Fields, MD. Both had received outstanding educations placing them at the top of the lists for jobs, but while Alexander had chosen to stay in Boston to practice, his good friend yielded to an unbelievable offer via a headhunter representing a very wealthy West Virginia coal mine operator. Alexander sat at his cluttered desk in his rather small den and unconsciously fiddled with the papers on his desk. His hand fell on the last letter from his son, David. He picked up the letter and reread it. The letter had was written at a time when his son was feeling particularly sympathetic towards the abused and weak and had written an exceptionally good essay on the plight of the underprivileged. Was it possible that David had developed a sense of unselfish compassion to go along with his top-notch medical training? The son's letters for the past year had included poignant narratives of the horror experienced by the civilians caught up in the Korean "police action" and how he was spending more and more time with them outside his military medical practice.

"Maybe, just maybe, my David is not suited to high pressure, big city practice," thought the father. "Only one way to find out; I'll write to him and submit the possibility to him."

So, he did.

Dr. Alexander Cabot pulled out an old, beat-up Remington typewriter and inserted a half-sheet of writing paper into the carriage. He began to type:

THE LETTER

July 15, 1953

My Dear David:

Your mother and I are thrilled with the prospects of your returning to the sensible use of your medical talents and training. That war in Korea has driven a wedge into the fabric of our country. Many of us were conservatively opposed to entering into another war at a time when we were beginning the healing process from the greatest of all wars. We had thought when our boys returned from around the world in 1945 that we were through with war. Well, on to the more cheerful news. In our last correspondence, you stated that you were uncertain as to what you would like to do once you returned stateside. You could, of course, begin the slow process of building

*a practice of your own or joining me. There is
another opportunity that has presented itself to
allow you to make up the three years spent in the
army. A very dear friend and classmate of mine
passed away last week. His death leaves behind a
successful and satisfying solo practice that requires
only a physician to continue. I understand that
until they find a replacement a very competent
RN is holding the practice together. Stan was
one year behind me at Harvard Medical. Our
paths crossed several times as we rotated through
the program. I assure you that you will find
his practice in more than a satisfactory array,
reflective of conscience, a physician who cares
about his patients. While in Boston*

Dr. Cabot rolled the first page out of the carriage, inserted a second identical half sheet into the carriage and continued to write:

*Knob, West Virginia he has been quite content.
He told me on several occasions that he could
not have made a better choice as to a place to
enjoy the practice of medicine. He told me that
the mountain people there brought him into their
families early on in his work and would have it
no other way than to be certain of his welfare and
comfort. They are mostly poor and uneducated
people, principally supported by the coal mines,
railroad or timber. He found their faith in God
and Country to be refreshing. He also enjoyed
their frankness in all matters as it pertained to*

logic. They believe the law is intended to fit only special roles and that certain rights are not fitted to the laws of Man if not covered in the Bible. Stan has been more than a physician; he had become the all-things- advisor and expert for townsfolk of Boston Knob, West Virginia. He even obtained a notary license as an aid.

Again Dr. Cabot reached the bottom of the page, rolled page two out of the typewriter and placed it face down on the desk. He then inserted the third page into the old machine and continued to peck away.

The phone rang.

Dr. Alexander Cabot promptly answered without delay as he always did. A voice on the phone announced that he had a home-bound patient in distress. Searching his desktop for something on which to write, he grabbed the second page of the letter to David that he had placed face down on his desk after that he jotted an address, folded it, placed it in his pocket and left the house hurriedly on his mission. That emergency managed, he returned home, and his letter writing with page two still in his pocket and page three— incomplete—in his typewriter. He continued to write:

He has developed a very loyal and generous following where finances have never been a concern.

I have checked with my lawyer, and he will gladly look into the estate and arrange for purchase if you are interested in taking over Stan's practice. Let me know your wishes.

The weather here has been typical Boston with the feeling of fall in the air. I hope the weather there is a bit more tolerable now that you have moved out of those horrible MASH tents that you have called home for the past two years.

We look forward to your arrival home and Godspeed.

Affectionately,
Father

The letter was complete. Father pulled the third page from the typewriter and placed it on top of the first page that he had set aside before going to the hospital. He folded them, placed them in an envelope, sealed it, addressed it, and put it on top of a stack of other letters in the outgoing mail. The second page was still in his coat pocket.

Chapter

Three

The link between Dr. Alexander Cabot, his son Dr. David Cabot and Dr. Stanford Fields of Boston Knob, West Virginia, was that they were all graduated from Harvard University. Dr. David Cabot was very proud of this heritage to the point that he was sometimes a real pain-in-the-butt snob. His exaggerated Ivy League diction had become more pronounced during his stint in the social poverty of the MASH unit in Korea.

Under that classical veneer, was a sensitive man who would cry when faced with a medical problem beyond all possibility of a solution. At times he was lulled into the unreal belief that his Harvard degree granted him powers that defied failure. When failure did occur, as it surely must, he took the responsibility upon himself and did not fully consider that some things are out of the control of human skills. This trait was sorely tested during the past months, but the end was drawing near. Truce talks that began in July 1951 appeared to be finally coming to fruition, but the fighting continued until July 27, 1953, when the negotiations at last bore fruit and the conflict ended in a cease-fire agreement. It was time for Dr. Cabot to go home.

Dr. Cabot's MASH Unit was awaiting orders regarding the redeployment of the personnel and facilities from their current location 'somewhere' in Korea; the 'war' was over, and so was the bloodshed requiring medical mechanics. The hospital portion of the MASH unit was gone. Only the quarters and dining facilities were still intact. Dr. Cabot and a Medical Service Officer (MSO) remained along with a skeleton crew of non-coms and enlisted support personnel. Dr. Cabot was bored beyond belief when a young sergeant approached him with a coffee pot in the mess tent.

"Could'je handle another cup of this battery acid, major?" he inquired.

"No thank you, Sergeant, but if you are as bored as I am I could do with a bit of congeniality," Doctor replied.

"Sure'nuf, Ah'm at your disposal. What do you want to talk about? How about my love life? That's an excitin' topic. Or maybe I could regale you with my military exploits as an Army Food Specialist MOS 95 somethin' or other. My wooden spoon handle is fully notched as a result of the causalities in mah kitchen. By the way; Ah know your name. Mine is Tom Duggan."

Doctor laughingly responded, "I sense a bit of the 'Old South' in your diction there, am I correct?"

"Ah reckon ah'm only partly guilty since ah'm from Rocky Gap, Virginia. Ah consider myself southern without the 'Ol South' hang-ups on who's God's chosen. You see ah have been called a 'rebel' not because of where ah'm from but for what I believe and practice. Ya' see I am a genu'wine conscientious objector and when I was drafted ah told'm to give me something to do that didn't require a gun. They did and here ah am."

Doctor Cabot related to this young man's forthrightness.

"You must have at least partially adhered to army regulations for most of your military time based on your rank. How long have you served?"

"Four years. Yeah, ah've been lucky, but you see, ahm kinda' sneaky, ah tend to my own business and ah don't hang out with people who I don't feel measure up to my standards."

"Your standards?"

"Yes sir, my standards. Take you for example. I know who you are. You are serious, honest, faithful to your profession, and if you don't mind my saying so, a bit of a snob. Now hold on before you bust me to a buck private for insubordination. I mean that in a good way. Aloofness is just one way of self-preservation in situations we find ourselves in a military hierarchy. The easy approach is to go with the flow and some time to compromise our morals and skills. You, Sir, are a tower of responsibility and competence in your profession. I hear all of the tales about the shenanigans that go on here even in surgery, and you never were a part of it although the rest of the officers called you a snob. I see it as restraint. Are we gonna be friends now? Can I tell you my deep dark secrets and know you will retain confidentially forever?"

Doctor Cabot laughed, extended his hand to Sargent and declared, "Yes, indeed, we are compatriots forever, or at least until we get out of this miserable place. You say you like to 'beat the system.' Entertain me with an example."

"Okay. Try this one. When I was in basic training, the obstacle course was a plaything for me because what was happenin' was what we did for fun back home. Mah task then was to figure out a way to get around the whole stupid routine but still come out ahead. The course was laid out in a big 'U' with a start and finish points about the length of a football field apart. The first-time ah ran the whole thing ah discovered that the very beginning and end both crossed a creek. At the beginning was a rope swing over the creek. At the end was another rope stretched across the creek that we had to hand-walk across. We had to swing across the creek as the very first obstacle and most of the city boys would not drop off at the high end of the outward swing but would hold on too late and fall somewhere short and then climb up the bank and continue. On mah second try ah intentionally dropped into the creek and walked along the stream until I came to the other crossover at the end. Every time I ran the obstacle course after that, I would drop off short of the first bank, climb down to the creek bank and wait for the rest of the squad to hand-walk toward me on the rope where I would be waitin' for them. I thought nobody had figured it out until the final day when an old-World War II veteran, serving out his last days before retirement, was waiting for me when I climbed up the bank. He offered me his hand and pulled me to my feet and declared, "Ah been'awatchin' you, boy an' all ah gotta'say is, if'n we'd had more boys lahk yew fah'n fer the south w'ed a'won that war."

The doctor expressed his appreciation at such ingenuity with laughter followed by a question. "An age-old rule of never volunteering must have caused you to assigned duties many times, am I correct?"

"Il n'est pas donc mon médecin. J'ai volunteered evert fo," Tom answered in passable French.

Doctor responded. "Ah, nous allons parler Français," Doctor answered in French. "So, you always volunteered?"

"In your words, 'yes indeed.' I had two ways of beatin' the system. First off, when I indicated my interest in cooking they gave me a direct appointment as an 'apprentice' cook and shipped me directly to Korea where I was assigned to a United Nations dining hall workin' for a French Chef. There I learned to cook and to speak French. Likewise, there I found out that the disdain for the French was so widespread that I would be ignored if I volunteered and spoke French. Second, I always volunteered for the odd jobs or the ones that other GIs shunned or didn't know how to do. For example, early on when I had KP, I would offer to sharpen knives. Another job I would volunteer for, that nobody else wanted to do, was janitorial at Post Headquarters. Very few of the people at headquarters were regular army, and they mostly ignored me if I seemed busy, so I would carry a broom and dustpan around all day in an air-conditioned building while all my 'equals' were scrubbing garbage cans or washing dishes. On top of that, if the officers had donuts, they would offer some to me."

The sound of a helicopter approaching broke into their conversation. They both attended its approach with different interests: Tom with curiosity, Doctor as a ride home. It landed, and the whoop, whoop of its rotors slowly faded into silence. They could see the pilot going into the orderly room carrying what looked like mail. Shortly after, the pilot came into the mess tent, flung a haphazard salute in Maj. Cabot's direction and called out, "Garcon, some victuals, se vous whatever," as he approached Tom. He then turned to Maj.

Cabot and said, "Ol' Tom here is my favorite army French chef. He can turn SOS into a truffle soufflé. Are you Cabot? You got a telegram in the mail pouch. Oh, by the way, get your gear together; I'm your ride home."

Maj. Cabot rushed to the orderly room where the clerk sat waiting with the telegram in his hand. He handed it over to the Maj. who anxiously ripped open the official envelope and began to read. As he read his face went from anxiety to incredulous to something like fear as he shouted, "Dear God in heaven above please tell me this is a mistake! Sargent, read this and tell me what it says!"

The young soldier took the telegram and read it. He then looked up and declared, "Maj., looks to me like the population of the Mountain State of West Virginia has just increased by one."

Four

The Flight from Korea to the only airport near Boston Knob was Bluefield, West Virginia/ Virginia; long and tiring, but certainly not boring. The first leg of his trip was from the chaos, via helicopter, of the dismantling of his MASH hospital and the deployment of its patient-load and staff. The MASH helicopter was also carrying two seriously injured marines to a stateside medical evacuation center where David hoped to hitch a quick ride to his new home. Since the wounded are on the skids outside the chopper, he had very little to do. Nonetheless, he felt that he was paying his fare to the airbase where he would likely find a slot on one of the two large planes used for medical evacuation. As a doctor, he was welcome on any of the large air-ambulances since medical personnel were in short supply for transport duty.

While waiting at the MATS Operational Center in Tokyo, he had exhausted the reading material that he had quickly assembled, while packing, back at the MASH unit. Alternately pacing and squirming in an uncomfortable chair, he watched the clock crawl forward. He stood up and then again plopped into the chair, glanced over to a side table where the only reading matter was a journal with a picture of a C-47. He would read anything to stop the image of his new home from dominating his thoughts. He picked up the magazine and flipped through the pages. He came upon an article on the aircraft used in the MATS service and found it rather interesting. The first plane that caught his attention was a featured article on the C-47 on the cover. It occurred to him that the second leg of his trip from Seoul to Tokyo was on a C-47 configured. For a medical evacuation flight. In this 'police action' and WW-2, C-47s served dual purposes on many missions. Supplies were to a combat area, and as soon as the aircraft unloaded, litters would be installed to help evacuate a large number of wounded personnel on the return flight.

After what seemed like weeks, Maj. Cabot was assigned to accompany severely wounded troops being airlifted to Hawaii on a C-118A Liftmaster modified for aeromedical evacuation. The 29th DC-6 ordered by the Air Force was adapted as the Presidential aircraft, designated the VC-118, and named 'The Independence' after President Harry Truman's hometown, Independence, Missouri.

Dr. David Cabot had flown in from Cincinnati to Bluefield via Charleston on a Piedmont DC-3, which was the civilian version of the C-47 that had carried him from Seoul to Tokyo. This C-47, however, bore no resemblance to the military version. He was deeply ensconced in plush leather seats and served a Coke in the classic glass bottle. He couldn't resist looking at the bottom of the bottle to check its home place since all bottles at that time were glass and bore the city and state of its origination. This one was from Roswell, New Mexico. Too bad he had no one to go-distance with; he would win for sure. The airline seats, unlike the military canvas ones, reclined almost into a bed. He was not interested in reclining as his gaze flitted from sight to sight below. It was on as clear a day as he had ever seen.

The pilot announced the descent into Charleston and almost immediately the sun disappeared as the plane dug into a cloud of dirty haze. The strong smell of the smog was strong enough to turn one's stomach. David's eyes began to burn.

He motioned to the steward and asked, "What is that smoke?"

The steward responded, "Don't worry about it. It's just Charleston. They're workin' on a solution."

The DC-3 plowed on through the nasty cloud and approached the runway. David watched for the ground below. When he could finally see it, he was frightened to see the side of a mountain rapidly rushing toward them. The thoughts of crashing churned in his head when suddenly, at the edge of the mountain, the plane smoothly glided onto the runway.

The only passenger deplaning at Charleston was a small, wiry man carrying a violin case and a small valise. He held himself with unease and walked with a slight slump. He caught David's gaze his way and specifically greeted him with a friendly smile and said, "Hi, my name is Bob Byrd and ah'm runnin' for the Senate. Vote for me if you can."

David thought to himself; "Good luck, Little Fellow. If you are elected, you won't last one term." Cabot would later learn that his exchange was with Robert Byrd, a member of the Democratic Party, served as a U.S. Representative from

1953 until 1959 and as a U.S. Senator from 1959 to 2010. He was the longest-serving Senator in United States history. Also, he was, at the time of his death, the longest-serving member in the history of the United States Congress. He became one of the Senate's most powerful members, serving as secretary of the Senate, Democratic Caucus from 1967 to 1971 and—after defeating his longtime colleague, Ted Kennedy—as Senate Majority Whip from 1971 to 1977. Serving three different tenures as Chairman of the United States Senate Committee on Appropriations enabled Byrd to steer a great deal of federal money toward projects in West Virginia.

They were on the ground just minutes before the door closed, and the plane began to taxi towards the end of the runway. No one boarded the plane in Charleston leaving David to muse the possibility that Mercer County was not a prime destination. David noticed as they taxied to the end of the runway that it ended abruptly on the edge of the mountains. The plane accelerated down the runway and lifted off towards the south. Out the window to the east, the derivation of the haze became clear. Large smokestacks were relentlessly spewing massive columns of unabated black smoke into the air. The plane continued to climb through the dense haze and suddenly broke into a brilliantly clear blue sky. David had just experienced the worst smog that he had ever seen.

The airplane followed the valleys gaining altitude only to cross a ridge. The view below was a mass of color. It was early October, and the colors were truly awe-inspiring. The pilot announced over the intercom, "They're saying that this is the best year ever for color." The color could not offset the unbelievable scarring that had been left behind by the process of "strip mining." One could see the sorry remains of the lovely Appalachian Mountains pushed into the valleys in an endless scene of environmental murder. He would learn later that the 'correct' regional pronunciation of the regional mountain chain was 'ah-pu-latch-chun' NOT Ah-pu-lay-chun.

The pilot on the flight from Charleston to Bluefield was as verbal as a tour guide. He kept a running discourse on the sights below. He pointed out the rudimentary beginnings of the West Virginia Turnpike that would run from Charleston to Princeton. He explained the large patch of black covering the side of one mountain and the smoke billowing from it. He opined that it was an 'eternal flame' honoring the mining industry's rape of the Mountain State. In reality, it was a slag heap, or debris, from mining that even heavy snow would not extinguish.

Finally, the pilot announced the approach to the Mercer County Airport built by pushing smaller hills into a valley—similar to Charleston but with far lesser dramatic results—between them to make a single runway. The DC-3 approached the airport from the northeast. One look to the south into Virginia revealed that those beautiful mountains had escaped the destruction done to their sister mountains to the north. "That," he thought "must be what West Virginia once looked like."

As the plane descended it followed the East River Mountains southwestward directly over the cities of Bluefield, West Virginia, and Virginia, then north again for a landing from the northwest. Small villages and farms, in the valleys and on the ridges, rushed past. One Irish green farm, with a large white silo and a herd of snow-white cattle lazing about, caught his eye and then was gone as the plane touched down on the runway.

Chapter

Five

The plane slowed and turned towards the small brick terminal. David caught a glimpse of a well-dressed redhead standing at the gate so lovely that she practically took his breath away. She was wearing a fitted two-piece suit that complimented her perfect figure pleasingly. Perched on top of the magnificent head of red hair sat a Beret made of the same fabric as the suite. On her lovely face was a near scowl that would have been unattractive on a lesser beauty, but on her added mystery of her charm. His eyes remained fixed on her even after the plane had come to a complete stop and the door was opened for its single passenger to deplane. The steward stepped back to David and informed him that, "We are here, Maj."

Snapping out of his fog, David looked again at the lovely mystery-lady and said to himself, "Oh, what a heavenly body. Could that gorgeous vision be waiting for me? Not likely since no one is expecting me. But I can dream."

Dr. Cabot stepped away from the plane and paused at the foot of the steps. He placed his military hat in its proper position and tried to brush away the wrinkles accumulated in his uniform before picking up his bag that an agent had placed next to him. Then he walked uncertainly toward the door that displayed a greeting sign that said 'Welcome to Bluefield, West Virginia, Nature's Air-Conditioned City.' The temperature in Bluefield seldom reached 90 degrees, and when it did, the city served free lemonade.

As he meandered to the gate, his 'dream' approached him with an extended gloved hand and simply declared, "You are Dr. Cabot. Ah'm Jenny Lou Stone. Folks around here call me Jenn. Ah'm your welcomin' committee and also your office nurse if you want to continue the arrangement ah had with Dr. Fields. Are you hungry? Ah have an early supper ordered for us at Frankie's but ah can cancel that if you don't want to go. Do you like chicken cacciatore? Mama Ferranti makes the best in the world. You can even have wine with it if you join the club."

David hoped he did not look as confused as he felt. He was at a loss for words both from her introduction and her striking beauty.

He finally stammered, "O...O Oh, y...y... yes, I most certainly should keep the arrangement." He stood looking at her in sort of a fog.

Jenn broke the awkward silence by inquiring, "Hey, you with me?"

"Oh sorry," David almost shouted. "Supper would be nice. How did you know who I was?"

Jenn retorted, "Well, ah don't know. Could be 'cause you're the only passenger gettin' off the plane in a uniform of the United States Army, or it could be my super observational powers. What a dumb question. Let's go," she snapped.

Chapter

Six

Jenn drove the car with graceful familiarity. He was to
find out later that the Packard Clipper she was driving
came with the new practice. Soon they were winding
down the mountainside towards US highway 52 that would
take Dr. Cabot to his new practice. The road flattened
and straightened somewhat, and he could see an attractive
example of a new craze sweeping the nation. The Skyway
Drive-In Theater sat in the juncture of the Airport Road
and Route 52.

Jenn turned right onto 52 at the community of
Brushfork. Route 52 was no better than the airport road.
The concrete, poured in 1937, was showing signs of disrepair
with broken pavement and unkempt, potholed, shoulders.
The road was barely wide enough to be called two-lane
and wound upward between two wooded mountains to
the community of Bluewell where the road leveled out
again. Along the road in Bluewell appeared a large, decrepit
greenhouse, Lynn's Drive-In, and a hodge-podge of rinky-
dink fruit stands with a wild abundance of fresh produce

housed behind chicken wire. Centered between two of the markets was a boxy red brick building bearing an elegant sign reading "La Saluda Club."

Jenn guided the car off of the concrete pavement onto a gravel and dirt parking lot full of deep holes filled with water from a recent, or maybe not so recent, rain. She parked the car so that neither she nor Dr. Cabot would have to dismount into a puddle. Looking about, David saw that others had parked their cars at odd angles, also, so that no parking scheme, except avoidance of mud holes, was obvious. As David stood from the car, he noticed that all of the other businesses had similar parking lots. Not a square inch of parking pavement was present. Carefully weaving his way around the puddles towards the restaurant, David was reminded of the time in Korea when he watched the rescue of a small boy from a minefield.

Jenn led the way to the canopy bearing the name La Saluda Club to a door displaying a small sign informing the potential visitor that this was 'a members–only club.' To the right was another door through which anyone could get a beer and a hamburger at 'Frankie's Restaurant.' Dr. Cabot approached the door apprehensively. Jenn practically barked, "Well go on in!"

He held the door for Jenn and followed her in to be surprised by rich aromas and smiling faces. His spirits lifted decidedly, and he practically shouted: "My heavens what a delightful place."

The inside of Frankie's was taken up by a long counter that turned 90 degrees to extend most of the way to the south wall and took up all of the north wall. The south wall contained wooden booths. The space behind the counters was an array of coolers containing just about every beer label available. There were no signs of hard liquor. To the immediate right of the entry stood a magazine rack containing nothing but funny (comic) books. Reading material was practically non-existent in outlying schools at that time. Delph School in Bluewell had no library. Books, at that time, were not provided by the state, but 'funny books' were plentiful and were a source of barter. Next to that were a single pinball machine and a large, very colorful, jukebox. A small tow-headed lad was perusing the funny books and offered the new entrants no more than a quick glance. A very blond attractive woman stepped through a set of curtains from the kitchen, smiling broadly.

"Hey, Jenn" exclaimed Mary, Frank's sister. "Where you been? Who's your friend? I bet he'sa the new doctor, right? Frankie, come out and meet'a the new doctor. He look'a like he a good one. Sit down, Doctor. You, too, Jenn. Are you hungry? We got'a your supper ready just'a like you say."

From a curtained door behind the counter, a very small smiling man emerged.

"Hey, Jenn," he likewise shouted in a thick Italian accent. "I see you drive'a the Packard; you do'a somethin' special? Why you have'a the big car?"

"She has the new doctor with'a her," Mary explained, "and they're hungry. You ready to eat?" Mary asked again.

Frank excitedly proclaimed, "You will like Mama's cookin'. You like somethin' to drink Doc?" Frank asked.

"I would love a brandy—a good brandy," David blurted out, "but all I see is beer."

With an exaggerated gesture, Frank smugly commanded, "Jes'a Follow me," which David did. Frank led them through the curtains behind the counter into a very large room taken up mostly by a hardwood dance floor surrounded by tables with white linen covers, mounded napkins, and properly placed silverware.

"In here is the La Saluda Club," Frankie said. "In'a here I give'a you brandy after you sign'a your membership card."

David was later to learn that West Virginia, along with most Southern States, was 'dry' and that only 3.2 beer was available outside State-run ABC stores. He was also to learn that this restriction on alcohol contributed to the colorful moonshinin' business throughout the Virginia's, Kentucky, North Carolina, and other states with restricted liquor sales.

Frank dug into a drawer behind a metre de pedestal and came out with a printed card declaring the holder to be a member of a private club. He then disappeared through the curtains and soon reappeared with a bottle held high in one hand and stemmed brandy snifters in the other. The bottle in Frankie's left hand bore a label with a large 84 centered below the word STOCK.

David conjured up an image of pure rotgut that an Italian-West Virginia-hillbilly would likely call brandy. He steeled his stomach to receive a liquid somewhat akin to kerosene but was pleasantly surprised to experience the most delightful warmth of delicious and most excellent liquor.

"My," exclaimed David. "I do believe this fine nectar to be among the best I have ever tasted. Surely, it's French. Let me see the label."

David's surprise grew, even more, when he saw that the brandy was of Italian vintage bottled in 1932 in Trieste.

"I am being served a 26-year-old brandy in a backwoods café in West Virginia," David marveled. "Not only that, it's good brandy!"

Frank asked: "You like it? My family friends, the Stocks make it. The old man, Lionello Stock, was my father's friend and made the best wines in Italy until The War. This bottle is from a shipment of 12 cases sent to me when I opened my restaurant here."

"Mr. Ferranti," David said. "You have now won yourself a new member of the La Saluda Club. Place my name on a case of that fine brandy, and I shall be a regular." They followed Frank to a table where they sat, and he sipped the brandy. His reluctant companion declined the brandy declaring, adamantly that, A'h do not drink!"

Dr. Cabot would learn later that her logic for that decision was impeccable.

Dr. Cabot, still a bit unsure of himself, finally said, "Well, I must say, this is a most pleasant surprise. White tablecloths and napkins, real silverware and cut-class water pitcher. The lighting is perfect for a dinner for two."

Jenn responded vehemently, "Don't get any ideas, soldier. It's this or Lynn's Drive-in, and I really don't like eating in a car parked beside a carload of teenagers."

David somewhat nonplused spoke more sharply than he intended, replied, "Forgive me, dear lady. I was commenting on the ambiance. No intentions implied. Do I sense a bit of hostility?"

Jenn sat rigidly still for a very long moment and finally retorted tearfully. "Now that you mention it, yes. You big city snobs think you can buy anything and anybody. You don't know anything about us, and yet you move in here with your money and fancy college degrees takin' the place of sweet and kind Dr. Fields. You can't replace him. Nobody can replace him."

The doctor stared at her with stunned silence. He was at a total loss for words or actions.

"Well, don't just sit there and look at me with that dumb look. I meant what ah said. You bought this set-up at auction and won. You were then, as now, ignorant as a new-born baby as to what you have here. You bought me like a cow!"

"Wait just a dam... confound minute," David practically shouted. "In reality, as it happens, I did not buy anything, most particularity you. My father and Dr. Fields were classmates and very good friends over the years. Dr. Fields, according to Father, had confided in him that if I were available upon completion of medical school, he would like for me to join him in practice. That letter led father to write to me about this, ah...opportunity, with the suggestion that I might consider it. I committed, and I will honor that commitment. I have no intention of forcing you or anyone else to continue with me. You are free to leave, but I must say, I would be a first-class fool to let you go. Selfishly speaking, what would I do? I have never had a sole practice in my entire life; I am among strange.... unique people that will probably be more skittish of me than you appear to be. Lord knows this transition has me petrified. I am more frightened of being here that I ever was in Korea. A little tolerance would be welcome!"

Jenn, sobbing almost uncontrollably, responded, "A'hm sorry. Ah've been a real bitch. Oh, ah shouldn't use that word but it's true."

David moved to her side to console her. She made no effort to move away from him. He quietly pleaded with her, "Forgive me if I appear insensitive. It's not my intention. You have lost a dear friend, and you fear for your future. Please give me the opportunity to show you that I am a sensitive physician...person... in spite of perceived social baggage that I may carry. I, too, am still grieving. I spent two years trying to prove my worth as a surgeon in a frontline army hospital, but I failed miserably. We went from battle to battle, trying to pick up the pieces of broken humanity but we all failed. I failed, in spite of my fancy degrees and schools. I don't want to fail here. I need you."

Jenn leaned into David and wept uncontrollably. He was shocked by the closeness of her. Cautiously, he took her into his arms, and she responded to his embrace. He welcomed the propinquity of her charms, but he was well aware of her very recent scorn for him and knew that this acceptance of his solace was only momentary and that she would bitterly regret her weakness when she recovered. Slowly he released her and returned to his chair across the table from her. She wiped the tears from her eyes and adjusted the Beret that had slipped and whispered, "Thanks for the shoulder. You are very good at consoling a damsel in distress. I won't ever forget it."

Seven

The mountain ride from Bluefield down to the coalfields was uneventful and silent. Jenn's attention was focused far away as she navigated the level roads of the community of Bluewell. That changed with an upward slope into progressively higher hills and deeper valleys. The road traversed the mountainsides first to the left and then to the right. To the left side of the car, one could view the colors of the treetops and to the right, looking upward, to the trunks. Occasionally, the near trees gave way to reveal the glory of the rugged color-covered mountains.

Around one bend an apparition of stone filled the whole of the view over the left fender of the car.

"My Heavens," exclaimed David. "What is that magnificent formation?"

"That's Pinnacle Rock," responded Jenn flatly.

"Pull over, if you don't mind," asked David. "I would really like a closer look."

The parking lot would probably hold 200 cars, but theirs was the only one there. The lot was delineated from the footpaths by endurable stonewalls punctuated here and there by stone steps and walkways. The main walkway led upward to an impressive stone building with arched openings. Inside were modern toilet facilities and large wooden tables and benches. A rear deck of stone looked out over the valleys and mountains to the south. To the east of the building loomed the namesake of the park.

Jenn launched into a travel log description of the park with a note of pride in her voice. "Just over the hill yonder is what's left of the Town of Bramwell built by the rich outsiders when coal was big through these parts. Bramwell had the highest ratio of millionaires a few years ago than any other city in the country. The WPA built the park; you rich folks probably don't know what that was, back in the depression. Ah'm told that there is a lake over the hill yonder with good fishin' if you care about things like that."

Eight

Boston Knob, West Virginia consisted of a row of mostly two-story buildings lining one side of Route 52. On the other side of the highway two train tracks and a coal-blackened river—the product of strip mining—ran parallel to the town and road. The town, the tracks, and the river were in a deep valley created by rugged mountains on both sides so tall and steep that it was doubtful to Dr. Cabot that the sun showed its presence more than a short time around noon each day.

Other roads likewise followed valleys, known locally as 'hollers', and creeks as they headed into the hills from the main road. As the Packard had carried him along the highway, Dr. Cabot had noticed huge structures mounted high upon the mountains with long covered chutes descending downward to a large building sitting over multiple train tracks. Jenn told him that they were tipples where slate was handpicked from the coal and then washed and sized before being loaded on long strings of rail cars that would carry the 'black gold' to markets around the world. Men standing beside conveyer belts spent their days sorting through the coal. Theirs's was the better job. Beneath them, under the mountain and in the deep pits, other men blasted the coal or loaded it onto the special trains to be hauled to the shafts or drift mouth. Others set timbers to hold up the roof that followed the route of the coal seam.

"This one has been here for a long time, and over a hundred men are workin' in that miserable heap," volunteered Jenn.

Jenn guided the Packard smoothly along the narrow street in the evening shade of the buildings when suddenly she swept the car into a side street and then again onto an incline parallel to the main drag just abandoned. On one side of the inclining street stood substantial houses with steep steps leading to large porches; on the other side of the street were similar houses but with porches on level with the street some with catwalks bridging the gap between the house and street. There were no sidewalks.

"I must say," mused David aloud. "These are not poor-folk homes."

"Spoken like a true snob," retorted Jenn. "Not everybody here is poor white trash."

Dr. Cabot was abashed. "Well, I am certain that every community must have its professional element," to which Jenn replied, "Why don't you just hush so as not to dig yourself deeper down?"

Eventually, the street leveled somewhat as the car approached a cove grudgingly given up by the dominating hills. The road curved into the cove through a pair of native stone columns. A narrow cobblestone drive led to a massive stone and beam house, nestled within a forest of giant trees. The architecture closely followed the Tudor style brought over by the British during the colonel days. Such an abode was not the humble housing David was expecting. It was a mansion. Unlike the mansions of his upbringing, this one stood out by the amount of natural beauty gracing the grounds and the organic nature of the architecture that caused the house to be a part of the surrounding environment.

It was difficult for Dr. Cabot to remain calm as the enormity of his 'inheritance' became apparent. He unintentionally gushed as he inquired of Jenn.

"What is the history of this magnificent edifice," he asked almost in a whisper.

Jenn responded indifferently. "Been here since the beginning of Dr. Field's practice. This area didn't have a doctor and couldn't get one so old man Jenkins who was as rich as Solomon, makin' his money from coal, sent a team of Pinkerton men up north to find the best doctor they could find. Part of the offerin' for a doctor to come here was a house, land and a complete medical set-up with protected money set aside in a trust to keep the Clinic goin' for a very long time. Whoever took the deal had to stay for ten years and then the whole shebang would be his plumb free.

On top of that, at the end of the ten years if the doctor stayed, was another trust fund that pretty much supported the Clinic for about a hundred years, according to the First National Bank that held the trust. Jenkins owned all of the lands around here including the place where a house built by a coal operator before the war between the states burnt down. He hired an architect to design a cottage to fit on the foundation of the old house, and that's what you see here. Jenkins lost everything in the Great Depression, but this house remained protected because it was in a trust. You like it so far? Wait 'til you see the inside cause you haven't seen anything yet."

Chapter

Nine

The front door of the house banged open and rushing towards him was a slender man with a head topped with the bushy head of disorderly rusty-red hair rushed toward them. He was an attractive youngster with freckles to match his hair. His smile was as bright as his hair and freckles.

"Howdy. You Doc Cabot?" he gushed.

"I am. And who might you be?" responded David.

"Ah'm Jim Corborn; I wuz Doc Field's all 'roun handyman. Ah us't to work at Woodlawn diggin' graves but Doc Fields said ah wuz too smart for that and give me a job with 'im. Hits a good job and I git a place to live, and all ah kin eat. Never had to worry none 'bout gittin' sick neither. Ah do ever'thang from fixin' tars on his car to makin' sure nobody needs nothin' ever'whar else. I guess ah work for you now that he's dead'n gone."

"Woodlawn. You mentioned Woodlawn. What is that?" queried the Doctor.

"Hit's a cem'tary. A rel'tive of mine runs hit. Hit has paved roads a'goin all through hit and all the kids ride thar bikes in thar. They's a great big reflection pool that we ain't supos'ta swim in, but we do anyhow."

Doctor Cabot was to learn later that Jim epitomized a real family of men who made up an important portion of the non-mine labor force in the area. The dialect, indigenous of much of the white population of southern West Virginia at that time, was nearly impossible to understand.

"And why would you assume that I will need your services, my good man?" David inquired.

"Only natchrul" said Jim. "No one else'll do it less'n you plan to do hit chur'self. Course you could git one of them laid off coal miners that don't know how to do nothin' less'en hits minin' coal. Anyhow, most'uv'em air near dead from the black lung and tabac'ie. An 'sides that, they all want union pay. Come on in and me th' rest'ath folks. Annie Turner was Dr. Field'es housekeeper an' cook. She'll take gud ker of yew if'n yew decide to keep'er on. She makes the best chickin' un dump'lins yew ever tasted. Her bis'kits beat any yew ever had. She's kinda' bossie but Dr. Fields put up with'er causin' she don' need no bossin'. She jes knows what needs adoin' and she does hit gud. Twix the two of'us yew don't be need'n to worry 'bout any'thang aron' cus we git to'hit a'fore you even know hit needs uh'doin'."

David scratched his head in puzzlement as he wondered what Jim had said. "I believe he is telling me I have another employee that comes with my new practice," he thought to himself.

"Well, Mr. Corborn, is it? Why don't we take a tour of the kitchen and meet this culinary genius that you hold in such great esteem" David responded.

"Whatcha say?" Jim asked.

"Let's go meet Annie," David simplified.

"Sure. Yew'll l'ahker."

Jim led the way into a large foyer that provided access to the rest of the house through rough-sawn beamed doorways. Most every opening was supported by post and beam construction whether needed or not. To the right was a massive great room with a double balcony, resplendent with books of all genres, including a bountiful array of medical books and journals, taking up one entire wall. The side walls were probably twelve feet high and supported by hand-hewn scissor trusses reaching heights of twenty-four feet or more, joined together with cast iron connector plates about one-quarter inch thick and secured with bolts. Wood was the only material visible in the room.

"Wh'cha look'n at is uh'house of nothi' but wood that come off'un this place rit'cher" volunteered Jim. "They h'ain't narry a piece'a store bought wall coverin' in the whole dang house. Th' floors air all oak an' the walls air either walnut or heart pine panel'un. The ceil'uns air two anch pine, an all the post un' beams air oak. They's even'down some cherry wood mixed in."

Jim continued to narrate the tour as they walked to the end of the foyer to a large glassed-in sunroom that seemed to serve as a distribution point. Above the windows directly in front of him was a long balcony/sitting room ending at a door and another to the head of the steps leading from a point near to where he was standing. A wide hall ran parallel to the steps and led to what appeared to be an eat-in kitchen and joined by a large dining room. A turn to the left in the sunroom led to three closed doors of lesser proportions than all of the other construction.

David inquired. "Where do those doors go?"

"One goes to the Clinic, and the other two go to suites, one on this floor and the other upstairs," interjected Jenn. "The Clinic is attached to the house but has separate entrances for patients, deliveries and such. Nobody comes through here to the Clinic except those of us people who belong in the house."

"Hum?" thought Doctor. "What does 'except those of us people who belong in the house' mean or imply?"

Chapter

Ten

A voice called out. "Anybody home?"

Jenn excitedly said. "That's my brother, Bill. Wonder what he's doin'' here? We're in here. Back in the sunroom; come on back," she called out.

Bill bounded down the hall and engulfed his 'little sister,' who was a year older than he was, in a bear hug. He always had declared that she was the slow one in the family in their frequent banter.

"Hey, skinny, how you do'in'? Busy bossin' our new doctor around? He inquired.

David retorted. "Call it bossing if you like, but I think I am in for a treat having her as a boss."

"Well now, Sis, you have done gone and pulled the wool over the doctor's eyes. You don't fool me none. It's your beauty that has caught the doctor's attention."

David turned every color of red in the rainbow and sputtered, "Her merits have nothing to do with looks. I mean…. she…." he wisely broke into silence.

Bill laughed heartily and hugged both David and Jenn with an arm around each and declared. "That's okay. I love her and so will you one day if you don't already," he added in a whisper aimed at Doctor.

David hastened to change the subject by asking, "William, I recall in an earlier conversation with someone that you have had architectural training. Perhaps you can recall the style of this house?"

Bill smiled as he welcomed the opportunity to display his educational prowess. "This house is an excellent example of Tudor revival architecture although I don't think the architect knew that when he designed it. The design was mainly to take advantage of locally available building materials. I'm sure you have noticed the wide range of woods used. They all came off the place. Historically this is a unique house sometimes called 'Free English Renaissance' loosely modeled after the more domestic styles which were cozier and quainter. It's associated with the Arts and Crafts Movement. I know the architect by the way. It was Mr. R.A. Sheffey of Bluefield who was the first local to practice architect in the area. He designed the 'Oaks" for a judge, one of the first very fine houses built on Oakhurst Avenue in Bluefield. It is reported to be the largest Four-Square house in West Virginia, 8,000 square feet. A doctor later acquired the house."

"My word," said David. "Your explanation reminds me of a young corpsman in Korea who asked me a question that I was reluctant to answer for fear that I would misdirect him. I told him to go asked the commanding officer who was known as somewhat of a 'know-it-all.' He looked at me sincerely and replied, "I don't want to know that much about it."

The tour moved on to the kitchen accessible by an extension of the sunroom that opened into another magnificent, wood-paneled, high-ceilinged room very similar to the parlor. A large table sat in a space that was a dining area surrounded by a hodge-podge of chairs ranging from Windsor, early American to even wooden barrels. The tabletop, made from no more than four planks of maple, stood on matching pedestals. All cabinetry was a mixture of walnut and maple.

They entered the kitchen to the halloos of a woman who could be thirty or sixty. Annie represents the many 'Mountain Mamas' who were the glue that held fragile homes together. They never slowed down, were a source of community energy that was always doing something for someone and, along with their children, filled the pews on Sunday morning. They were full of metaphoric expressions such as "Never be seen on a galloping horse, Hollow in the butt cleaning and too much sugar for a cent." She wore a flowery dress down to her ankles. Over that was an apron large enough to serve as a surgical gown. Her broad smile revealed a healthy set of teeth of which spoke to her self-image.

"Come on in. Ah'm uh, bakin' bread for tomair'e. Since nobody much'es been roun' I ain't been doin' no bakin'. Fresh hot coffee's on th' stove. Hep yer'self. Cream's in the ah'ce box an' sugar's on th' table oar thar. Now do'n you worry none cause ah'll take good keer of yew jus' lah'k ah done for poor ol' Doc Fields a'for he up and died. Wha'ca lahke to eat? I kin fix al'mos anythang if'n you jes tell me what it is yo're awantin'."

David had an instant fondness for this unassuming woman. He decided right then and there that she was to be a continued member of his extended family. In the meantime, Jenn had poured coffee in cups with saucers that David recognized as Havilland's Amaryllis that he had seen at homes of Boston Old Money. Such quality was not Montgomery Ward merchandise. He gingerly took the cup and saucer from Jenn.

"Well, take it," she snapped. "And, don't get used to bein' served coffee by me. It's not a part of my job description. Annie keeps a fresh pot going most of the time, and you can help yourself."

Annie piped up. "Now Jenn, that ain' no way to be a'talkin' to the doctor. Now you tell him yer sorry an' git him a piece of that chock'lt cake out'n the ah'ce box."

Strangely Jenn followed the request almost meekly. Could it be that Annie ruled more than the kitchen around the house?

Chapter

Eleven

The very first thing that David decided he needed to do was to parse the dialect. He never had in his life experienced such mangled usage of the King's English, but yet, marveled at its rhythmic beauty. While he found the language harsh to the ear, he also found it full of basic color. In trying to find an algorithm, he decided that comparing the dialect to a painting worked best. If the dialect were a painting, the artist would have been Monet. The dialectical painting was full of overlapping strokes requiring the eye to fill in the details. The colors were not true to the actual word, but yet the substitute offered more of an artistic fulfillment than the actual. The result was a canvas filled with broad, bright-hazy images, breaking all of the rules of the color mix, but still leading the viewer to grasp the intent of the painter. Mountaineer impressionism: a unique art form lived on the ridge, up the holler, or in town. Education, too, was a determinant of grammar and dialect. The differential was evident even in those having a high school education. The one constant was the long "I" **/ɑ:/** instead of the general American diphthong **/æ/.**

Latching onto an opportunity to delve deeper into the regional dialect, Doctor prodded Jim to continue talking by asking, "Where did you go to school, Jim?"

"Ah /ɑ:/ went ta Delph School up in Bluewell."

"Who was your teacher? Was she well educated?"

"Well educated?" Jim inquired with surprise. "Well, heck yes; she was a teacher wa'nt she? Her name was Miss Jam'son. She drove'uh real fancy car cus her paw was a big x'tive in the Bram'ul Bank uh'fur hit went broke ah hear'd. He did okay cuz he did'nt own none of hit. He owned a hotel and after the depress'un let up he went to work fer a bank in Blue'fil an that's when she wuz air teach'ur. We lah'ked her 'cause she give us pres'uhns. If'n we did'n miss no skul for one week she give us a ten-cent prize. Course, we had to have come to skul on mundi with clean clothes, havin' took a bath an' air har combed uh'for we got anythang. If'n we did that fer a whole month, she give us a twenny five cent prize. Course they wuz only twelve of us in'a whole room. One tiem Mz Jam'son gave us a Chirs'mus party and guess what we had?"

"Let me see," pondered Doctor. "A surfeit of ice cream; lots of ice cream?"

"Naw" chortled Jim. "Strawberries! Strawberries for Chris'mus! Kin yew believe hit?"

The first of the two more articulate folks who were to play major roles in David's new world was Jenn, the gorgeous young woman so stunningly beautiful that David lost his ability to articulate in his typical Bostonian suaveness. This magnificent red-head, in the most pleasing way, made it quite clear from the outset that she, and no one else, not even the Doctor, was in full control of the Boston Knob Medical Clinic. The second was the tall male carbon copy of the gorgeous redheaded nurse-in-charge at the Clinic who was becoming his close friend and confidant. William had already proven his mettle by dealing with all of the legal matters regarding Dr. Fields's estate. Of course, there was little to do since Dr. Fields had meticulously arranged the disposition of his estate before his demise. Amazingly, there were no funds required from Dr. Cabot That seemed strange, but he didn't contest it. He was not going to, as the locals would say, look a gift horse in the mouth. He had asked William what that meant and got the following explanation: "When a person buys a horse it makes no difference what the seller says about it, there is a routine to be followed, kinda' like kickin' the tires on a car before buyin' it, that reveals genu'wine facts. A horse's teeth, along with the condition of its hooves can be a good indicator of its age, health and bone condition."

"Oh," responded David. "I will take heed of those truths when I buy my next horse."

Bill said laughingly, "Now who's being a smart mouth?"

Annie was another enigma introduced into his new life. She too held a senior position in the 'clan' that he had inherited along with Jim.

Twelve

The door in the middle of the three emanating from the sunroom yielded stairs leading up to an amazing suite of rooms designed for a man. The curtains, the bedspread, and the chair covers were of a striped brown and tan rugged fabric that no women would have chosen for herself or her house. The room was spacious with one corner serving as a miniature office centered on an antique roll-top desk of massive proportions. The top was up, and a new supply of pencils and paper, neatly arranged, on the writing surface. Stacked to the side were several medical charts with a tag spelling out that these were the patients to be seen on his first days' work.

Next to the charts was a stack of X-rays corresponding to the names on the individual charts with a note written in precise cursive, "These are the only nonsmokers I could find without going deep into the files. Please don't think I am bossy. I know that most of your work over the past three years was different from what you are mostly going to see here." There was a total of eight X-rays and attached to each one in cursive was the notation 'non-smoker.' Also, with the films was a medical book opened to a section titled 'Black Lung Disease.'

Dr. Cabot flipped on the X-ray box sitting on the desk and glanced at the X-rays. He was relieved to find that he could make a diagnosis from every one of them since the common elements of each were low set diaphragms and hyper lucent lung fields that were also common findings in emphysema and other obstructive pulmonary diseases. He was grateful for the filtering Nurse had done, hence making his first visits on a new job a bit easier. Additionally, she had scheduled about one hour for each patient allowing him to carry out a full evaluation and history without being rushed. He appreciated her apology immensely and would remember to thank her for her consideration of his new environment.

He rose from the desk and took another look at the room having not spotted a bathroom when he first entered. He swept the room visually again and still could find only one door in the room, and that was the entry door. Glass doors were opening onto an outside deck but no bathroom door. Surely, he thought, a room of such bounty would contain a bathroom of equal luxury. As he scanned the room again, he noticed that most of one wall had no furniture placed against it. He approached it and began to search for cracks that would indicate a door and low and behold he found one. He pushed inward near the crack, and the wall opened. He had found the bathroom and much more. In the large room were closets, a dressing room complete with a full mirror and modern plumbing fixtures including a shower and a separate bathtub. Behind another similar opening was a small but complete kitchenette. It was obvious this was not what was available in the original construction, but an update, evoking a recollection of the main kitchen. It too had been updated with all new appliances and equipment. As he took it all in he was overcome by the efforts of "his people" to make him welcome and comfortable. He reminded himself to find out who made the revisions and the source of the funds.

Feeling the need to move about Doctor drifted downstairs where he found Annie working in the kitchen.

In a clumsy effort at camaraderie, Doctor blurted out, "Don't you ever rest?"

Annie laughed and with the ease of a mother to a child responded. "Never. Ah've got a family ta'feed. Come on'n. Want some tea er som'n?"

"Tea would be nice."

"Cream'n sugar?"

"Just sugar, please."

Annie placed a teapot on the new electric stove offering the comment. "Ah'm havin' trouble with this here new-fangled stove. They done gone an' taken'out all'uh the gud kit'shun thangs and put in this mod'urn junk that takes a mine engineer to op'rate."

David broke into genuine laughter. "How long have you worked here, Miss Annie" Doctor inquired.

"Long tah'm. I come here to he'p when the lady of the house tuk sick. They wuz a ol' black man pertendin' to cook then. When he up and died uh the black lung hit was only nat'curl that I tuk over."

"A black man? Are there many here in the State?"

"Not many. Most moved up here for work. Some to escape the KKK. That bunch of no-gud white trash have got plum'outa' han' some places. We hav'em aroun' here, but they don'n bother the black folks none. I think the leader here is a self 'pointed preacher who thank's he's better'n most. Last year the KKK burn't a cross'un whupped two white girls cause the preacher said they wus....whores. That kind'a mis'chuf's what they do here. Silly foolish stuff."

Annie quickly glanced at the doctor and put her hand over her mouth. "Goodness, Ah've done gone an got out'a line. Please excuse me, Doctor, Ah should'a kept my mouth sh'et bout thangs lik'at. Ah wuz plum'outa order."

"Never you mind. I admire people who speak out against social maleficence," Doctor assured her.

Chapter

Thirteen

'His People': This was the first time he considered such a personal relationship with the population he was destined to serve as their primary care physician. Coal was the lifeblood of southern West Virginia and had been for well over one hundred years. The Coalfields were active before the two 'Great Wars' not too many years following the Civil War. The coal market had grown primarily to support wars. His People were a mix of immigrants from Poland, Hungary, Italy, and Greece and they came in large numbers from Ireland and the Post-Civil War South.

They might have been diverse, but they had one terrible commonality: Black Lung. The insidious black-lung disease was an evil byproduct of coal mining. Miners accepted the breathing of coal dust was a part of their job. Large dust particles settle in the tracheobronchial tree, the passageway from the mouth to the interior of the lung, causing mucus that can be coughed up efficiently at the outset but worsens with continued dust or smoke aggravation. Smaller particles, on the other hand, are another issue, causing emphysema and its devastating consequences on the quality of life. Doctor Cabot mentally reviewed his studies of pulmonary diseases. He knew that Black Lung was not a new disease. Ever since humans first started mining minerals of any kind thousands of years ago, those who worked in the mines breathed in the dust that destroyed their lungs. He also knew that the widespread and excessive practice of smoking tobacco was mimicking the black lung, both becoming epidemic, and both included in the diagnosis of chronic bronchitis and emphysema. Neither was likely to subside in the near future because' King Coal' was the absolute economic lifeblood of West Virginia and tobacco was a part of 'manhood' that even pre-teen boys rushed to indulge. The obviousness of coal as an economic factor in Bluefield was an enormous sign that stood at the intersection where Federal Street ends at Princeton Avenue at the juncture of Federal Routes 52 and 460 and State Route 21, all primary roads in and out of Bluefield. Route 52 was the major road to and through the West Virginia Billion Dollar Coal Fields.

Chapter

Fourteen

The morning was young, and Doctor Cabot had not had breakfast. He arose from the clutter of his new desk in his new office which looked to be ages older and in no way measured up to the quality of his new home. He correctly assumed that this was intentional on the part of those involved in the remodeling of the complex. However, it had all of the appurtenances of a well-managed medical office. He moseyed up the steps to the kitchen and found Annie casually working around doing whatever she usually did. As he entered the room, he felt a presence behind him. He turned to see a happy-faced canine of the Terrier breed, furiously wagging its long tail, looking up at him.

"Git, Bo, you sorry, gud fer nuthin' houn' dawg," she yelled. The dog ignored her and continued to favor the Doctor who uncharacteristically bent and scratched the dog's ears. From that day forward, for reasons only known to the dog, Doctor had become Bo's forever buddy and companion. Bo learned the Doctor' routine and followed it as his own.

Annie announced, "Yew'r brek'fes air ready. Set'ch'self-down and ah'll brang hit to yew. How do'ye wan'cher aigs fixed?" she asked as she set a steaming cup of coffee in a saucer before him.

"Over easy if you please, ma'am," He responded.

"What breed of dog is Bo?" Doctor inquired.

"Ah've been tol' that his is'uh Jack Ras'kul Terr'or, but'at don't mean nothin' ta'me. As fer as Ah'm concerned he's jist uh dang dawg. Ah ain't seen none like him any whar else, ever."

Dr. Cabot smiled at the use of the pet name often given to the energetic nature of the Jack Russell Terrier. He had heard of them and had even seen a few of the breed in action since the JRT was a favorite of the wealthy elite who engaged in fox hunting.

"I have seen the Jack Russell Terrier in action on the estates that take pleasure in chasing after foxes on horses with dogs chasing the fox ahead."

"A'a Sha'. Menfolk aroun' here fox hunt but they don't use little pet dogs like Bo. They use honest'ta'goodness big fox houn's that know how to hunt. All the hunter has'ta do is sit by a far (fire) and wait fer the houn'dog to brang the fox tu' them. They say the fun is bein' able to tell by the dawg's bayin' who's dawg in headin' th' pack."

The doctor smiled and changed the topic. He was well aware of when a superior foe had defeated him.

The coffee was excellent, and while waiting for the eggs, Doctor refilled his cup.

"Tell me, Miss Annie. Where do you purchase the sumptuous foodstuffs that grace our table every day?" Dr. Cabot asked while furtively slipping tidbits to Bo.

"Off'n th'farm here." She answered as she placed a large plate of hot biscuits on the table followed by a platter of three eggs and country bacon. Already on the table was a plethora of, obviously, homemade jams, jellies, and other condiments.

"A farm? Here?"

"Did'n cha know they's a farm on this place?"

Annie laughed. "Yes'sir'ree bobtail. Been here since a'fore the civil war. The 'rig'nul farm was mos'ly on the t'thr side'uh the hill an' had nothin' ta'do with coal, Woud'cha believe hit? Th' way Ah hear'd it sev'ral fam'lies came up the New River an' struk'out west prop'bly followin' the Bluestone 'til they found a flat spot tha'had pro'by been burn-clear by Injuns fer farmin' and settled in intendin' to be a stop-over place fer the large number of folks headen' west to claim land u'ther own. It had sev'ral nat'ural sprangs fer gud water makin' hit a perfect spot. The springhouse they built is still here 'long with the bot'um hafe of a blockhouse. We have a typ'cal hill farm wif cows, hogs, horses, sev'ral gard'un plots, wild berries an' apple, peach, cherry an' plum trees; ever thang yew wud want on uh farm. Hit's all yourn! Yew need to go look at hit firs' chance yew git. Jenn will take yew, I bet."

"Um, hum. I suppose," Doctor mumbled.

"Now hits been said that this here house was built on'th foundation of the ol'house that was 'built by the first people to move here. Well, that ain't so. First'uv all, this here's a big house that wud no way fit on that tiny spot. An' in the secn' place, hit warn't built by them but instead by the man who opened the first coal mine here'u'bouts a lil'after th'civil war. Hit burnt down long afore ol' Man Jenkins bought hit. Ya wan'some more coffee?" ended Annie's historical dialogue.

"May I inquire as to where you live and about a family?" He asked as he sampled a small bite of everything on his plate along with a biscuit or two slathered generously with wild strawberry preserves and home-churned butter.

"Ah ain't uh'shamed to taw'k bout my fambly. I live in'a house here on'th place with my sick husbun' and my retard' dot'er. My husbun' is near daid with'th black lung that jus about ever man aroun' here has. Yew'll meet him t'day since he's down to see you in yer office."

"Thank you for telling me that. I'll want to learn all about your family. They sound nice," as he pushed away from the table and commented. "You cannot feed me in this fashion on a regular basis," he proclaimed. "I will swell up like a balloon before you can say, Jack Robinson. How is that for my use of the local vernacular?"

"Believe me, yew'll work hit off jes kep'n up. Hit ain't easy tend'in to the folk up here."

"I'll do my best," he said earnestly.

"Miss Annie?" He said cautiously. "About your daughter? You said she was retarded? Would I offend you if I ask you to be more specific?"

"Heck no. Hit ain't nothin' ta'be 'shamed'uv. Ah'v hear'd a lot'sa talk about hit from lots of people. I went over'ta Bluefield to a healin' preacher one tahm to see if'n he could cure my baby gurl. Hit was my cousin, Bobbie's, ah'dee. She wuz a nurse, well, not really, she jus' worked in a hospital. She's a reel strong-will' gal. One tahm back when Bluefield switched Fed'ral and Bland streets tu'one way, she kept git'n in tru'bl cause she wod'nd pay no nev'r mind to the one-way sahns. If'n she went the rahgt way she had'da stop at two stop laht's, one a'goin' uphill. So, instead, she still went the wrong wayever' day on Bland Street, a'gin traffic so'ns not to have to go through the laht's. Th' same po'leec'mun stopped her ever' day and she jus' kept'on a'goin' the wrong way, ever' day. Whur'wuz ah? Ah wandered off'n mah way. Oh, Th'heal'in preacher. That thar preacher man did'n do nothin' but go 'roun col'ectin money in a bushel basket and, you know what? He filled'um plumb up and had to empt'um a'for goin' back fer more. He said hit was the work'uf th'devil. Now ain't that thu'berries?"

"Speki'n of Bobbie, her and Lula tuk their boys up to that big hospital up North to see a doctor who was supposed to be a expert with kids with probl'ms. I don't know wahy cuz, Sonny didn't have enythang a'wrong with him except'n as'mee. Course, he cud'nt read wur'th a hoot, yeah, none to gud, if'n at'all. I guess though, if'n yor an expert, findin' a new ailment that nobody,s seen a'for is yor job He said Sonny had that dis'lex'uh. Bobbie's boy, too, as ah re-clet."

"Well," Annie concluded. "Yew better git'ta work. Yew gon'na be buzy today an ah hav'ta give this here house at least a holler in the butt clean'un. Yew git now. We both have work ta'do."

David, pretending compliance, meekly replied "Yes ma'am," and proceeded towards the Clinic door with his new-found friend, tail wagging furiously, trundling along behind.

Chapter

Fifteen

Dr. Cabot went from the kitchen by the 'front way' meaning he used the steps from the sunroom hallway. He paused in the sunroom to see a clear day with storm clouds building up to the north. Jim was busy working in the yard doing what, Doctor could not detect.

He arrived at his office that was situated next to a flight of stairs going directly to the kitchen instead of the sunroom which he supposed was to give him an exit from the Clinic without being seen. Hanging on a hook to the right of the door was a blindingly white lab coat. He assumed it was for him and he knew for sure when it fit him perfectly. He turned to his desk and was surprised to observe the charts and films had preceded him thereupon. His curiosity piqued as to who had made the transfer. His face flushed with the thought that Jenn had been in his bedroom, but he dismissed the thought as being insignificant since she appeared to have the run-of-the-house by somebody's authority. Curious.

He had gotten situated in his chair only briefly before Jenn knocked and entered the room.

"Good mornin'" she said expressionless. "People are waitin.' Ah have scheduled only black lung patients today," repeating what she wrote the night before.

"What's Bo doin' in here. You want me to take him out?"

Bo acknowledged his name by thumping his tail on the floor.

"No, leave him alone. He isn't bothering me," David said.

"I have some walk-ins comin' just in case you finish up in less time than ah have scheduled for the black lung people. Ah'm sure I misjudged with the times given; you are an accomplished physician, but I didn't want to rush you in any way. I will get better at scheduling as we get used to each other. We can set up a scheduling book to fit your wants or I can do them, and you can change them anytime you want."

"Nurse Stone, Jenn, as Clinic director, 'Boss' as your brother William calls it; I certainly cannot surpass your abilities to manage the practice. I am a klutz in matters of organization. So, please, don't let me interfere. Tell me how I fit into your management style, okay?"

Jenn manages a tiny smile and did an abrupt about-face and said in parting, "Okay, your first patient is in room one. Oh, you should know if you don't already. The girl up front, the receptionist, Shirley is her name, has been here a long time. She's good at her job and knows everybody by their first names. She can be a big help to you if you need anything and I am not around."

The patient information needed for his visit with the doctor was in a wall-mounted box just large enough to hold a standard file folder stuffed with clinical notes and X-rays. Dr. Cabot collected the file, stood at the door to "room one," took a deep breath, and then entered. Sitting forlornly in a chair was a medium height youngish man who could not have weighed more than 110 pounds. He wore a blue work shirt underneath a pair of oversized bib overalls that made him appear even smaller. He clutched an old misshapen Fedora firmly in both hands as if it might attempt escape.

"Mr. Spradlin?" Doctor inquired.

"At's mah name al'raht."

"How are you feeling today?"

"Tol'r'bol, thanks."

"Breathing okay today?"

"Hit h'ain't no worse, h'ain't no better. I got'th black lung, Doc. Hit don't change none."

"Mmmm. Let's have a look."

Doctor Cabot took another look at the chart in his hands. It became painfully obvious that Dr. Fields had not updated his knowledge of current medical practices. Currently, in most medical settings, the basic evaluation of lung diseases skimmed over the implications of one disease or another different one as being pertinent. Not one of the records of the patients scheduled today mentioned co-occurring diseases associated with black lung, diabetes being a major one; pulmonary hypertension resulting in heart failure being another along with kidney disease and blindness, but the diagnosis is primitive at best. He knew that glucose levels depended on urine tests, showing only an increase of blood sugar. Heart attacks were common in 50- 60-year-olds because there was no known treatment.

"Well," he said under his breath. "Maybe Dr. Fields knew more than I thought he did. Sometimes when one is fighting a losing battle, facts become meaningless, so why bring them up?"

After the pause for reverie, he began his evaluation including those areas excluded by Dr. Fields, or perhaps in spite of Dr. Fields. Then a second revelation struck him; maybe, just maybe, nurse Jenn is more astute than he had anticipated?

Chapter

Sixteen

David learned just how in control the gorgeous redhead was to be when the phone rang on Friday afternoon at 4:00 and she began to issue do-it-or-else orders to the new doctor.

"They're callin' from the camp up on the ridge that there's been an accident up on Buzzard's Roost," announced Jenn. She pronounced "accident" with the emphasis on the final syllable: ax-uh-DENT.

David looked at her with a questioning expression expecting more information. Instead, he received a rather impatient command.

"I'd go with you, but there's too much to do here. Well, don't just stand there; get ready to go while I get your bag. And don't let that dog go with you."

"Is an ambulance on its way?" inquired the doctor.

"Of course not," retorted Jenn. "A Company Doctor has to make the referral and right now you're the closest thing to a Company Doctor we have. So, get goin'. Go south down 52 about a mile 'til you come to a dirt road going west to the sawmill. You'll come to a creek with a wood bridge over it. Go left up that road, and you'll find the sawmill. They'll meet you there. Go!"

Dr. Cabot did as ordered. The excitement emitted by the redhead beauty sent him scurrying to the parking area where there were the Packard and a jeep station wagon. Giving no thought to local terrain and road types and conditions, the Doctor slid into the Packard ignoring the sturdy jeep.

All day rains had made even the best of the mountain roads difficult to travel. He easily found the turnoff from Route 52 as well as the wood bridge heading up to the logging camp. But here things fell apart. It had started to rain again as he turned left at the bridge and instantly discovered the road to be a pair of muddy ruts cut deep by trucks laden with mine props. The rain became a torrent and the thunder and lightning transcended into nightmare proportions. The Packard gave a valiant effort, but the road was destined to win. Finally, the car bogged down and would go no further.

The situation bore down on Dr. Cabot to the extent that he was emotionally returned to a harrowing experience during his service during the Korean War. He and his driver, Sargent Walton, were trying to reach an isolated group of wounded British soldiers trapped by enemy mortar fire. The weather precluded evacuation by helicopter.

The lightning and thunder were fierce and continuous, causing David to become agitated and more withdrawn from reality. His movements became erratic as he screamed and pushed the car door open and tumbled into the mud.

"Get out, Sargent, they're killing us. Crawl to those rocks, follow me, we can make it. No, you can't be hurt. I need you. Get up. Get up. Stop it, damn you. Stop it. Stop it."

"Git up doc. You're ok. Hit's me. Stop fighten' me doc. You ain't hurt," someone was saying.

"What? Where? Who are you? Where is your uniform, Sargent? Who are you? I have to get up to the ridge. There are people injured. Help me up. I've got to go. Where is my trauma kit? Get it for me. Why am I covered in mud?" David inquired out of his confusion.

A man was trying to lift David out of the mud onto the rain-soaked grass beside the mud-ensconced Packard. David continued to fight as he slowly became aware of the situation. "Thank you. I think I'm recovering now. Who are you? I thought you were my Sargent from Korea. I was dreaming."

"Ah'm one of the Hicks boys. Yew ain't never met me, but ah know who you air. Yew okay now? Yew need me to go with yew? Ahm here't tell you they's been a axe'dint up on the ridge. Yew want I should go with yew?"

"No" replied David. "I believe I am sufficiently recovered to proceed on my own. Just point me in the right direction."

David decided that his only alternative was to proceed on foot. He walked about fifty feet in the roadbed when he realized it would probably be better to walk alongside the road where the leaves and grass afforded a more stable surface. He had walked about a half a mile when he encountered what looked like a road leading into the woods, and he decided that this probably led to the logging camp. He was now wet and cold, but he slogged on. He had walked what seemed like miles when he spotted a pickup truck sitting in the middle of the road. He called out but got no answer. He looked inside the truck and saw a pile of clothing in the floor. He opened the door and discovered a pair of very dirty but dry coveralls, a military-issue field jacket, and a pair of goulashes. There was also a sweat-stained hat that looked inviting since he had left the Clinic without one. He pulled off his jacket, and tie, and donned his new wardrobe including the hat placed jauntily on his head. Now, more appropriately attired, he struck out up the road thinking that he would soon find the camp. He was in for quite a surprise.

Seventeen

Now warmed by the borrowed clothing, he found himself enjoying the walk through the bright fall colors of the heavily wooded area. The rain had stopped, and the thickness of the trees had protected the blanket of bright leaves covering the forest floor so that they rustled as he pushed his feet through them. The ambiance was so pleasant that he imagined the aroma of fine cooking brushing his nostrils. Soon he realized that the wafting olfactory delight was not his imagination but rather quite real. He decided it was bread; bread. He headed towards the smell when someone spoke.

"Stop rat th'ar and pu'cha hands whar I kin see'em," pronounced a voice from nowhere. "Ah swar I'll shoot'cha if'n yew don't."

Dr. Cabot quickly complied but answered the voice by declaring who he was and why he was there. "My good fellow," he said, "I'm Dr. David Cabot from town looking for an injured man up on the ridge."

"Yew ain't no Doctor. Yew'r, a dadblamed gov'ment man. Ah ain't no fool. If'n yew'r a doc whar's yer bag? Sides, no self respectin' Doc's gonna be caught dressed in duds like yew'r a' wearin'." He announced with certainty.

"Hey, Bootjack," He called out. "Ah got me an intruder claiming to be air new doctor."

A second man emerged from the direction of the cooking smell and slowly studied David.

"He's right, June Boy. He is air new doc. I seen him the day he come to town. What'cha doin' dressed like at?" he asked David. "At hat looks like the one belong'ta Daddy. Whar'chu git at' hat?"

David's thoughts illogically flickered to the popular song "Where did you get that hat," but he realized joviality was not in order at the moment.

"I found it along with the rest of these ... uh, duds, in a rather disreputable vehicle that I believe you folks refer to as a pick-up truck, down the path," he responded.

"They air Daddy's. But whar's he? Did'n'chu see him down the path?" asked the one called Clarence.

Before David could answer, a third man broke through the underbrush and enthusiastically greeted the doctor. "Hey Doc! Good to see yew. Hit was me what tol' them to call you 'bout the tree fallin' on June. He's ok so you don't need to worry none. Come in'ta the camp and have a snort to warm you up. I ges we can trust you as one of us to not spread the word aroun' as to what we be doin' here. Name's Riley; That'n's Clarence, he's June Boy, and I'm Chance," said the old man pointing a bony finger towards his 'boys.'

David followed behind the one called 'Paw' expecting to see a cabin of some sort. What he finally saw was so unexpected that he involuntarily explained, "My heavens, I've lived with one of those for almost two years in a MASH tent in Korea!" recalling the still his tent mate's operated.

It was a moonshine still. The apparatus was nestled deep inside a large cavity left where the roots of a fallen red oak tree had been. Saplings between the outside rim of the hole and the roots resulting in a dome roof. Covering all of this were several tattered tarps that had probably salvaged from some mine operation. The still was centrally located on a well-packed dirt floor. Makeshift stools constructed with greenwood frames and thatched seats stood around the still. A firebox fashioned from flat stones stood close to a spring-fed stream running close by. A sluice, made of split hollow logs, zigzagged downwards from a rudimentary dike and carried the spring water through the still house and dumped it further down the hill where it found itself back into the stream. A long section of copper tubing, beginning at the top of the still contraption and extending to the sluice, ran submerged in the cold water for a length of about eight feet and terminated into a half gallon Mason jar. This ingenious design negated the need for a coil above the still body.

Paw invited the doctor into the still house and instructed him to "pull up a cheer (chair)."

David complied and sat down on one of the homemade stools close to the friendly fire glowing in the rough stone firebox. Paw dug into a gunnysack and came out with two bunged up tin cups that he proceeded to fill part way from the dripping copper tube.

"Yew boys git'ch yer own, these air for the doc and me," instructed Paw, passing the clear warm brew to David. "Hit may be a mite raw comin' straight from the tube like this, but it'll warm up your innards."

David took a tentative sip and found the product to be surprisingly mild. Just as he was preparing to take a second apprising sip, the world around him turned into a hornet's nest.

"Federal officers; up with your hands," shouted the first man in, brandishing an enormous double-barreled shotgun. Others followed shouting various commands suggesting arrest was underway. One lifted a booted foot into the air and kicked the still into a pile of rubble. Steam spewed from the fire where the mixture from the cooking pot had spilled. Paw and David, immediately cornered, remained fixed, but June Boy and his brother had managed to make their way into the woods to avoid arrest.

David was stunned but not into silence. "How dare you," he cried. "I'll have you know that I am a respected physician! How dare you! How dare you!"

"And I'm President Truman," responded one of the agents. "Shut'cha mouth and keep your hands up."

David, along with Paw, was unceremoniously loaded into the back of a rugged vehicle with huge tires and hauled to the Mercer County Jail in Princeton, West Virginia where he was incarcerated like a common criminal.

Dr. Cabot had exhausted his lamentations of being in jail. No one seemed to care that he was a Harvard Medical School Graduate and that the Cabot's were amongst the first families of Boston.

"Pa, what possessed you to engage in the manufacture of illicit whiskey, uh, Pa, by the way, what is your name again? I can't go on calling you Pa," exclaimed David.

"Hey, I ain't possessed. I'm a God fearin' church-going man an' nobody's going to accuse me of havin' the devil in me, an' my name is Chance Riley. I wuz a'goin to tell you that early on. Don'cha listen when folks talk to ye?"

"No, no" David quickly backtracked. "My inquiry had to do with your choice of profession. No reference to your religiosity was intended."

"What in tarnation does that mean? I never know what yew air a'talkin' about."

"Why do you make moonshine?"

"So's I kin put food on the table. Why else do people do thangs tha'make money? They's not a'nuff jobs in minin' since all them newfangl'd machines wuz brung in an' they ain't 'nuf timber to har all of us and they ain't nothin' else reg'lar nuf to feed a dog much les'un a fam'ly and they ain't no shortage of buyers. We kin sell ever drap we kin make, jus' like at. Hit ain't nuthin' wrong with makin' it. Hit ain't none of the gov'ment's biz'nus but they done went an butted inna air lives in pert nur ever' way yew kin emagin.'"

Chance fell silent. David watched the old man with a sense of understanding. He, too, had had his life 'butted into' by a government dedicated to political expediency and corporate greed. He had been plucked from a potential medical practice in Boston to be unceremoniously dropped into a primitive hospital in the middle of a war (police action?) to attend to young men being slaughtered in the righteous fight against communism. His resentment of that incursion upon his life would never end; he would always carry that resentment within. David found himself wanting to know more about this gentleman who wished no more than to lead a simple life protected by the mountains around him.

"Chance," asked Dr. Cabot gently. "Tell me why you feel so strongly about your occupation. Is it something you grew up with similar as I with medicine?"

"I ges you cud say that" answered Chance. "My grandpaw was the first man ah re'member runnin' a still up these hollers. He did it much different than us today. He tol' me that back in 'em days they wuz called blockaders 'stead of moonshiners. He said that the name come from when the early set'lers started, they wuz called free-traders who wuz fightin' for rights against being taxed by the King of England. We ain't no diff'rent today. All we want is to be left alone. We ain't got nothin' agin nobody. We leave other folks alone, why can't they leave us alone? We always bin law abidin', church goin' people who jist want to be left alone without the inner'ference of outsiders. Well, Ah'm jist foolin' myself. Ah know why. They want air coal. We don't git none of the money fur the coal. Hit all goes outside to rich folks. Look up air at Bram'el. More millionaires up air than any place in the world. All we do is dig the coal and git air'selves kilt with nobody giv'n a gol'durn if'n we live'er die. Well here's one feller that ain't going ta die down thar in them dirty pits."

"Tell me how you make your whisky," prodded David.

Before Chance could respond, the cell door opened. Dr. Cabot looked up, and his jaw dropped in amazement. Standing in the door, next to a uniformed law officer, was Jenn's brother, William.

Chapter

Eighteen

"Well, this is a fine way to establish your name in the neighborhood," said the young man with a bit of a twinkle in his eye. Dr. Cabot recalled his brief earlier encounter at the home-place. Home-place: For the first time in his life the concept of a 'place to call home' with family around resonated as more than a place to live. He summoned up his best glare and responded to William. "It was absurd and uncalled for to treat a man of my station like a common criminal. And who do you think you are to assume such familiarity?" asked David with his nose high in the air.

"I'm your lawyer, I suppose." Bill appraised the doctor for several seconds and finally laughingly said, "Yep, your attire is that of a proper Bostonian."

David had forgotten what he was wearing. He looked down at the dirty clothes and glanced back up with a look of disdain on his face that finally morphed into one of amusement. "Under the circumstances, I am indeed pleased to accept your offer as my attorney. Perhaps we can better complete our discussion outside of this place? If the local constabulary has no objections might we be on our way?"

"You can thank Sheriff Hare here for your release. If it were up to the feds, you would be on your way to Charleston to face a federal judge for moonshinin'. You're still not out of the woods on that account. Let's get out of here."

"At the moment, William, all else is inconsequential. What I need are a bath and some decent clothing, plus I am near starvation since I have not eaten one bite since being seized by that bunch of federal hoodlums. Where might I acquire something suitable to wear that does not smell of wood smoke and sweat?" pleaded David.

"We can get all of that in Bluefield," said William. "I know the folks at the West Virginian Hotel and any one of them will gladly give you a place to clean up while I go across the street and get you something to wear. You wear about a forty, long don't you?"

"My dear boy," David haughtily retorted. "I have no idea of my size since I have always had my suits fitted by the best tailors. Are you suggesting that I obtain a suit off of the rack?"

"Oh, you'll be fine. The store I sometimes use will send a tailor along, and that's saying a lot since we have shops here with top brand clothing. You can't do any better." William informed a befuddled David.

They departed the jail through the front door. David was not impressed by the City of Princeton. It was like thousands of other county seats all over the country. But after an unimpressive ride of ten miles, he was not prepared for the City of Bluefield.

They had been traveling across ridges and down into valleys for several minutes when the road sunk down between two tree-covered mountains. On the left side of the road situated on a piece of rarely seen flat-land, sat a gigantic, bright red building with the name 'Hillbilly Barn' emblazoned across its front.

"My, my," exclaimed David. "Isn't that the most vivid reflection of the area? Hillbilly Barn where fiddlin' and'a kickin' is alive and well in them thar hills of West Virginia."

Suddenly, Bill swerved across the oncoming lane and skidded to a stop in the dancehall parking lot. He turned angrily to the doctor and firmly declared. "Okay now! I've had a belly full of your sanctimonious holier than thou, upper-crust rich Yankee bull malarkey. For your information, the Hillbilly Barn is just a name in no way reflectin' the type of music played there. The best representation of the quality of music served up there is the bands of Duke Ellington, Glenn Miller, Woody Herman, Sonny Brown, Tommy and Jimmy Dorsey, Robny Goodman, even Spike Jones and his City Slickers, as well as many others.

Furthermore, there may be some country-western music performances there, but not Hillbilly! And for your further information, we don't hold well to bein' called Hillbillies by self-righteous outsiders. Maybe if you work hard and learn some humility, you might just earn the title of Hillbilly as an honor of being a valued resident of these glorious mountains. And while ah'm on the topic of music, a least four times a year we have performances from such respected groups as the New York City Ballet and the Metropolitan Opera right here in this hick town. My nephew played a supporting role in La Traviata when the Met was here a couple of years ago. He sang and even danced the waltz; would you believe that?"

The ensuing silence was deafening.

Dr. Cabot's thoughts went back to the luncheon with Jenn and thought to himself, "This is the second time since I have been here that I have been 'chewed out' over an observation someone considered offensive. Perhaps mountain folk are a bit paranoid or could it be just the one family?"

Bill slowly put the car in gear and returned to the highway where they gradually emerged from the darkness of the deep valley onto the side of one of the mountains. David could see a steep drop off to his right. To his amazement, a wide valley opened up to reveal train tracks covered with long strings of open gondolas filled with coal.

David, seeking to break the silence and to show Bill he understood his outburst said, "My heavens what a spectacular display. I assume that is all coal."

Bill, taking the cue softly replied, "Yep, and you're lookin' at a slow day. More coal goes through here than just about anywhere in the world. It's why Bluefield is one of the best shopping towns this side of New York. Wait til' you see what you can buy here. Then you won't feel so bad about being isolated here in West Virginia. The wholesale market here is such that if you order a particular refrigerator, I forgot which one, in New York City, Bluefield Supply Company has the franchise.

"Wesley, my sister Lula's husband, has a little grocery and feed store in Bluewell and all of his family can go into just about any wholesale house, and there was a bunch of them, and buy with cash, at a discount, just about anything possible. Bluefield has five movie theaters with first-run movies going on all the time. Let me see if I can list them: The Colonel, the Granada, the State, the Rialto that usually show movies like the "Outlaw" that the others would not, and the Lee in Bluefield, Virginia. The West Virginian Hotel is 12 stories tall and has a very nice dining room. My favorite place, though, is Kresge's where they have an automatic doughnut machine. I like to watch the machine spit out the dough from the spout into the hot fat and push it halfway around before a thing comes up and turns it over and then picks it up and dumps it into the sugar. I used to leave art lessons in the Coal and Coke building just across the street on my way to the Consolidated Bus Terminal. You'll see the buses with the slogan: "Serving West Virginia's Billion Dollar Coal Fields' on the side. I'd stop in and buy a fist full. They're still only a nickel uh-piece and taste just heavenly. Doughnuts are absolutely no good unless they are right out of the fat."

"There are two hospitals here in town, and you will no doubt be invited to join them both.

"As your lawyer, I'd advise you to be on staff at both. The bigger of the two has branches in Welch and Richlands which gives you a good network of coverage. Another reason to join the big one is that they put on a very nice staff party and dinner at Christmas every year. There're two architectural firms here, and Lula's boy worked for both of them. If you look across the tracks, you can see the college sittin' up there on the mountainside. You can enter that building on the fourth floor on one side and exit it from the first on the other side. You'd never guess that to be a Negro college, would you? Well, yes you would; who would put a white college on a hillside like that. Besides, that side of the tracks is where the colored folks live, and you want to be sure to keep them over there, so the best place to put their college is on the colored side of the tracks; and yes, that comment was tainted with sarcasm. BC is a fine college, and the white folks are beginning to recognize it and are beginning to attend classes there. The composer or I guess you would say, songwriter, who wrote *Sweet Georgia Brown,* Maceo Pinkard, was born here in Bluefield and graduated from what was then the Bluefield Colored Institute. *Sweet Georgia Brown* became the theme song of the Harlem Globetrotters basketball team. Another great song of his you will probably remember is a song you still hear today: *Them Their Eyes* was recorded by Bing Crosby and Jenn Holiday and the bands of Louis Armstrong, Robyn Goodman and Duke Ellington and others I can't recall."

Finally, Bill lapsed into an unexplained, almost embarrassed silence. After Bill's long rambling soliloquy, David realized, for the first time, that this young man was decidedly worthy of his friendship.

William, or Bill to his long-standing dismay, was an educated man. He studied architecture and finished a law degree from The University of Virginia. His education was a result of the GI Bill that provided many a World War II veteran the opportunity to attend college. The government had paid for his architectural degree, and he worked as an architect for the Charlottesville, Va. firm Lorentz to complete his law degree. The architectural degree was a long-time dream, and the law degree was so that he could go back home and serve his people. More realistically he needed a profession that would provide some degree of income reliability given the failing economy in his beloved West Virginia Mountain Home.

Dr. Cabot was to develop a strong and lasting friendship with Bill, first by refusing to call him "Bill," and secondly through many long discussions from politics to religion. Music was to become a strong bonding agent since both enjoyed the classics. The term 'classic,' however, definitely bore different translations for each of the two.

Chapter

Nineteen

David was okay on the violin. He fancied himself to be far better than he was and could be a bit overbearing in discussions centered on stringed instruments. Bill, on the other hand, was a mountain virtuoso with a fair ability on several instruments including the fiddle, banjo, Dobro and a brushing familiarity with just about any component found in folk, country, or Bluegrass band. As more of a joke than anything else, Bill invited David to "sit in" at one of the music sessions.

"Why don't you bring your violin and join us one night in one of our practice sessions?" Bill invited.

David was ecstatic, although he doubted the ability of the local musicians if you could even call them that, he was sure that he could take this bunch of yokels and turn them into a presentable chamber group. Most of his sheet music was still in storage so the selection would be limited to a few of his favorites that he kept in a loose-leaf binder along with his record collection. He came upon a violin arrangement of Beethoven's Ode to Joy and pulled it from the folder. He also had a well-worn 78 RPM recording that he had played along with many times during his tour of duty in Korea — much to the dismay of his colleagues who were forced to share his austere living quarters.

"This," he said to himself, "Should be simple enough for the uninitiated locals." A couple of weeks after he had delivered the music to Bill, Jenn asked if he was free for Sunday dinner followed by a music session with Bill and his band of musicians.

"Yes," he enthusiastically responded. "I have been looking forward to this for some time. Tell me when and where and I shall be there."

The following Sunday, after a delicious meal of roast beef, twice baked potatoes, black-eyed peas, cornbread, and peach cobbler, the band gathered in the parlor for music. David was somewhat aghast when he saw the instruments emerging from their cases: A banjo, guitar, bass violin, fiddle, and mandolin and, "what is that peculiar device?" he almost said aloud.

He got his answer without asking the question.

"Dr. Cabot, you probably recognize all of the instruments except that guitar-looking thing with the shiny plate underneath the strings. That's a Dobro, and Walter's a master on it. It's played with a slide so that every note is infinite, kind'a like the violin. Are you ready to lead us into a little Classical Mountain Music? We have been rehearsing Ode to Joy so that we could at least start somewhere on an equal footing with you. Just speak up if we do anything wrong. We'll depend on your direction."

"Fine," David said. "I'll direct you first so that you can feel the gentleness and solitude of this particular piece. Remember, this is a song of love; your instruments must whisper with the gentleness of a butterfly's touch and color. My selected piece of music is not foot-stompin' ho-down but the essence of sweetness that evokes tears of joy. Now— let's start; one, two three, all together with feeling."

The music started with all of the instruments quietly supporting David's better-than-average violin solo through the entire piece. Once David brushed the bow to fade away for the ending as written, the others did not follow suit. David was first annoyed that these hicks would dare to interpret Beethoven on these crude hillbilly instruments, but something caught his emotions along the way. The guitar and mandolin had each played a run, followed by the five-string banjo, after which the Dobro took the lead. Bill then turned to David and indicated that he was to take his turn on the violin. But David did not respond. The mournful sound of the Dobro gliding through the sadness of the music itself brought visible tears to David's eyes. He could only stare at the players with a look of puzzlement on his face. He had experienced this feeling in the great concert halls of the big cities but how could this small band of hillbillies cause those emotions to rise, on a Dobro for heaven's sake! Truly, the piece belongs to the dobro. Beethoven's Ode to Joy had never sounded better to David who sat motionless for several seconds and quietly whispered, "A-men."

Chapter

Twenty

Dr. Cabot's calls were often for traumatic and medical events caused by the excessive use of alcohol. It was a scourge of the mountains, particularly in those of Irish descent. The Italians, for the most part, were not abusers of hard liquor, or even beer, since their culture of wine-use mitigated the continuous guzzling of beer in quantities enough for inebriation. He found Annie to be an expert on the behavior of drunks and alcoholics. She said she was well acquainted with both and summed up her view, "They's a diff'runce between a out'raht drunk an' uh man uh'dict'ed," she opined.

That bit of wisdom lay dormant until one wintery day a heavy snowstorm shut down the community. Doctor, Annie, and Jim were at loose ends there in a home with little to do so they sat around the large kitchen table drinking coffee and chattering contentedly on matters of no particular concerns, generally nonspecific and generating periods of long silence.

Jim broke the silence. "Doctor Dave, wuz th' war hard fer yew? Whut ah mean, yew wus'nt a sol'jur lahk all them others so hit had'a been diff'runt, rah't? M'ah 'spur'unce has taught me that ever' thang we do learns us some'thn new. H'ain't that right for yew too, even in'a war, right?"

"Jim, you are a wise man. You are correct in your observation about 'learning from our experiences.' But it is also true that we are destined to often relive old experiences in a new situation or environment, thus only changing the characters. Don't you find that true, Annie? I recall a conversation we had one day some time ago when we were discussing alcoholism. You differentiated between a 'drunk' and an 'alcoholic'; that observation has led me to numerous reflections on how to deal with the abuse of liquor. While in Korea, addressing your question about the effects of war on me, Jim, I observed a focus...no; fascination is the word; not focus...on obtaining some form of alcohol at every rank level, possibly attributed to boredom or anxiety. Rank was often the differentiator as who could drink hard liquor, or beer and indeed, who could drink at all, considering the stupidity of a policy that a young man could be demanded to give his life for, more often than not, politic expediency and still be too young for a 3.2 beer or glass of wine with his meal.

"Every installation with roots for any period had an officer's club with a bar. The enlisted grunts could sometimes get a beer at the service clubs or by going to the invariable 'gin mills' always, historically, popping up around a military encampment to exploit the troops. Therefore, it appeared to me that alcohol was ingrained in the military way of life and likewise in our everyday life. Thus, anytime we encounter stress, fear, anxiety, loneliness..."

Doctor lapsed into silence. His mind was regressing to a rumor following the Korean War that the MASH units were going to Indochina where another war involving the United States was brewing. The fear felt by those whose lives would have been inexorability impacted forever, led to a couple of suicides and promises to defect to North Korea or China by others if the rumor proved to be true. Fortunately, it was a rumor, nothing more.

"Wake up Doctor," Jim was saying. "Wha'ch mean 'don keep me here,' you want to leave us?"

"No, no. Please excuse my lapse into the past. I was thinking of our present activities in Vietnam and what a disaster it could have been for me, and you, too, Jim. What is your status with the draft board, Jim?"

Annie quickly jumped in, apparently to protect of Jim, "That h'ain't of no concern. Who wants som'thun ta'eat?"

Both Jim and Doctor responded in the affirmative and food became the immediate focus.

Shortly Jim said, "Doctor Dave, yew di'nt answer my question. Jis what did yew learn in tha army that hep's yew today?"

"Sorry for my relapse, Jim. My past fears–induced reverie momentarily placed me under a state akin to hypnosis."

"Wh'cha say?" Jim queried.

"Never mind. I'll finally get around to answering your question about what I learned in the army. First, I learned that no one wins a war. Second, I learned the war begins when it ends."

"Dang, Doc, that don't make no sense a'tall. Hit shor'nuf is over when all the boys come home, don'hit?"

Annie injected a thought into the dialogue with the observation, "Jim, ah'm a'thinkin that the doctor is talkin' about what the war did ta'those who did the fight'en, ain'ch doctor?"

"Indeed, I am, Miss Annie. We were discussing alcoholism earlier, and I am sure you have also noted the link between those in dangerous professions and the abuse of alcoholic drinks. I saw it in their eyes in Korea, and I see it in their eyes here. In Korea, many times soldiers of all ranks, ages and levels of education were brought to the hospital because their psyche could no longer tolerate the fright, the mayhem, the noise. What spirit they brought with them was broken, sometimes unrepairable. Sometimes controlled by numbing the psyche with drink or drugs."

"Wat'sa psyche?" Jim puzzled.

"The psyche is the totality of the human mind and soul. It abides within the 'whole-human' in harmony with the world around him so that he can peacefully provide for himself, his family and community through the boundless gifts provided by the good earth. Man, though, through greed and lust for power, has for many centuries attempted to systematically destroy man by crushing his soul through wars that have exceeded nature in its destruction of natural resources and humanity. So far, they have failed, but they keep trying. Hitler......"

"Hey, Doc. Ah know a gud story 'bout Hitler. Yew waz' a'talkin' 'bout drafti'n men inna army-? Well, my gran'pa tol me about a man up tha road a'piece that di'nt pay no 'tentsun to his draft papers that come in the mail. So, one day th' Feds come after him an' ast him wahy he did'nt com to jine the army when he got his notice. "Wha'cha need me fer," he as't'm? "Tu'hep us git Hitler," they tol him over. Wahl, ya'll don't need no army ta take keer of jes'one man, the thang to do is ta wait fer him to come out'n on the porch fer his mornin' piss and shoot the sum'bitch."

Annie exploded. "Jim, they's a lady an'uh Doctor at this here table. Don't yew be a'usin filthy language with us!"

Dr. Cabot said, "He has a good point, Miss Annie, but, Jim, she is right about the presence of a lady."

"Well, they's never a mistake in behavin' right." Annie opined. "Reminds me of a story my cousin's husband tol us about misbehavin'. He was born an' raised in Indi'un Valley, Virginia whur so many of the folks aroun' Bluewell come from. He tells the story of a weddin' they had up there a long tahm ago and a man wus a'playin' an ol' banja and a'drink'n way too much bootleg liquor, showin' nary uh'bit of goud sense. He decided he awanted a dance with the bride over the groom's objection-? Well, them two fool drunks got in'a fight, and the banja player swung at the groom but missed and hit the bride and kilt'er. He, the banja player, tuck off a'runnin' and landed just down the road near here an went'ta workin' in the mines. Sev'ral months later, the shurf uv Floyd counti', he wuz a uncle of th'bride, showed up and shot that fool banja player dead right thar in his sleep. He drug him out and put him in his po'leece car and tuck him back to Indian Valley whur somebody finally buried'm outside the family cem'tary."

'Hey, Aunt Annie," Jim called out. "Yew air u'tellin' me not to do bad thangs? Tell me if what me and Sonny did back a'ways wuz bad. We wuz a'sittin' on a flat rock up'above the road jes a lil bit down from whar Mr. Miller had his garage, yew know the place. Hit's whar Mr. Surface put in his firs' fruit stan' in Bluewell-? Well, whil'st we war a'sitten' thar a car come a'tearin' down 52 a'headin' t'ward Pinn'cle rock so fast it'd make yer head swim. All of a sud'nt hit stopped smak'dab down below us and hid two five g what they wuz. We did'n even check ta' see. We went straight to see a man we knowed down on Lortin's Lick and tol him we would tell him whar the cans wuz if'n he'd give us fifty cent uh'piece. Now we seen a crime and we reported a crime. Wus'nt that the right thang ta'do?"

Annie sighed, shook her head and said, "Now don't that beat all?"

The doctor turned as if to look at the snow with a big smile on his face. After a short pause, he said, "looks like the snow is letting up."

Chapter

Twenty-One

David had been exposed to the Episcopal Church in his early years and had little contact with organized religion since then. As far as he could tell the only reason his family attended the church that they did was because it was "the" place to go. During his stint in Korea, he had occasional conversations with the Catholic Priest at the MASH Unit but other than that his exposure to faith-based activities was limited for a man of his intellect and background. It was with disdain that he was inundated with invitations to visit the many congregations found up and down the many 'hollers' in his new hometown.

As the pressure to attend church increased, he was surprised to receive one of his father's infrequent letters with a strange request.

> My Dear David:
>
> We are well, and I hope this letter finds you likewise. We are busy as usual with the mundane activities of the big city. We

attended the opera last Friday evening and ran into your cousin, Melvin, who, as you might recall, is an editor for the Globe. He has been toying with an idea of a special feature on religions of America and suggested that you might be in a unique situation to contribute some material on the mountain folk. Let me know what your inclinations might be.

You mother is calling me to dinner, and I will sign off for now. Let me hear soon.

Love, Father.

David's first reaction was "never in a thousand years," but upon reflection he considered the possible intellectual challenge to be worthy of his abilities. On several occasions, he and William had approached the topic of faith-based activities, and he recalled that the conversations proved to be stimulating, at least to a degree. They had never really gone into any depth on the topic of religion; maybe now would be a good time. Several days later the opportunity for discussion presented itself when William dropped by just as Dr. Cabot had finished with his last patient for the day.

Bill and Jenn were engaged in some sibling banter as David entered the breakroom of the Clinic.

"Let me ask the two of you a question," David ventured. "How would one go about assessing the religious bent of the mountain folk around here?"

"Go to their church," the doubles responded in unison.

"An obvious answer but not so easily executed," argued David a bit testily. "Don't you think I haven't already considered that possibility? However, I cannot just insinuate myself into their midst without proper prelude. Of course, many of them have been inviting me to attend their services, but I don't feel comfortable by showing up without an invitation."

Jenn, sensing a long-winded exchange, not to her liking, excused herself pleading charts to organize and glided out of the room under David's surreptitious glance, leaving the two men to their discussion.

"Tell you what," Bill said. "Buy me a couple'a hotdogs, and I'll set up a plan for you."

"My man, you have yourself a deal. Shall we go up to Frankie's?"

"No, not this time. What I want is from Alex's in Bluefield. You haven't had a hot dog until you have tasted one of his. Alex is Greek, and he opened a three-stool one booth restaurant across from the post office when I was just a little feller. He has always managed to feed anyone who came in no matter that he only has seats for seven people. My uncle, GC, ate lunch there every day of his working life. Every Saturday my cousin, Joe, and me would go to the Granada to see a western and would eat two hot dogs and an RC cola before. There might be better hotdogs, but I don't know where. The secret seems to be in the meat sauce. Well, I call it meat sauce, but it is no more than meat flavored hot sauce that soaks into the bun. He doesn't ask what you want on it. You get it his way loaded with onions."

"William," declared David. "Don't you ever have a short answer to a simple question?"

"There's no such thing as a simple question," Bill retorted. "Let's take your car. My pickup doesn't ride as nice."

Twenty-Two

The time for the Sunday visit to a local church rolled around, and Bill had decided that the Union Church in Bluewell would be the wise choice for the first excursion into the Appalachian religious culture where no division of beliefs (overtly) separated the membership. Membership was probably not the appropriate referent for the mixture of pew sitters turning to see this new person entering the front door.

All eyes focused on Dr. Cabot until one parishioner exclaimed, "Well I will be dogged if'n it ain't the new doctor from down the road in Boston Knob!" With that declaration, all of the pews emptied as everyone dashed into the aisles to welcome the newcomer.

The pandemonium ended when an older dignified gentleman dressed in a severe black suit entered the door and approached the handmade pulpit and sat down in one of the two chairs provided for the leaders of the service. Bill whispered into Cabot's ear that the gentleman was the preacher who was the president of Bluefield College and also, on a rotational basis, served three churches around the area.

The service started with announcements followed by a protracted prayer offered by a white-headed gentleman of advanced years whose speech was affected by severe stuttering. On he went with the dysrhythmia tromping through Cabot's organized mind that longed for an end to the mounting appeal for the blessings of the Lord on everything possible in the minds of this humble gathering. Dr. Cabot was probably not the only one heaving a sigh of relief when an "A-A-A-A men" finally reverberated through the rafters of the small building.

With no introduction a quartet made up of two young girls, a young boy and an older gentleman moved next to a well-scarred upright piano where a stylishly-dressed young woman had begun to hammer out a jazzy version of "Take My Hand, Precious Lord." Following the introductory rift, the quartet's smooth harmony encircled the congregation reflecting a surprising influence of good musical training. While they were singing a couple of men passed through the congregation with collection plates after which the song finished, and the pastor took his place behind the pulpit, bowed his head and exclaimed, "Grace be to you, and peace, from God our Father, and from the Lord Jesus Christ, Amen." This preamble followed the reading of the Gospel and causing David to take pause because the pastor had used a phrase common in liturgical churches.

David, more attentive now, fixed his focus on a rather large man in black who presented total dignity in all respects as he stood beside the lectern preparing to deliver his sermon. He lifted the book to where it was almost touching his nose and the coke-bottom glasses thereon. He began to speak.

"Paul, writing to Titus, is part of the New Testament of which most of us are familiar. Titus, as you recall, was one of the church leaders whom Paul was instructing in the duties of the church as he anticipated the end of his ministry. Paul writes in Titus, chapter three, verses four through eight:"

> *But after that the kindness and love of God our Savior toward man appeared, not by works of righteousness which we have done, but according to his mercy he saved us, by the washing of regeneration, and renewing of the Holy Ghost; Which he shed on us abundantly through Jesus Christ, our Savior; That being justified by his grace, we should be made heirs according to the hope of eternal life. This is a faithful saying, and these things I will that thou affirm constantly, that they which have believed in God might be careful to maintain good works. These things are good and profitable unto men. (KJV Titus, 3, Vs. 4-8)*

Barely whispering, but still, with emphasis, he looked up from his Bible and said, "Oh, what a powerful message embodied in these words."

He looked first to the congregation and then to the heavens to which he raised his voice to a near shout: "That being justified by His gra-a-a-ce, (long pause) we should be made heirs according to the hope of eternal life! Not by works of righteousness which we have done, but according to his mercy he sa-A-A-ved us!"

Dr. Cabot angrily thought to himself, 'Oh shucks. Here it comes. He's going to saAAve us with some old-fashion-hones t-to-goodness-hellfire-brimstone-Jesus-saves-preachin'!

David was steeling himself to bear such an affront to his moral beliefs almost to the point of deliberately getting up and leaving the church. However, the next words took him totally by surprise.

"In 1517 Martin Luther preached a sermon about grace that planted the seed that grew into the Protestant Reformation that led to our protestant beliefs whether they be Lutheran, Methodist, Presbyterian or, yes, even Baptist! Luther took Paul's words to Titus to mean that no amount of human virtue or righteousness, replaces the GRACE of God."

For the first time, Dr. Cabot suddenly became curious about the man in the pulpit. He leaned over to William and asked, "Who in that remarkable man?"

To which Bill jotted down on a scrap of paper found in the book rack in the seat in front of him, "Dr. J. Taylor Stinson, past President of Bluefield College."

Confused, David responded in kind "I thought that was a Negro college?"

On the same scrap of a paper, Bill wrote, "That's Bluefield State in Bluefield, West Virginia. His is a two-year Baptist College in Bluefield, Virginia."

David muttered, "Confusing."

The preacher continued. "Luther introduced his 95 theses or proclamations, or perhaps we should call them his interpretations of the Words of the Holy Scriptures, or more specifically, the behavior of those entrusted with the task of preaching the Gospel. Luther declared that our Lord Jesus Christ willed the entire life of believers 'to one of repentance.' Luther denounced the practices of the church of the time that placed the priest between God and man and, indeed, even allowed the selling of indulgences."

The preacher paused at length, took off his glasses and walked a short distance from the lectern. Pinching the bridge of his nose with his head down he continued.

"Now.... an indulgence was a way of buying an exemption for punishment, they called it penance, from the church for minor sins. Purchasers were mostly those who feared that if one of their sins went unconfessed, extra time in purgatory would be required. According to the history books all of this happened because the Crusaders risked dying without the benefit of a priest's doing the final rites, so, they gained automatic forgiveness for fighting to free Jerusalem from other faiths. Church leaders preached that good works earned salvation, and making Jerusalem Christian was 'good works' so, therefore, paying money to support good works was the same as doing good works."

The preacher put his glasses back on and began flipping through his Bible finally settling on a page he began to read.

"In Paul's Letter to Titus, chapter three verses five through seven, He speaks against the practice of 'good works' serving as salvation. He says,

> *Not by works of righteousness which we have*
> *done, but according to his mercy he saved us, by*
> *the washing of regeneration, and renewing of the*
> *Holy Ghost; Which he shed on us abundantly*
> *through Jesus Christ our Savior; That being*
> *justified by his grace, we should be made heirs*
> *according to the hope of eternal life. (KJV Titus*
> *Vs. 5-7)*

He took off his glasses and continued to speak softly. "These words tell us that only God is the source of salvation, free of good deeds, assured by the gift of his only Son and cleansed by God and His grace. Then, why do we continue to demand good works? From this very pulpit, a man setting himself as a preacher told you, 'if you love me give me a dollar. God loves a giver.' He was telling you, in the very face of the scriptures, that by giving him money, you will receive God's grace. What blasphemy!"

"No Church, Synod, Convention, diocese....no organization.... can put a demand or price on the grace of God. No priest, preacher, bishop, deacon, can take the role of providing you the grace, or forgiveness, of God. No one can sell you what you already have."

Dr. Stenson placed his glasses on the lectern before him and looked to the congregation through the visible dimness of severe cataracts. He paused for long seconds and finally spoke in a volume so soft he could barely be heard:

"Jesus IS the Word, and the Word IS God that, through him and by Grace alone we are saved..........AMEN"

The sermon wound down as the clock approached noon. David relaxed in anticipation of a benediction and a rapid exit when Dr. Stenson announced: "Turn to hymn number 198 in your hymnal and as we sing those beautiful words if you have not welcomed the gift of Grace you are invited to come forward and accept Christ as your personal savior."

The piano began quietly at the beat of a dirge. The congregation began to sing: *Just as I am....

Just as the last of the first verse line faded away, the preacher began to speak in a most pleading voice: "Jesus is bidding you to come forth. The Lamb of God is offering you salvation. Truly his blood was shed for you. The road to his presence is right next to you and leads to the altar of God. All you need do is take that road as we sing the next verse."

Just as I am, ….

Again, the preacher interjected his extemporaneous plea: "Doubt and conflict can be washed away by the blood of Jesus if you just come forward and accept his plea. Don't put your salvation aside for another day. Accept Him now. Be washed of your sins in baptism. Come forward and receive his Grace!"

Just as I am, …

"Jesus is welcoming you with open arms; yes, yes, his open arms offer you his power of grace to cleanse your soul and troubled mind. Come forward now and accept his WORDS OF PROMISE!"

As the next verse began, David saw people moving toward him. William secretly shielded him. He made a mental note to ask William what that was all about.

Just as I am, ……. I come!

* Text: Charlotte Elliott, 1789-1871
Music: William B. Bradbury, 1816-1868

"Thank Goodness that's over," thought David but his thankfulness was premature. The Preacher pulled a one-more-time on him as he practically shouted, "LET'S REPEAT THE LAST VERSE AS WE OFFER THE GRACE OF GOD AND THE LOVE OF JESUS TO SINNERS ONE MORE TIME."

Finally, it was over, and David and Bill made a hasty exit trying hard to avoid well-wishers. They successfully dispersed to the front yard of the church, and William stopped Dr. Cabot by pointing toward the back of the church into a flat area of ground between the church and the back of Sunny South Market over on New Route 52 and said, "See that flat spot right there? I've got a story to tell you about that so don't let me forget to tell it to you sometime."

With that, they returned to the car and rode away to David's mixed thoughts of chagrin, downright disgust, and genuine curiosity filling his mind. He questioned William about what was going on when he blocked the church members away, during what he had learned was the invitation, to which Bill replied, "They intended to save your soul."

To David, the invitation was an oxymoron to the sermon offered by Dr. Stenson. His sermon was educated, well delivered, thoughtful and as worthy of delivery as a homily in any Liturgical Church anywhere. Why then did the deliverer of such a sermon pull a pulpit Dr. Jekyll/ Mr. Hyde? The preacher went against his litany of 'Grace being free' and put a very specific condition upon receiving it.

Twenty-Three

Dr. Cabot stayed busy in his practice with days turning into weeks and weeks into months with nothing but routine to fill his mind. Well, that wasn't true. His proximity to Jenn was a constant distraction. She went about her business oblivious to her beauty's effects on people around her, and most certainly, Dr. Cabot.

David approached her many times intending to invite her out for a nice meal and a movie but always reversed his actions because of their working relationship. In no way did he want to give Jenn the impression that his interests were anything more than friendship, or professional. So, he arranged a Clinic party that included his professional relations. That meant Bill, Jenn and himself. He mentioned the plan to William who suggested that he bring a date that would help solve the imbalance but David felt that this would make it appear that Jenn was along as a date for himself. So, being the dignified coward, he was, he canceled the whole plan.

Dr. Cabot was cognizant of the dangers of the mines. He was soon to see the reality of the true impact on the lives of his patients. In random conversations with those around him he had learned that since January 21, 1886, 2394 miners had lost their lives in West Virginia in the coal mine industry with all but about 21 of those a result of violent methane gas explosions. He was anxiously aware of the potential for a mine accident; the question was not 'if' but 'when.'

He knew he would most likely be called to assist in his role as physician and surgeon. True to expectation, that call came at about 2:00 AM, on a cold, wet, miserable, moonless night. He did not think to ask the name of the person on the phone since the shock of the possible number of deaths had practically frozen his ability to move or think. 134 men were working approximately 400 feet underground in a giant mine extending from an elevator shaft on the Virginia side to a drift mouth on the West Virginia side about three miles away.

Dr. Cabot's MASH experience had not fully prepared him to face the trauma of violent injury and death in a situation where the family was at the scene before others. The Korean War had been a laboratory for improvements in the care of the wounded from injury to treatment. Here, in the isolated mountains of West Virginia, hospital facilities were miles away, reached only by road, in double-duty hearses, used mostly for mortuary transport sans even a Band-Aid. Here he stood by, helplessly, waiting nervously for bits of news from the rescue team, along with the wives and children of the men still underground. He feared the prospect that he could suffer a flashback experience that would defeat his ability to be useful in the present situation.

Doctor's long wait finally ended as a chain of mine cars rolled slowly from the drift mouth entrance on the West Virginia side, bearing the dead and living bedraggled rescuers. Now he knew what the term "drift mouth" meant. He had heard it mentioned from time to time; it simply meant a flat direct entry into a mine where rails could bring the coal out to the tipple. Now it was disgorging human misery.

Rescue workers, some who had just escaped the explosion, their sad faces blackened with the interminable "black gold dust" they removed from the mountain for a miserable living, rode on the cars, accompanying the bodies of their friends and relatives. David could not hold back his horrific memory of a massacre that occurred above the village of Tunam, South Korea where thirty unarmed, critically wounded United States Army soldiers, and an unarmed chaplain, were killed by members of the North Korean army following the Battle of Taejon. Troops of the U.S. Army's 19th Infantry were cut off from resupply by a roadblock established by North Korean troops. To avoid the roadblock, they attempted to evacuate their wounded through nearby mountains only to become stranded. There they were discovered by a North Korean patrol that executed all but the medic who managed to escape.

Dr. Cabot, the escaped medic, and other medical personnel were ordered to return to the scene and document the incident including identifying the victims.

Dr. Cabot desperately shook off the negative war images and tried to focus on the current situation. The bodies of the miners were being unloaded from the coal cars and taken to a mining company building where they were laid in rows so that Dr. Cabot and the other physicians and the county coroner could begin the grim task of establishing identification and, believe it or not, the cause of death. The examiners agreed that most of the first victims brought out of the mine died from suffocation rather than the force of the blast. The lack of physical trauma in many of the deaths probably saved David from being overcome by the scene's similarity to war. However, he nearly lost his composure when the last bodies brought out had been buried under piles of slate brought down by the explosion, as well as the explosion itself. The task of identification was carried out mostly by process of elimination since one miner was missing most of his head and others were unrecognizable from burns.

David became overtaken by the condition of the dead miners triggering MASH memories. He rushed outside where he bumped into Jenn on her way into the building. He spontaneously burst into tears and extended his arms out to her. She responded by falling into his arms and returning the embrace. They remained so until Jenn slowly extricated herself and spoke to him as if he were a child. Dr. Cabot was so overwhelmed that he was unaware of his physical contact with Jenn.

"There, there; you'll be okay. Just remember what and who you are. You're a fine physician, but first, you are a fine human bein'. Now stand up straight and get on with the unpleasant job you know how to do. Later on, we can sit down to a quiet talk and work ourselves through this. It might appear to be amongst the worst you've seen but, believe me, you will see worse many times before you end your days as a doctor, especially here in the mountains where violence sometimes appears to be a way of life," Jenn consoled.

Chapter

Twenty-Four

True to her word, two weeks later Jenn invited David to be her guest for supper at The La Saluda. Of course, Jenn would dress up since it was a 'dinner out;' it meant that Jenn would be spiffed up in her Sunday best and that was almost more than David could handle. Her in something more than the day-to-day nurse's uniform conjured up mental images of every fancy dress he had seen in the most beautiful movie stars. He unconsciously avoided her at work for fear she might change her mind. He discussed the date with Bill as if he was facing a Major Event. As if! Dinner out with Jenn WAS a Major Event. Bill was not very sympathetic since, after all, Jenn was just a sister and certainly not special enough to cause the torment that David was experiencing. "Hey, Buddy, she's just another girl. If you like her, speak up. She'll appreciate it. Like any girl, she wants to be noticed and complimented."

David took offense at William's dismissal of Jenn as being 'an ordinary girl.'

"I beg your pardon," David practically shouted at William. "Under no circumstances is Jenn ordinary. Haven't you looked at her? She is the loveliest creature I have ever seen in my life. She is perfect."

Bill glared at David with a look of puzzlement that suddenly changed to astonishment. "Well, I'll-be-dog-gone. You're in love with her," Bill declared.

David's face turned to bright crimson. He sat as if frozen. He tried to speak, but nothing happened. He tried to laugh casually, but he couldn't make it happen. He finally said in a whisper, "perhaps you are correct."

"Well, dang it man, do something about it," William demanded. "I think you would make a swell brother-in-law and truth be told, Jenn has no inkling of your hidden adoration. Jenn has never been around boys very much, and the ones she has been are...well...just not her type, boy's already doing a man's job in the mines or...well, you know...I'll say it: poor white trash! She's as dumb as a post about courtin'. I taught her to dance, and I am the only person she has ever danced with until I went away to school. Sure, she went to nursing school at the St. Luke's program in Bluefield, but even there it was all women and old and older doctors. You are here providentially for a community needing a doctor. Don't you think that same providence might be a heavenly match up for Jenn? She is too precious to be wasted on 'old- maid-hood' if that is a word. Let me tell a story of a beautiful woman who lost out on the joys, heaven help me for saying this, of marriage."

"Up on the ridge, there were two 'old maids' living in a very nice house with no one but the two of them and an orphan nephew. One was a very sweet, kind, gentle, accomplished, registered nurse like Jenn. The other was as

crooked as a barrel'a snakes and just as mean. I'll call her
Miss Mean. The nice one, I'll call her Miss Nice, was our
go-to person for minor injuries; Miss Mean was a flim-flam
artist. She was the reason Miss Nice was never married.
She was the oldest, dependent on her younger sister for her
livelihood, and a gatekeeper to keep men out of their lives.
Miss Nice had a boyfriend at the hospital, but Miss Mean
started rumors that he was…well… queer, causing him to
leave to another state. Miss Nice was broken-hearted, and
Miss Mean got meaner."

"Miss Mean was my brother-in-law's nemesis as well as
my nephew, Sonny. Miss Mean flimflammed both of them
big time. She got Sonny and Joe first. She had a small field of
hay, probably about three acres, that she hired Sonny and Joe
to 'put up' in her barn. Sonny was only about fourteen at the
time, and Joe was two years younger. They used Wesley's
Studebaker half-ton pickup to load and haul the hay from
the field and unload it in the hayloft of the barn. It took two
days and a tank of gas. Pay time came, and she gave them a
dime apiece for work that was worth at least $10.00 even in
hard times, not counting the cost or the truck."

"She flimflammed both of them again the very same
year. Wesley decided to put Sonny to work doing something
useful until time for school to start. Sonny was hauling
wood from a sawmill up on the ridge and stacking it at the
barn to sell by the pickup load. He had hauled about 20 loads
at the cost of fifty cents per load plus the cost of gas for the
truck. Miss Mean came to Wesley and asked how much the
wood was, and he told her two dollars a load. She paid him
the two dollars, and the next day while Sonny was in getting
more wood and Wesley was at work, she showed up with a

two-and-a-half-ton tandem wheel truck and hauled away the entire woodpile in ONE LOAD!"

David said, "I think I comprehend the first story as being a paradigm of unrequited love, warning me to not shy away from Jenn for fear she will sense rejection and therefore become an old maid. But the moral of the second story lacks not even a vague relationship to the first. Can you enlighten me?"

"They're not related. I was just on a roll, so I thought I'd tell you a bonus story while I was so wound up in your affection for my sister. I'm on your side, man. Don't lose her by being as shy as she is," Bill chuckled.

"Laugh if you will, you infantile nitwit. I will become your brother-in-law just to torture you," David countered with laughter.

Twenty-Five

Thanksgiving Day was approaching and with it came numerous invitations to Dr. Cabot for a multitude of functions ranging from family dinners to institutional organizations including the Bluefield Country Club and the Elks Lodge also of Bluefield. David had no priorities except for one; he wanted to be wherever Jenn was. Of course, he did not make that wish known to her, but he did drop a hint to Bill.

He and Bill had lunched together at Frankie's a couple of days earlier. David tried subtly and unsuccessfully to "weasel" information out of Bill on possible family gatherings to which he just might be included, but in the words of Bill, there was nothin'-a- peckin'. Bill did invite him to go to a Turkey Shootin' matchup at Hale's bottom run by the Hale clan. "Hey, how'd you like to go with me and Wesley, my sister, Lula's husband you remember, to a Turkey Shoot next week? We have lots of fun and Wesley and I nearly always win."

David, aghast, answered with abruptness. "No, of course not. You of all people should know that I am not amenable to the killing of animals for sport! Poor turkeys: subject to slaughter by a bunch of men bearing rifles."

Bill, laughing, said, "We don't shoot at turkeys, and we don't use rifles. We shoot at targets with shotguns.

David adamantly proclaimed, "I saw the movie about Sgt. York of Tennessee and they showed a Turkey Shoot there. They positioned a turkey behind a log, and the contestants waited for the turkey to protrude its head and the one that hit it won the contest."

"Well, maybe so, but that's not the way we do it. Bill countered. "The turkeys are the prizes and have been dressed for cookin'. Here's how it works: each shooter pays a fee to shoot at a target provided by the match sponsor that he has marked with an X and shoots at it from the same distance same as all the others who have marked their own targets. The shooter who gets the closest to the X wins the turkey. If the amount of money put up by the shooters goes over the cost of the turkey the winner gets the 'back draw.' That's the real reason for the contest is to get the back draw money. Nobody wants the turkey but if the back draw is part of winnin' the turkey then it isn't gamblin', and gamblin' is illegal. Got it?"

"Yes, I do indeed get it. Just another way you good mountain folks have devised procedures for avoiding the laws of your great state. First, it was the private club to serve liquor and now a Turkey Shoot. What will it be next?"

Bill laughed and said, "I don't know but try this one on for how to beat the law. As you have experienced, not too happy as I recall, only the government can sell hard liquor and wine in West Virginia made by controlled companies who are taxed at the point of shipping and receiving. But if the booze is made at an illegal still, it must be delivered some way because not everybody is handy to a source. So, moonshiners use bootleggers as their delivery system. Bootleggers may be locals on foot or mobile by way of specially built cars. Now, there's a difference between a bootlegger and a moonshiner. One makes, and one distributes. There is a social difference between the two as well. A moonshiner is higher up on the social scale than a bootlegger who is often a low-life peddler pushing illegal liquor to hard-drinkin' people who are cheap drunks, or to alcoholics who want to hide their drinking problem or churchgoers who don't want to be seen goin' into a state liquor store."

David, exasperated, said, "Good Lord, man, quit rambling and get to the point."

Bill whistled and said, "My, my, ain't we testy. Okay, well, the motorized bootlegger in this part of the state can plan his route to cross the West Virginia and Virginia State lines several times in a few miles. Such a plan puts up a barrier to the State Cops since they can't cross state lines in chase that gives the bootlegger a chance to stop and wait or to find another back road to where they are goin.' That didn't work after the state boys got radios because all they had to do was stop at the state line and call ahead for a BOL, that's 'be on the lookout' for you city slickers, thus causing the bootleggers to find other routes within their own states. The local constabulary doesn't care, or might be customers themselves, or have family members in the business. Another thing…."

David interrupted emphatically, "enough, I have had enough for now. Besides I need to get back to the office or your sister will have my hide, as you frequently comment."

The day of the Turkey Shoot arrived. The snow was falling sporadically. Bill and Doctor approached the site of the activity leaving behind telltale footprints in the pristine snow. Bill said, "There's Wesley over next to the fire barrel."

There, beside the requisite fire barrel, a fifty-five-gallon oil drum, stood a cluster of heavily jacketed men laughing and sharing a bottle. Two men stood, slightly apart from the drinking population, engaged in a conversation of their own.

"Over there," Bill said pointing, and then added, "Well, dog bite it, if that isn't Sonny with his Daddy!"

David responded enthusiastically, "Splendid, finally I get to meet the famous Dotson Boys."

Their approach was detected, and all eyes turned to see Bill and his mystery guest. Wesley spoke first declaring, "Well, look what the cat drug in" extending a hand of greeting.

Bill grabbed Wesley's hand and pulled his top-rated-in-law to him for a manly hug.

Then he said, "Wesley, I want you to meet Dr. David Cabot; he has taken charge of the medical clinic down at Boston Knob."

As they were shaking hands, Bill continued, "And this long drink of water is his son, Wesley, Junior, better known around here as 'Sonny.'"

"How are you, soldier?" The doctor inquired still holding Wesley's hand. He extended his left hand to Sonny and apologized, "please excuse the left hand."

"It's Airman... and Ah'm well, thank you, Doctor. And the left hand is, after all, the best since that's my dominant one."

"Oh, no wonder you bear the title of a family rogue. Do you, or have you ever had problems coping with authority figures or persons?" Doctor ventured.

Bill and Wesley simultaneously burst out in laughter, and Bill inquired, "Does a bear shit in the woods?"

More laughter and the topic appeared closed but not before Dr. Cabot addressed Sonny with an observation. "As a physician in the military, I encountered an inordinate number of left-handed young men of apparent high intelligence who could not seem to fit the mold. I would like your viewpoint on that observation. Will you have time over your leave to visit with me?"

"Why, yes, Ah would be glad too. How about you come by the house so you can meet Mama at the same time? Mama fixes the best-fried chicken in the world." Doctor recalled a similar claim about Annie's chicken.

Twenty-Six

After the Turkey Shoot, the snow had fallen in earnest and had blanketed the area with about six inches of pure white. Here away from the mining it would remain so for several days. As he drove by the tipple, the snow was already blackened. The very efficient State Road Crews had cleared Route 52 and covered them with cinders. Jim was 'chauffeuring' the Doctor today so that he could take the opportunity to visit his mother up on Red Oak Ridge.

The Dotson House sat on an artificially flattened area in the side of the hill above Old Route 52 just at the point where State Route 20 left 52. Snuggled within the juncture of the two routes was a small building with a large sign declaring this to be the 'LW Dotson Store, Groceries, Feed, Hay.' A sign in bold letters on the door declared, 'No Script Accepted.' Dr. Cabot was aware of script as a company-specific form of currency usable only in the store owned by the issuing company, just another way to control the miners. The store was open. He entered.

The first sensation he experienced was the unique aroma of a small country store. David looked to his right to see a ceiling-high stack of one-hundred-pound sacks of cattle and hog feed contained mostly in colorful flowered fabric. Hanging from the ceiling was a stalk of green bananas. To his left was a homemade counter with ceiling-high shelves behind full of canned, boxed and bagged products of all kinds. Directly ahead was a meat case filled with rolls of baloney, boxed cheeses, and soda pop. On the countertop was boxes of Moon Pies, both round and square, and like-choices. In the middle of that chaotic display stood a pot belly stove putting out a warm glow. He was the sole occupant of the building. Just for the novelty of it he went behind the meat case and retrieved for himself a twelve-ounce bottle of RC Cola. He then sat down on the stack of feeds and sipped his drink. Again, he surveyed the scene and further identified one of the dominant smells. A bright red painted square 'box' with a hand pump mounted on top contained 'lamp oil' according to a sign hanging from the pump. It briefly concerned him that the combustible liquid sat so close to the blazing stove. Next to the kerosene stood a wooden barrel of 'salt fish.'

The environment relaxed him. The ambiance was pungent but pleasant. He waited. No one came. Finally, he placed his empty bottle in a wooden departmentalized pop bottle case, left the store behind and walked up the hill, traversing the fairly steep incline by way of steps created with large flat stones. He topped the hill and advanced to a large, two step-up, roofed-over porch that would take him to the front door. Directly in front of him, taking up one end of the porch, was a windowed room resplendent with live plants. True to this expectation the front door was there. He knocked.

His encounters with similarities reoccurred as a near-carbon copy of Annie, but more concerned with appearance answered the door.

"Hello, Doctor. Come in. Ah'm Lula. Welcome." she greeted with the same type enthusiasm as her brother William. "We've been waitin' for you. Are you hungry? I've put the chicken on so we'll eat as soon as you say. Everybody's in the kitchen. Come on in."

David followed her through curtains into an unheated dining room, then through a two-way swinging restaurant style door into a wonderful old fashion kitchen. There at a large table sat Wesley and Sonny with coffee cups in front of them. The aromas were intoxicating. On a wood-burning cook stove, sitting forty-five degrees in the inside corner of the room, sat a cast-iron skillet, over an open flame, alive with the sounds of frying chicken. Pots with potatoes and home-canned beans were boiling away, and homemade biscuits were going into the oven.

David was told to "sit" and was given a fresh cup of coffee and directed toward sugar and thick, thick cream. He dipped the cream into his coffee and watched the butterfat drift to the top, to which he thought, this, must be what they mean by 'dessert' coffee.

An abundance of food appeared on the table with instructions "to eat."

To his surprise, there was no table grace offered. Conversation while eating centered around the snow, wintertime drops in milk and egg production, and how he was enjoying West Virginia, coming from the North.

As the main mean wound down, out of the oven came a piping hot apple cobbler to be placed in bowls and smothered with sugar and the very thick cream. Sonny polished off two bowls but refused the offer of more. "Eat it while you can, 'cause you won't get any more for a while when you go back to Roswell his Mama chided."

There was a knock on the back door that turned out to be a customer of the store. Wesley departed take care of it. Dr. Cabot and Sonny went to the 'front room' and sat in chairs close to the Heatrola Stove and visited.

David broke the ice by asking, "Do they often leave the store unattended?"

"Seldom." Sonny responded with no further explanation then, leaning toward Dr. Cabot intently asked, "Do you think there is something wrong with people like me?"

"I assume you are referring to my observation of left-handers?"

"Yes. Tell me what you have noticed."

"Of course. But first, let me state my hypothesis. It is my thinking that left-handedness is a neurological phenomenon affecting logic. Primarily I must say that, as a group, your mistakes are not the results of stupid behavior as is so often considered in reported infractions of the multiplicity of illogical rules we all encounter, but rather the reaction to stupid expected behaviors based on 'that's-the-way-we -have-always-done-it' demands. I should point out that in medical school we were exposed to very little on the works of psychologists. I do remember a lecture or two about brain dominance differences of left and right-handed people. The theory is that disorders, such as stuttering, may be caused by mixed brain dominance. Well, I am beginning to sound like your Uncle Bill. I will ask him a question, and he tells me the history of the Roman Empire as part of the answer. Forgive me for rambling on.

Sonny alertly responded. "No sir, you have my attention. You have noticed that Bill stutters sometimes, haven't you? Neurological, I think; something I will look into some day. Bill and I have been very close. He and my Aunt Pauline have been so close to me that I don't refer to them as uncle and aunt but by their first names. And Bill has always been a talker. Pauline, by the way, was my fifth-grade teacher who finally got me to reading."

"And, I understand, you also are a bit legendary in your exploits," said Doctor.

"I don't see anything that I have done as 'exploits' but rather the act of taking advantage of opportunities. An example, right after the war was over, the WW2 that is, not Korea that caused me to go into the Air Force, an Italian family moved here in Bluewell, just beyond the schoolhouse down in the bottom. Where the moved from was unknown. They had no family here and all of the local Italian families that lived here for a long time tended to have nothing to do with them. A couple whispered that he might be running from the 'Mafia.' A few days after they moved in a brand-new Chrysler Convertible appeared under their carport attached to the garage. It just sat there; never moved. I had to know why so I went to their house, knocked on the door and this is how it went down.

The door opened, and I said to the man who answered, "Fine looking car you got there, mind if I look at it?" I knew enough Italian to know that he said 'wait a minute' and 'speak English,' so I waited."

"Shortly a pretty blond about my age or a little younger came to the door."

She said, "I know who you are. My name is Bonita Cordusio. I've seen you up at Frankie's, and Mary said you are real nice. I'm listening to my record player. Do you like to jitterbug? I don't know how. I'm glad you stopped by. I haven't made any friends yet. The girl just across the road there and I have met, but she has other friends."

Her English was northern and with not a bit of Italian accent. I asked her if it was alright for me to look at the convertible.

"Oh, sure," she told me. "You drive, don't you? I think I've seen you drive to the house across the road."

"Yes," I told her. "I have a driver's license."

All of a sudden, she said, "I've got an idea, wait here."

In a minute or two, she came back with her Papa and introduced me to him in Italian. She then turned to me and said that she had asked her Papa if I could drive the car for her and he said, "Yes," after he took a look at me. I smiled my most winning smile and waited for an answer that came after they had a brief exchange.

After looking me over and asking Bonita several questions, he finally smiled at me and said, 'Va bene' followed by what I didn't understand and then the word 'dollari' that I recognized as money. She was very happy and told me he said it was 'very good' and that he would pay me twenty dollars a week until school started. For almost three weeks I chauffeured Bonita to the swimming pool, to the show, to the drive-in; everywhere. Then, one day right before school started, Bonita told me that they were moving. She did not know when or where and for me not to come anymore. So, that ended that. I missed her, but I missed that convertible even more."

"How are you faring in the Air Force?" Dr. Cabot asked.

"Okay. I'm in a very unmilitary setting. Most of my work responsibilities are to civilians of the Corp of Engineer personnel or retread officers who are engineers. I have had only one encounter with being disciplined and that officer turned out to be one of my best friends and an excellent teacher."

"That sounds intriguing. Tell me about it."

"I am, and was at the time, a well-respected architectural draftsman in demand for my ability to take a project and go with it uninterrupted, only to discuss changes, not of my doing. We had a brand-new Second Lieutenant right out of college and ROTC who was unaware of the protocol, albeit unconventional militarily, that existed in our squadron. Lt. Little came to my workstation the first week he was there and ordered me to empty his trash can. No big deal. I said 'Yes sir, I'll get to it shortly.' In just a minute or two he returned and yelled, 'Airman, I gave you a direct order to empty my trash can. Now get to it'. That time I was not so polite when I told him to 'empty it himself or get Airman Bice, who's assignment that was.' I informed him that I was working on a deadline that preempted all other assignments. Well, the Squadron NCO who works directly for the commander, came in the back door soon after, walked directly to my workstation, and kindly told me to keep my mouth shut and go quietly to see the Colonel. I did as he suggested and reported, in good military fashion to the Colonel who was also a retread structural engineer who was pulled from a major national engineering firm to serve in the war. I approached his desk and snapped to attention and said, "Airman—"

"Aw, hell, Dotson, don't do that crap with me. Just tell me why you thought you could tell an officer where to get off."

"I tried to answer him, but he cut me off and quoted the old military saw about the uniform, not the man in it, assigned me the task of washing all of the windows in the entire squadron over the weekend. I left his office and went directly to the firehouse located in our complex. I had done favors for most of the firemen since I had access to the photo reproduction unit, and who are air force like me, and borrowed a firetruck, with the crew, for Saturday. That Saturday I went and got my crew, and we went to work. I sat on top of the tank while the fireman directed the hoses to every window that I was ordered to wash. My heart sank when the Colonel's car entered the complex, and he got out and walked towards his office. As he approached, he gave me thumbs up and entered the building. The next Monday morning there was an official letter from the NCO that said,' 'The Colonel said if there were a next time he would be more specific as to how the task was to be done.' I figure next time, every step of the command will be spelled out."

Chapter

Twenty-Seven

The invitation to the family gathering came from Jenn and not Bill as David had expected. The invitation had been offered shyly, as if from a little girl, in a small unsure voice. Nonetheless, it was received excitedly by David. It was for the Monday before Thanksgiving Day and was Dr. Cabot's first visit to the 'home place.'

Jenn greeted him at the front door wearing a red and white striped flared skirt dress with box pleats ending just above the knees. The buttons led to a 'V' collar low enough to reveal a modest view of cleavage that challenged David's ability not to stare. He quickly focused on her face and said, "Lovely dress you are wearing."

Jenn demurely placed her hand on the top button and gently tugged on it lowering the neckline a small increment but enough to reveal further evidence that she was taunting David. She aimed a coquettish smile at him and asked, "Do you like it? I made it especially for you."

David was mesmerized. He tried to speak, but nothing would happen. Bill saved him, appearing behind Jenn and addressing David. "Well, I see my sweet sister is practicing her wiles on our innocent sawbones. Or should I say that love is busting out all over? Why don't you two admit that there's a mutual attraction and start courtin'?"

Jenn turned to Bill, struck an inquisitorial pose and declared, "For once you have uttered a profound question to which Ah say, why not?" She turned to David who just looked back at her with a silly grin on his face. She took his hand, placed it on her waist and said, "Come on. Dinners ready. Ah've saved us seats together next to Mama. She wants to see you close up."

Grandpa Stone sat at his usual kitchen-end of the big dining room table with Grandma at the opposite end. Except for the children, who waited second table. Scattered around the table were the balance of the clan on benches and stools down the sides. David politely answered the less than polite questions thrown his way by a rowdy bunch of quarreling, bickering and happy brothers and sisters and some outsider in-laws. The kitchen staff consisted of Lula, who provided most of the food and Virginia, Charlie's wife, an out-of-place Yankee in-law from Detroit, who wanted so much to be embraced by a family as one of them. The seating arrangement was always the same. Grandma sat sideways at one end of the table in a position engrained by years of holding a child in her lap, as it turned out, facing David who sat at the end with Jenn to his left.

Grandpa sat at the end opposite Grandma and, as usual, provided the Blessing: "Our Father, we give thanks for these table comforts, forgive us our sins, in Jesus ….. AMEN," at which time he grabbed for the cream pitcher always placed in front of him, taking a healthy swig, followed by Grandma shouting, "Joe," and him responding with a happy, hearty, snicker.

As the food dwindled so did the folks at the first table. Routinely pairs collected in various corners, rooms, sheds and even the outhouse for in-family gossip. The second table was for the food preparers and children. Bill rescued David leading him to the front porch even though it was a bit cool. They sat quietly for a while looking at the remainder of snow on the northeast side of a sixty percent grade hillside not too far from them. After a while, Bill broke the silence with, "Hey Doctor Dave; you remember the time when we were leaving the church, and I told you to look at the bottomland behind the church, and I would tell you a story about it later?"

"I do" replied David. "Please proceed."

"Well, it was a mean trick my two nephews pulled, but I still think it's the best prank I ever. Anyhow, that flat lot between the church and the Sunny South Market was a favorite place for evangelical tent meetings. Throughout the summer there's no tellin' how many might set up there. One time a group set up for a revival right between the Bluewell Union Church and no more than 100 feet from the back of the dance hall. The revival started on Thursday night and was just getting warmed up on Saturday night at the same time the joint was jumping over at the dance hall. It was a hot August night, and all of the windows were open at the dance hall to let in some of the cool air for the revelers. At the same time, the churchgoers were getting wound up and were speakin' in tongues so loud that the dancers complained that they could not hear the jukebox.

It just so happened that the Bluewell Union Church was havin' a Singing Convention on that very same weekend and, they too, had all of their windows open, and the tent meetin' was disturbing them as well. Well, let me tell you, Sonny and his cousin, Joe, were men of action! Right after the Union Church let out, they decided to curtail the tent meeting annoyance by bringing in the power of the Holy Ghost. They went over to Wesley's store and borrowed a couple of banana knives. Their strategy was for Sonny to go up one side of the revival tent and Joe up the other, cutting the taut ropes holding the tent in place one at a time, while the congregation was engaged in tongue-speakin' and praisin' the Lord with shouts of joy! In their gleeful discussions of the plan the perpetrators imagined that the tent would collapse onto the activity within, reducing the sounds of joy into screams of fright; but alas, that's not what happened! The tent collapsed at the sides, okay? But the center poles didn't! The Rollers began to roll out from under the partially-collapsed tent looking for the source of the interruption while my two nephews made a rapid departure to the woods, where they hid in their tree house for hours after the event. The next day Aunt Sara, an honorary name for an old woman who had no relatives, and was one of the tent meeting attendees, came visitin' Sonny's mother, my sister, if you recall, and proclaimed that 'she knowed who done h'it but she warn't gonna tell.' Lula knew, too, but she just laughed because she knew Sonny-boy could do no wrong."

Twenty-Eight

A normal day was progressing at the Clinic with patients complaining of the usual cuts and bruises, gout; earaches sat patiently in the waiting room. Jenn efficiently performed triage, sorting the most needed judiciously in order not to appear to be favoring one over another.

Suddenly the door burst open and a frazzled old man shouted, "Hoot Turner jist kil't his'self."

Jenn went into action and explained to the waiting patients, who had already heard what was going on, that they would have to wait or come back later. By then Dr. Cabot had heard the ruckus and stuck his head out of exam room door and asked. "Is there a problem?"

"Yes," said Jenn. "A man has shot himself, and you are needed, probably to pronounce him dead."

Without being told Jenn brought the car around to the front and waited for Dr. Cabot to emerge from the building. Her reasoning was twofold: First, she knew the way and second, a severely damaged young man could evoke bad war memories in the doctor, and she didn't want him being alone in that event. She knew he would protest and she was right.

"I don't need a babysitter," he declared.

"Ah'm nobody's babysitter; Ah'm a nurse, and you are a doctor. The nurse's role in medicine is to assist the doctor," she said.

"You think I can't handle a suicide, don't you," he blurted.

"How can you be so dadblamed stupid not to see when somebody might care for you? I care what happens to you. You are special to me...I mean us...and I...we...want you to stay with us and be a part of us," she pleaded.

Dr. Cabot was stunned into silence. Jenn started the car towards Butt Holler. She took route 52 to the point where it intersected with the old route 52. They passed Hatcher's Mill where the locals had their grain ground and followed the paved road for another mile or so. Then she turned onto a well-cared-for dirt road that dipped down into a valley. The house they were looking for sat downward from the road decorated with multi blooming bushes and wildflowers. Jenn drove the car onto a natural lawn where the scene of the shooting became apparent. Dr. Cabot jumped from the car and rushed to the spot where onlookers had gathered. Jenn followed close behind. Dr. Cabot pushed his way to a body slumped over a barbed wire fence with the hands touching the ground and the feet on the other. Doctor rebounded as he saw the condition of the man's head.

"Lord help us," he cried. "What possesses people to do this to themselves; he is dead, and there is nothing I can do. Call the undertaker," he demanded.

Jenn quickly moved to his side after having observed his unsteadiness. She took his arm as casually as she could and 'walked' him back to the car.

They sat there in the car for several minutes before David quietly said to Jenn, "Perhaps I do need a babysitter after all."

Chapter

Twenty-Nine

Bill had dropped by to see David delivering legal documents for signing that could have more easily been sent by mail. So here he was, in Annie's kitchen, enjoying the fare of the day along with a cup of the world's best coffee. They discussed how the trees were the brightest and most colorful that had ever been and how the October weather was probably the best of the whole year. Silence fell.

"What did ya'll do on Halloween up there in Boston where you were born and raised?" Bill asked.

"Nothing out of the ordinary in the secular world. In our church, All Saints' Day, is celebrated as a Holy Day when the Church honors all 'Holy Ones, known and unknown,' with Holy Communion said to be the *'Communion of the Saints,'* explained David."

"Well, Halloween is a holy day in the hills, too. It has been civilized by the introduction of 'trick or treatin', but it wasn't too long ago it was trick only. No prank— short of causing damage or hurt—was out of bounds. Turning over outhouses had been an age-old requirement but President

Roosevelt's Work Progress Administration, fondly referred to as the WPA, dealt a blow to 'toilet tippin' by building the floor and stool out of concrete with metal strips embedded to provide an anchor for the main wood-constructed enclosure. Therefore, alternate pranks would have to suffice. For example, once a group of boys 'acquired' detour signs from the county road department and put one on the route 52 and 20 intersections in Bluewell directing all traffic to Red Oak Ridge. At the intersection of Route 20 and the Littlesburg road, then sent to Brushfork where still another sign directed traffic to Route 52, right back to start in Bluewell. Those tricked by the detour awarded cider and gingerbread cakes."

Again, David looked daggers at Bill and exclaimed, "Get to the point you windbag!"

Again, Bill pretended hurt feelings and continued: "Okay, sorehead! Sonny and Joe were, like many children in America, keeping track of my World War Two assignment on the B-29 Superfortress and set up a bombing raid of their own. By the way, there was no way of knowin' at that time that Sonny would serve in an adjunct role of the 509th Bomb Wing that dropped two atomic bombs on Japan. He was in the 812th Engineering Squadron that designed and built the facilities used by the 509th at Walker AFB. That's where he got all of his experience that allowed him to get jobs with the two architects in Bluefield after he got home."

"Bill," said David in exasperation!

"Okay, okay," said Bill as he continued with the story. "Route 20 from Bluewell east was carved out of a steep bank. An older road also carved out of the same hill, ran above the current roadbed, about twenty feet higher. They were so close together that the boys often cut grapevines from the trees growing between the two roadbeds and swing out over the new road."

"You understand me on this?" Bill inquired of David. "You have seen kids swinging on ropes over a river and then lettin' loose and fallin' into the river. Well instead of fallin'—

"Yes, Yes. They were swinging out over the lower road from the upper road. I get it. Proceed."

"Alright; you don't have to bite my head off! Okay. On Halloween night Sonny and Joe got a batch of over-ripe cantaloupes from Sunny South and used them as bombs by holding them between their feet and swingin' out over the road and lettin' go just in time for them to splatter in the road. They sat quietly in their imaginary B-29 and waited for a car to come up the lower road. Their wait was short; Sonny opened up the bomb bay, put a cantaloupe between Joe's feet and gave him and the grapevine a great push out over the road below. Joe was in great form and released the bomb just in time to splatter all over the windshield of Constable Purdue's windshield! By the time Joe swung back to the upper road Sonny was gone! Joe found him hiding in the ever-present treehouse hideaway."

"Why... the little deviants" exclaimed Cabot. "Did the Constable apprehend them?"

"No, but the next day he scared the living daylights out of Sonny. Joe had already gone back home to Bluefield. Sonny was leanin' against the pop case watchin' Mandy fix popcorn when the door burst open and who should appear but Constable Purdue! He stopped and stared for several seconds at Sonny; he said nothin', just kept looking and finally said, 'Hey, Boy, come here!' Sonny was so scared that he almost didn't make it over to the Constable Purdue. When he finally managed to get close enough to be reached,

Constable Purdue handed him a dime and said, with a grin, 'git us both a bottle uh pop.'"

The dignified doctor broke into laugher, a real hee-haw belly laugh when Jenn walked out the door and gave him a quick, light kiss on his forehead exclaiming, "My goodness it is so good to see you act human for a change." For the first time, David had experienced two emotions that had generally escaped him his whole life, sheer joy and reassurance of love.

Thirty

Months later saw everybody resisting work on a magnificent spring day. The outdoors beckoned. Wild Rhododendrons bloomed everywhere. The Dogwood and Redbud trees added their profusion to the mountain ambiance as gentle breezes carried the perfumes of spring to every shade tree promising solace from winter's cloistered imprisonment. David had decided that it was a perfect day for a picnic, and he had steeled himself to invite Jenn to Pinnacle Rock for a basket lunch, that he had asked Annie to prepare, knowing the teasing that would occur, which of itself required robust fortitude of its own, and as expected, by his lovable domestic gendarme.

Dr. Cabot was particularly chipper having made a giant personal decision. His spirits were instantly dampened when he walked into the Clinic and found Jenn wearing her professional attire and an all–business attitude. She had her back to him as she dealt with an elderly patient who was having difficulty following instructions. He stopped and admired the manner in which Jenn eased the tension; but as she turned, he noted something about her face that he had only seen once before—tears. He rushed to her, but she placed a hand on his shoulder and held him back. Suddenly the hand moved and encircled his neck into a hug as Jenn whispered, "I am so sorry, there is bad news from Boston!"

"What is it? David asked.

Jenn quickly snapped back into her professional role, backed away from him and responded. "It's your father. He passed away last night."

Thirty-One

He purposely planned to take a train, rather than a plane, to have time to think, (and perhaps mourn?) before facing his mother. She was a kind person, but she hid in every way from the world giving an impression of coldness. When he faced her, she would be in complete control, and he needed to face her in kind.

So, here he stood with his old army B4 bag packed with his best clothes. His best clothes; he was learning from his New World that best clothes meant that you had one set other than work duds. Age didn't matter. It didn't matter if the lapel or tie was wide or narrow; it didn't matter if the fabric was wool, cotton, had a collar, was "high waters," had a cuff or a shiny seat. Many of the dresses and shirts he saw were made of feed sacks or cut down from bigger dresses to make smaller ones. Bib overalls were the required attire for both men and boys who often had no other trousers. During the depression, feed mills realized that women in the Appalachians were using feed sacks to sew clothes for their families. Consequently, mills started using flowered fabric for their sacks. The manufacturers' labels were removable by washing.

The Dotson family could afford to purchase clothing, but Mama still made clothes out of feed sacks for Sonny. One reason had to do with large quantities of feed they used resulting in an abundance of empty sacks; another was because of the 'waste-not-want-not' philosophy. Four 'white' feed sacks sewn together made one bedsheet; most of my ever-day clothes were feed sacks as was Mamas. Only Mister and sister Dorcas's drew the line on wearing feed sacks. Mama's conservation philosophy was active in the kitchen as well. Country people raised their food and killed and dressed their chickens. When a chicken reached, the table, every part was cooked and put on the table. Everyday quilts were made of feed sacks and used for warmth since there was seldom heat in the bedrooms. Fancy quilts were made of scraps of mill fabrics and were hand stitched with designs.

Packing complete, David drifted to the Clinic to say goodbye. Business was moving on in spite of his absence. Nurse Jenn would handle many of the routine clinical maladies in his absence, but he still felt he was abandoning his responsibilities. 'His People,' as he now referred to his patients, were the most generous and understanding people he had ever encountered. Without a doubt, they thought well of him and had accepted him into the fold

Jenn saw him, stopped what she was doing and asked, "Are you ready to go?"

"Yes," he replied. "Would you find Jim and tell him I need a ride to the train station?"

"Ah'm going to take you," Jenn informed him. "Let's go."

It was a short and silent trip to the station. Jenn aimed the Packard toward a curb marked 'passenger parking' and switched off the ignition.

"Ah'll walk you to the platform," she said as she exited the car.

David followed suit and fell in stride beside her as she moved toward the platform. They took up a position a distance from where several other prospective passengers waited.

"The weather looks good for travel," David opined.

"Yes, it does," replied Jenn.

"Jenn," David said and fell into silence.

"What," Jenn questioned.

As if reluctant to speak David began again. "Jenn, I.....I want to say......

Again, Jenn inquired "what?"

"Jenn, I ..." David was interrupted by the noise of the train approaching. Suddenly, Jenn leaned into him and kissed him—solidly and lengthy on the mouth—quickly turned and ran off the platform toward the parking lot. A mixture of excitement and depression overtook David as he followed her with his eyes as she walked away.

Dr. David Cabot stood forlornly still watching the parking lot long after Jenn had driven away. He became aware of another person standing close to him and turned to see a very dignified, well-dressed gentleman, with an impish smile looking at him. As Cabot turned in his direction, the man queried, "Your wife?"

David looked back at the parking lot and replied dreamily, "No, my nurse."

The gentleman laughingly said, "That was no nurse's kiss; that young lady likes you. Do you share her feelings?"

David slowly turned his vision to the gentleman. "And who might you be to presume into my emotional state?"

"I'm sorry for my forwardness," the man laughed sticking his hand out in friendship and announced, "I'm Rob Bateson. Who might you be?"

Thirty-Two

At that moment they both turned at the sound of the mournful train whistle that David had learned to love. That sound had unique properties; it had the power of assurance that all is well plus it was an excellent weather forecaster. The black smoke spewing from the engine gave further notice that their train was just around the bend already beginning to slow for its short stop at the station. Both picked up their bags ready to board without a word. They gravitated to a group of vacant seats and sat down together as if by prearrangement.

Rob was the first to speak. "Well sir, as I said earlier, I am Rob Bateson from Bluefield, Virginia. I work at the Power Company, and I am on my way home for the weekend."

David was a bit taken aback at the forwardness of his seatmate. One thing he had learned about the people he had been experiencing for the past year was their willingness to engage in conversation, anytime, anywhere, so long as there were no uppity attitudes; that would put a halt to any friend exchange. That's not true; Republicans, in the minds of the

Majority, weren't smart enough to talk about anything since the State of West Virginia was as Democrat as it could be.

David wondered if Rob Bateson was a Democrat and then he wondered why that thought even came to mind. His recent experience with politics indicated, to him, that most Democrats were uneducated, otherwise ignorant, and of fundamental religiosity and, but perhaps not all, looking for a handout many blamed on President Roosevelt's New Deal. He decided not to ask, but it turned out that he didn't have to. The two riders talked companionably about politics, religion and more intensely, the just-ended war in Korea and the brewing conflict in Viet Nam. Rob had a son in the National Guard serving in Germany and a son-in-law in the USAF serving State-side. He spoke proudly of a brother-in-law, Elder, who served in the Second World War as the Executive Officer of the14[th] Airforce, stationed in China. One of the Major's activities assigned to the "Fourteenth" was flying supplies, mostly gasoline, over-the-Hump to the shark-faced nosed Flying Tigers, piloted by volunteers from the US Army Air Corps, Navy and Marine Corps, recruited under presidential authority and commanded by crusty ol' Claire Lee Chennault.

As the smoke-spitting train meandered slowly through the valley between tree-covered mountains, the switchbacks were so severe that the end car was visible from the rest of the train. Rob knew every twist, turn, bump, and village along the way and was as free with his travel expertise as he was with his political editorializing; David felt every twist, turn and bump as his stomach was doing some editorializing of its own. He knew he must be showing signs of motion sickness as the track began to follow the meanderings of the Bluestone River.

"Believe it or not that creek you are looking at is the headwaters of the Bluestone River. It passes through Bluefield, Virginia at the end of my street." Rob said glancing over at Doctor and noticing his discomfort.

"Tell you what. If you stay on this train all the way to Lynchburg, you're in for a rough ride. Let's see. It's 11:30 now. Why don't you get off at Bluefield and spend the night at the West Virginian? We'll meet you there for supper at the hotel dining room. You can have a good night's sleep, and you can leisurely catch the Powhatan Arrow in the morning at about ten thirty that's non-stop most of the way to Lynchburg where you make your connection north. Besides, I want to show you off to my wife, Irene; she loves sophisticated professionals."

"Sounds like an ideal and restful time to contemplate my reason for this trip," interjected David. He was not looking forward to his home visit since he had no idea what to expect. Maybe this purported twin-city of New York had so much to offer it might prove to be very interesting. "I accept your generous invitation!" He said. "This is another example of the most wonderful Southern Hospitality that I have been experiencing in this magnificent hill country," he added.

Thirty-Three

Rob had gotten off the train at Bluefield, Virginia with promises to meet David at six. The train barely had time to get started when it began to slow for Bluefield, West Virginia. David departed the train wondering if he should seek a taxi cab but after discussing the options with a porter, he decided to walk instead. The porter told him more than he wanted to know. He advised David to go west on Princeton Avenue passing by the Colonial Theater and the Matz Hotel, continue until he came to Federal Street, then turn left and the hotel is three blocks south.

The weather was suitable for walking, and his B4 bag was not heavy since he had packed sparingly. He crossed Princeton Avenue and soon came upon the theatre where 'From Here to Eternity' with Burt Lancaster and Deborah Kerr was playing and 'Roman Holiday' with Gregory Peck and Audrey Hepburn scheduled next, both first-run top movies. Back toward the train station, the Rialto Theatre was showing 'The Outlaw" with Jane Russell. He wondered what talent she had to offer. He strode along noticing the variety of stores on the street including a large Woolworths until he came to Federal Street, his turning point when he abruptly stopped. There in front of him, on the corner of the next street, Bland was a classic example of the Romanesque architecture that had been a part of his early days in Boston. It occurred to him that the style was similar to that used by Boston Architect H.H. Richardson who had designed Sever and Austin Halls on the Harvard Campus and Trinity Church that he had attended with his parents as a child. However, he was also aware that it was a massive 'fad' design used in many cities around the world. (The building, the old People's Bank of Bluefield, corner of Bland Street and Princeton Avenue built in 1895, was one of the finest Victorian Romanesque structures in West Virginia. The architect was probably E. C. S. Holmboe of Chicago who had had a branch office in Bluefield. Holmboe was heavy into Romanesque characterized by semi-circular arches. This style is seen in reduced form in many structures, including houses, in and around Bluefield and extensively in Bramwell.

Dr. Cabot vowed to find out more about the bank architect. His curiosity piqued, he decided to check into the hotel and find a source of information on local architects' past and present. He continued south on Federal street and was amazed at the degree of commercial, professional and financial activity condensed within a couple of blocks ahead of him. From where he was standing he saw three banks, The First National, the Flattop and the Commercial, two department stores, Thornton's and A.W. Cox, two Kresges within a block of each other and a Montgomery Ward. The West Virginian stood next to the Commercial Bank.

As he reached the entry of the hotel, he noted the Woodlawn Florist and the Pinnacle Restaurant making a mental note to pick up some flowers for Rob's wife.

At the appointed time David drifted down to the lobby of the hotel to be with the Bateson's. As he stepped off the elevator, a well-dressed gentleman left the front desk and approached.

"You are Dr. Cabot? He asked in a southern dialect typical of the upper-class West Virginian. "I'm T.P. Cole. Rob made reservations for the dining room, and your table is ready if you would like to go ahead and be seated? By the way, Irene is a cousin of mine on her mother's side who was ironically a Cabot. Her father is a long-standing businessman of Graham. Let me take you to your table." TP led David to a very nice table quite properly set as one would expect from a first-class establishment. He saw that Doctor was seated and then, to Doctor's surprise, and pleasure sat down for conversation.

"I gather you were with Rob long enough to get acquainted?" TP asked as a primer.

"We rode from Welch to Bluefield on the train just yesterday" David answered. "He appears to be a very knowledgeable man."

"He and his brother have worked their way up in the Appalachian Power Company quite well, and they did it as relative outsiders. Their Dad was a well-respected miller in these parts. He was associated with two or three flour mills in West Graham and Princeton, had several patents, I believe."

"Talking about me, I'll bet," loomed a voice from the door.

"Now Rob, be nice," Irene chided. "How are you, TP, Doctor Cabot," directing her attention to him, "so glad to meet you. Are you enjoying Bluefield? Isn't this a lovely dining room?"

TP pushed his chair back and announced, "I'll have Hayes take care of you. He is one of our best. You might remember him, Irene," and walked away without receiving an answer.

Immediately a smiling gray-haired gentleman came to the table and dispensed menus. He inquired as to their comfort and informed them he would give them time to "pu'ruz" the menus. Hayes would be a black man. At that time there would be no women or white men waiting tables in higher class restaurants and the hotel's barbershop.

Mrs. Bateson returned to her dialogue. "I have always found the roast beef with mashed potatoes here to be dependable. Is everyone ready to order?" and hailed the waiter without an answer.

Dr. Cabot noticed and thought 'She's ready therefore everybody is ready, just like my mother,' then turned to Hayes and inquired. "My dear fellow, I think I am going to have the country ham for the second time in my life. What do you advise?"

"M'ah advice," said Hayes laughing, "is if'n you have had it'afore they ain' no time lah'k now to try it agin' since the cook here does the best job of almost anybody in fixin' it. On top'a that, ah know the man what cures our ham and he knows how to keep it from dryin' out. You'll need some fix'ns to go wid that an' ah su'gust some sweet tater kas'rol and red eye gravy that ain't on the menu to sop up our very good bread. The bosses here are real gud wif bread."

"Perfect." declared Doctor.

Rob took his turn and said, "I'll have what she's having."

Chapter

Thirty-Four

Dr. Cabot was delivered to at the train station just in time to board the sleek, streamlined Powhatan Arrow albeit still a coal-burning engine. The trip to Boston was mostly a daze. He slept some and snacked each time a vendor passed through hawking his wares at the infrequent stops. He would rouse only when the train passed through big cities. Ultimately, the trip was coming to an end as he entered the surrounds of Boston. The depressing vestiges of decaying neighborhoods that too often were doomed to fade as a result of their rail-side juxtaposition and a shifting demographic saddened him. Strangely, he felt a sense of home-sickness. That melancholy was replaced with a sense of dread as the train glided into South Station that seemed to have shared the deterioration of the rest of the rail-related scene. He assured himself that being reunited with loved ones he would feel better but this was not to occur. Instead, each encounter just exacerbated the depression.

His mother and her brother, Uncle Thomas, who was a retired physician, met him at the train station with stoic solemnity. His mother greeted him with a brief hug while Uncle provided a weak handshake. The conversation on the drive to the home-place was stilted if not formal. Uncle Thomas prattled on about the advantages of a Boston medical practice while his mother focused on the lives of his social peers, mostly female.

"David" she hesitantly began. "I have arranged for a special reception of those close to you and your father after the funeral tomorrow at the country club. I don't suppose you brought suitable attire with you? I assumed not, so I have arranged for a fitting for you tomorrow morning. Several of your old friends will be there, and they are anxiously anticipating visiting with you. You remember Gloria Higginbotham and Suzan Cunningham, don't you? Well, they have both acknowledged their intent to attend. You will want to look your best for the reunion."

His first thought was that his mother was meddling, but he dismissed his disquiet as a result of his depression, so he decided to remain silent. The event did, however, evoke thoughts of Bill and what his response to Mother's declaration would be. Bill would say that "He smells a rat."

His depression deepened as the house of his childhood came into view. While the 1906 vintage home was of excellent design and construction, it, like the balance of the surrounding homes, was showing signs of deterioration or just plain neglect, a result of creeping de-gentrification. It was obvious that the urban renewal activities taking place in communities all over the country were approaching the old home place. There was little verbal interchange as the small party entered the house. His mother opined that he was probably tired and suggested he retire to his old room to rest and "freshen up" before dinner.

Thirty-Five

Dinner was at a modest restaurant situated in a cluster of upscale chain stores featuring affordable clothing, shoes and hobby supplies indicating a change in residents' income for the area. David, his mother, and Uncle Thomas entered the eating establishment, and David noticed the absence of a requisite formally dressed Maître de, but instead was greeted by a pleasant, simply dressed young woman who escorted them to a table for eight. David, turning to the hostess commented, "There are only three of us. Don't you have a smaller table?" To which his mother quickly responded, "This is suitable. Others will be joining us, thank you. "David, having not be informed of his mother's plan. reverted to a bill'ism thinking 'Now my hackles are up.' Before he could confront her, an assemblage of five well-dressed persons approached the table.

Uncle Thomas rose to introduce the individual members of the group by identifying each one with an open palm-up hand gesture. "David, you know Suzan Cunningham, here on the left, And Dr. Tom Endicott and Nancy in the middle and Dr. Dwight Eliot and Ellen here on the right. They are here to bring you up to date on the status of medicine here in our little community. Now if all will be seated, we can order drinks."

The group separated and places around the table. Suzan moved directly to the chair beside David. Although she could have more easily seated herself from the left side where no one was seated, she, instead, chose to enter the chair by squeezing into space next to David, brushing him casually. She immediately launched into a disconnected conversation ranging from her early association with David to her present situation as an available divorcee. Her physique, attire, coiffure, and most certainly the scent of a very expensive perfume drew his attention to her. He flushed to the warmth of her closeness as she had moved her chair to touch his. Suzan was assuredly desirable, but instead of being drawn to her he amusingly recalled the words of Jenn back at Frankie's La Saluda Club when he had suggested the ambiance to be romantic, and she boldly replied, 'Don't get any ideas soldier. It's this or Lynn's Drive-in, and I don't like eating in a car parked beside a carload of teens'. David began to laugh out loud to the dismay of his mother and the bewilderment of the rest of the table.

Coffee was served indicating that the meal was winding down. Doctor Eliot pushed his chair away from the table and inquired of David. "Well, David here you are back home for the first time since you were mucking about in that war in Korea supposedly practicing medicine. What are your plans now?"

David remained silent for several seconds while his thoughts went to "The cat is coming out of the bag." Eventually, he spoke. "What do you mean 'What am I going to do now'? I will continue with my practice in West Virginia, I suppose."

Dr. Endicott, in a rather condescending tone, interjected, "Come now, Son, surely you don't intend to honor that spur-of-the-moment fluke? Now that your father's successful practice is yours for the taking, it would appear logical that you would return home and take up your legacy. Your mother desperately wants you to return to be with her, and we are here on her behalf to implore you to comply with her wishes."

David again remained silent while he thought, 'Who in blazes are you to assume to call me, Son?'

Firmly, he spoke with a tone of voice that would have frozen a hot poker. "Am I to understand that you believe that I made a foolish decision in assuming a viable medical practice among people who are considered by many to be inferior to us?"

"No, no, nothing like that" responded Endicott. "As I said, your father has provided you with a far superior opportunity for a healthy financial future which would probably not be the case in such poverty as we hear about in West Virginia. Tell you what; why don't you take a look at your Father's set-up and give it some thought. Now, it's time for us old folks to settle down for the evening. Why don't you and Suzan have a glass of brandy and visit for a while?"

"Slick" though David. "He just finessed my ace of trumps." Suzan was thoroughly enjoying herself and making her presence known. David was loath to admit that he was enjoying her company. They had both enjoyed a brief flirtation many years ago before he entered medical college and her dashing off to marry money from a wealthy Boston Name. At the moment her history meant nothing to him.

She was providing attention he had not experienced for many years and bearing on his thoughts about returning to Boston. The brandy and the lovely, willing girl were influencing his sense of judgment, and he hesitatingly agreed to call it a night—at her place.

Thirty-Six

He awoke the next morning with a headache and a return of melancholia. His memory of the previous evening was somewhat vague. He stumbled downstairs to find his mother sitting primly on a kitchen chair waiting for him to appear. She was wearing her uniform of the day that consisted of a gray pencil skirt and one button blazer with a simple blouse. Her shoes were the usual chunky heel black patent leather pumps accompanied by a matching purse, her hat was a simple black satin pillbox, and she wore the required white gloves. The presence of the hat, gloves, and purse was the only hint that she was prepared to go out. Otherwise, she was dressed for a day at home, prepared for drop-in visitors. "David, I want us to go look at your Dad's office. His receptionist is maintaining the office and will be there to show you around and to answer your questions. Now, you go get dressed and have a cup of tea and a quick breakfast before we go."

His first inclination was to rebel but he thought better since the visit was inevitable, they should face facts. "Mother,

I don't drink tea for breakfast anymore. Is there coffee?" was his childish way of exerting a bit of willfulness.

"Do we call a taxi or do you have that planned out as well?" he inquired petulantly.

"We will take the family car if you can still drive" she responded in a motherly tone.

Sure enough, the gleaming black 1951 Studebaker Commander Land Cruiser sedan stood elegantly in the garage set apart from the house. David held the door for his mother and moved around the front of the car rubbing his hand along the stylish protruding "bullet" nose that was unique to the post-war Studebaker. He found that the car easily accommodated his larger than average frame. He situated himself in the comfortable cloth seats and turned the key. To his surprise, the big 8-cylinder engine sprung to life with a single press of the starter. The trip to the office was silent and uneventful.

Both the receptionist and the nurse were there to greet the mother of their old boss and their potential new boss. The entire facility was spick and span, but no amount of soap and water would be able to erase the effects of age. It was immediately evident that nothing had been updated in some years. The waiting room furnishings were worn and shabby. The walls needed paint of a less drab color, and the worn-out tile floors were free of pattern. The clinical tools and apparatus were up-to-date as far as they went and were limited almost entirely, to pre-war vintage. It was obvious that the clientele of this facility was no longer among the elite of the city.

He wondered why his father's old colleagues were pushing him to assume charge of such a pitiful scenario and out of the blue, it hit him. They were finagling him to take charge of his mother! It was obvious. His father was gone, and Mom had no one to care for her. She had always been dependent on father for almost everything, and now she was helpless. Uncle Thomas, even if he was young enough, had enough problems of his own without taking on an aging niece.

For the first time since being home, David looked at her from a different perspective. He had always seen her as too reserved, if not cold, domineering and self-centered where, in fact, she was simply frightened.

Thirty-Seven

It was a lovely day in Boston, and David was decidedly against any future tête-à-tête with Suzan. His thoughts were far too removed from his present location to consider other women. His mother was going through the motions of beginning the preparation of breakfast, but it was obvious that her thoughts were elsewhere as well.

"What are your plans for the day?" she asked vaguely.

"Oh. Nothing," David responded equally as vague.

"Isn't Suzan expecting you for dinner tonight?"

"Oh? Oh, right. I had forgotten. We were going to Michael's at Suzan's' choosing. I am not one iota interested, but I suppose there is an obligation, at least family wise. But, mother, it's time for you and me to discuss more pressing problems. I know it's not a fancy restaurant but Shony's serves a good breakfast, and there's one just up on the main street. Why don't we go over there and eat so that you are not distracted with preparations? I really must be thinking about returning home and to my practice as I have only begun to work through a very heavy schedule."

"Oh, home is it?"

"What? No, just a slip of the.... Yes, by heaven, HOME! West, by God, Virginia is now my home. I have friends and co-workers who care for me, and I am beginning to understand their ways. I have a wonderful home where I don't need to lock the doors even though hundreds of people live in poverty but are too proud to steal. I am providing a valuable, necessary service that is appreciated and too often paid for with chickens, a sack of potatoes or maybe no more than a genuine 'thank you' straight from a humble, broken heart shattered by the shame of it all. I am offering up my skills; maybe it is shocking for me to say it, in the service to God. And last, but by all means, not least, I have found a woman that I intensely admire. Yes, I need to go home."

The topic had finally been breached. David did not doubt that his mother was fully aware of his intentions. He knew that he must bring forth his must diplomatic forces to overcome the entrenchment of a mother from her familiar enclave. He steeled himself for the inevitable resistance.

His mother looked at him with the understanding that only a mother can muster and whispered, "Yes, you need to go home."

"Yes, I do. I apologize for my abruptness, Mother. My irritation is not with you. But we do need to discuss your future. Here you are in a decaying neighborhood in a home that was my home, and dad's home, as well as yours, for many years. When dad started his practice, the inhabitants of the neighborhood were professionals who could afford nice homes and country club memberships and all of the upper-class, heaven forgive me for making a distinction, niceties that only first-family status and money could afford. That is no longer the situation here now. Filling the driveways are pickup trucks instead of Buicks and Packards; the women are wearing short shorts and tee shirts instead of dresses and skirts. Break-ins are reported daily on the radio and in the newspapers. I cannot leave you here as a lonely, or maybe I should say, lone widow. Uncle Thomas is, sadly, well, let's admit it, getting old and lives clear across Boston from you, and additionally, has problems of his own. You know as well as I do that his situation with Aunt Helen's family would preclude any help from him."

He reluctantly looked his mother in the eye. He had expected to see a sad face, but instead, he saw peace. His mother had an expression one would associate with beatitude. She sat silently for a long moment and then reached for his hand, gently squeezed it with both of her frail hands and whispered, "If you are working up to inviting me to go home with you let me ease your mind. "When do we leave for our new home together? Do you think I'll be able to learn to be a good hillbilly?"

Thirty-Eight

The die was cast. His mandate was clear. His cluttered mind wrestled with details but, at the same time, was at ease. His thoughts drifted back to the times his MASH unit had to 'bug out' as enemy combatants threatened. The rapid deployment of a full surgical hospital appeared to be chaos. Yet, every member of the team knew exactly what needed to be done, and the outcome was an organized departure. The only emotion was fear. The here and now presented a different scenario. Here was an accumulation of forty years' worth of memories and collectibles. The memories are somewhat easy to transport; collectibles not so easy since they consist of a house and all of its appurtenances. The house itself has but one solution: sell it. The contents, then, become the real issue: what to take and what to discard.

They still sat in the kitchen without eating breakfast. Mother looked up at him and asked, "Well, are we going to sit here all day and worry over the future or are you going to take me to breakfast at Shony's?"

David jumped to his feet, bowed deeply and mockingly said, "Your ladyship, I am your servant. May I escort you to the local pub for grits and bacon?"

"Grits?" Mother giggled. "What in tarnation, see I'm already using the lingo, are grits?"

"Mother, I have learned that 'grits' is singular and you will learn that sometimes, in your home to be, they are the only food available for breakfast. Yet, the uppity folks eat them as a side dish, sometimes with cheese added, or even as cereal with cream and sugar. As they say back home, 'grits is good.'"

"Let me get my hat, and we will be on our way. I think that we are ready to start moving. There I said it. You can now put your mind at ease, and for your information, this has not been an impulsive decision brought on by your wise commentary. I have been considering what to do ever since your father died. I was only waiting for you to make a decision and, yes, an invitation."

David gave her a long loving stare and remarked. "Mom, you are a sly one. Here I thought I was in control. Speaking of being led down the primrose path!"

At the restaurant they sat in a booth, another first since her early school days, she eating pancakes and him bacon and scrambled eggs, she tea and him coffee, discussing tactics of the move. The final decision was determined to be a quick and clean break. He told her about the house and how it had been designed with two suites along with separate guest rooms to accommodate both long and short-term users. Her suite was on the ground floor with access to the library, sunroom, living room and, best of all, the kitchen that was active all day long from early morning to early evening, and all night if so desired.

Mother decided to cull treasures and leave the house and everything in it, including the car, to an estate liquidator. She decided a quick and clean departure would be less of a trauma. "Why linger over 'things'?" She asked her son. At first, she thought that the car might be needed, but David assured her that she had a car and driver at her disposal at any time.

They completed the arrangements in a few days. Travel plans were made. The 'bug out' began.

Thirty-Nine

As Dr. David Cabot mounted the steps into the waiting train with his mother in tow, he felt exhilaration greater than when the Korean War ended, and he found out he was going home. Again, he was going home to West Virginia, West, by gosh, Virginia. The realization hit him that Boston was receding behind him and his mother and would cease to be their physical home. Was this happening? The source of his early pride was fading in favor of a different society? With his sophisticated society mother beside him?

He had anticipated that Mom, as he had begun to call her as a part of the transition, would be somewhat of a reluctant traveler, but instead, she was as excited as a child on the way to a circus and almost as difficult to control. She wanted a full travelogue of each station through which they passed. David opted for a Pullman Roomette for his mother while he settled for a coach. That way he could make her comfortable, and he could easily check on her. In the space of this short reunion, he had developed a new protective fondness of his mother-child. She also seemed to be content with their new relationship.

The train left Boston, South Station at 6:00 PM during a front pushed by an Atlantic hurricane. His mother was frightened by the intensity of the storm, so David stayed with her until she declared she was tired and ready to go to sleep. With the help of a porter, Mom was left on her own until breakfast in the dining car while the train roared on to Washington's Union Station, leaving the storm behind, after passing through New York while she slept.

Soon after leaving Washington they entered Virginia, passing through Alexandria and Charlottesville heading to Lynchburg where they would change to the Norfolk and Western lines that would take them through Bluefield, then home in Boston Knob where he expected Jim to meet them at the station. He had notified his 'colleagues' of his return and had specifically asked for Jim to be there.

The train route from Radford, Virginia to Glenn Lynn, Virginia/West Virginia meandered along the New River providing picture book viewing. The road was quite curvy requiring the train to move at a rubbernecking speed. Harriet Cabot was thrilled with the abundance of flowering shrubs and trees. She had a pleasant exchange of conversation with a young lady going home from Radford College for spring break; she was further fascinated that the train stopped at a house alongside the tracks for her host to disembark and run quickly into a thicket of a million blossoms to a fairyland house. As the train began to move again, Mrs. Cabot looked back to see the front door of the house open, and a lovely grey-haired matron emerge before the view was lost by the accelerating train moving towards Bluefield, its next scheduled stop. There, from the train window, David exhibited his new-found knowledge of the city by pointing out the West Virginian Hotel where he had stayed the night on his trip to Boston and the First National Bank. He focused on the Bank building because of its architecture that mimicked many of the buildings his mother was familiar with in Boston including her church, Trinity, and a couple at Harvard, his school, Sever and Austin Halls. He promised his Mom that he would bring her to the "New York City" of West Virginia for a shopping trip and dinner at the West Virginian. Next stop, HOME!

Chapter

Forty

The train began to slow. The blossom covered mountains were lovely but beginning to become tedious, David thought. He watched for the station platform to come into view where he expected to see Jim waiting. Instead, the platform was overflowing with people. The parking lot was full, and cars sat along the road indicating that this was no spontaneous party, but was a planned activity. David dug into the possibilities and concluded that some dignitary was on the train and the gathering was for him. Assured that he had an explanation, he helped his mother into the aisle and proceeded to the exit. He carefully helped his mother down the steps watching carefully to assure she took each step without stumbling. Then he followed still looking downward.

Suddenly a great din erupted startling him. He abruptly stopped and was amazed at what he saw. Across the top of the station door, was a sign that declared 'WELCOME, DOC'S MOM.'

The town's mayor stepped forward and presented her with a document declaring her an 'official' resident of the State of West Virginia surrounded by a beautiful hand–made wildflower wreath. David, too, received a warm welcome. His heart did flip-flops when Jenn approached him and welcomed him with a generous hug and kiss on the mouth. He stood there stunned and speechless. William, standing close by shouted above the noise, "Well, don't just stand there with that silly grin on your face. Hug her back. She's glad to see you."

Jenn grabbed his hand and led him towards the inside of the station to hoots and hollers and teasing shouts as the crowd parted to let them pass. David felt like a teased little boy of having a girlfriend. He was thrilled but too embarrassed to enjoy it. Someone shouted, "Is they gonna be a weddin'?"

David wanted to melt into the floor as he entered the building where a bluegrass band was pounding out their version of 'Happy Times are Here Again'. He looked around for his mother and found her wearing a gold crown and carrying a magic wand thoroughly enjoying the party and, yes, the attention. What a crazy and new world for her.

Ultimately the party melted away. Jim approach Doctor with the question, "Y'all bout ready ta'go?"

"Thank you, yes, Jim. Come and meet my Mother."

"Tha's her rat thar?"

"Yes, I'll introduce you to her. She will depend on you a great deal. Is that satisfactory with you?"

"Sho'nuf. If'n she's enythang lahk yew. She's a fahn person."

They walk across the room where his mother was exchanging niceties with a group of people, and to his amazement, showed every indication that she was enjoying herself. The group included Jenn and Annie. When he saw Annie, he became a bit concerned because she was, for certain, the matriarch of the existing clan, including him. It occurred to him momentarily that she might consider Mom as an intrusion. However, all reservations melted as he approached close enough proximity to hear the conversation.

".......ah'n you kin hep aw yew wan'ta be uh'doin er yew kin pick wha'cha lah'k ta'do, mak's no mat'er ta'me," Annie was saying.

"Well, bless your sweetheart," Mrs. Cabot said boldly. "Perhaps I can relieve you of some of your chores and make myself useful."

He never had, in his whole life, never, heard her use the expression, "bless your heart." Was she assimilating that rapidly? He hoped so. He had been anticipating a reluctance from her to tolerate his new clan, let alone to accept it. Was the compliance for his sake or will she truly blend in and be a part of the family? His doubts faded when Jenn pointed to his Mom and gave him a great big wink and nod.

Jim helped by voluntarily approaching Mrs. Cabot with a cheerful "Hah'de ma'am. Mah nam's Jim and I ah'm at chur al'aroun' service. Wh'ever yew need yew jus call me an' hits dun. Ah'm a gud safe drah'ver an I kin fix anythang. If'n you wan'uh far in yor farplace, ah kin keep hit up fir yew. Jis ast, okay?"

Mrs. Cabot's response was again, "Why bless your heart," as she gave him a motherly hug. Jim took her by the arm and escorted her to the Packard where he opened the door politely for her and averted his eyes as she slid into the plush seats. He carefully closed the door and went around helping Jenn enter from the other side. Jenn laughed to herself because he had never held the door for her before. Jim was working hard to impress Mom. Jenn's approval rating for Jim jumped several notches.

The drive to the house was extraneous dialogue until they reached the entrance to the property. Mrs. Cabot suddenly sat erect, and her comments were excitedly favorable, as she viewed the serenity of her new home. When she first saw the house her only comment was a whispered, "Oh, my."

Chapter

Forty-One

The daily routine returned to normal with Mom readily fitting into the mix. Annie was thrilled to have her in the kitchen, and the two became fast friends. Additionally, Annie now had a 12 hour-a-day audience for her tall tales and family recollections.

The medical Clinic was running smoothly with a steady flow of appointments and the usual walk-ins. The number of hospitalized patients increased rapidly requiring daily visits. He did not mind for it gave him the opportunity to return to surgery, that being his primary training and military contribution. He never went into surgery without Jenn even though the hospital supplied a full complement of surgical nurses and technicians.

One day following the completion of their hospital activates with time to spare, Jenn inquired of Doctor, "How brave are you?"

Such a question was so out-of-the-blue that David was not sure how to answer.

"Well, I spent about two years of my life performing surgery near or under hostile enemy fire or threat of fire. Does that qualify me as brave?"

"Not entirely," Jenn retorted. "Since we have some time I would like for you to meet my Aunt Nan who lives down the river from Maybeury. It's just a mile or two out of our way, on the Bram'ul road, if you have the guts for it."

The gauntlet had been thrown down. Who was He to refuse a challenge from a mere woman? Well, maybe 'mere' did not fit in Jenn's case. Anyhow, he bravely, if not arrogantly, declared his acceptance of the implied dare.

"You're on. Lead the way to this daring venture," he replied with gusto.

Jenn, who was driving, guided the Packard through the winding road until she came to a turnoff from Route 52 where the Bramwell road, The N&W railroad, and Elkhorn Creek ran side by side for several miles. A clearing to the right came into view with two poles about three feet apart standing sentinel over their side of a suspended bridge across a deep gorge containing the Elkhorn Creek and two identical pole pairings standing on the other side. Each set of poles was secured by guy cables that were also the suspension cables for a wooden plank bridge swinging precariously across the gorge. The opposite end of the bridge terminated at the railroad. A path ran across the track, to what looked like a million steps, then ascended to a neat little house on the side of the mountain.

"That's where Aunt Nan lives. Up There."

"You don't expect me to risk my life crossing that.... that.... thing?" David moaned.

"You took the dare, you wimp. Come on. There're hand cables as handrails. I'll go first. Just do as I do," Jenn teased as she blithely stepped on the swinging bridge with a tantalizing 'swing' of her lovely derrière as she sashayed in sync with the bridge.

"You will be the death of me, he shouted. You cannot assume that I will risk life and limb just to please you. Your charms may beguile me, but that does not make me a fool."

From the other side of the bridge now came a taunting song. "Sissy, sissy, cut and run. Sissy, sissy, never has no fun."

"How dare you. I am your boss." Doctor shouted. "You are no longer in my employ, you hear me. Fired for…. disrespect of a superior officer, or something akin to that." David shouted back suppressing a laugh.

"Okay, you asked for it. I am crossing now solely to do harm to your bod." David threatened as he proceeded cautiously. As he approached the end of the bridge, Jenn backed away from him and began to run as if to escape from him. He had no difficulty catching her by the hand. She responded by turning and placing a generous kiss on his lips. He spontaneously returned the kiss but suddenly broke away and said, "I thought we were here to see your Aunt Nan. Is this visit a personal call or a professional call?"

He was still holding her as she replied, "personal."

"Right," he said and returned the kiss. The bridge proved to be dangerous after all.

Forty-Two

Their visit with Aunt Nan had gone well. They returned to the Clinic with hardly a word spoken. He invited her to stay for supper, but she shyly declined using laundry as an excuse.

"Please, stay. You have not been to our table since my mother arrived and I think she would enjoy meeting you again, especially.... now."

She relented since she was hungry and also because she was curious to see if Annie's cooking had changed since she had a new mouth to feed. And, so she could sit next to him while they ate.

As soon as they entered the house, Jenn excused herself to 'go freshen up.' When she returned, she gave a new meaning to the expression 'freshen up.' Her beautiful hair was no longer up in the knot that she usually wore at work, her face was red from scrubbing and embellished by a nominal application of makeup. But what caught David's attention was the dress she wore. It fit her perfect figure like the proverbial glove yet it was not provocative. She wore a shirtwaist dress with a fitted skirt made of pink cotton checked gingham. He could not resist asking her where she got it. She answered, "Thornton's in Bluefield. You like it?"

"Of course, I like it. But I didn't mean from what store originally. I meant where you got it here and now?"

"Oh," she smiled sheepishly. "I have had a closet in Annie's house for a long time since I served as Dr. Fields's hostess after his wife died. I can continue if you like."

He did not have a chance to respond since Annie, in her best hog-calling voice, announced that supper was ready. He took her hand in his momentarily and then tucked it under his elbow to escort her to the dining room.

They gathered around the table with Annie seated in the 'jump seat' at the end nearest the kitchen. David usually sat at the other end, but the evening he announced that he wanted to be on the side facing the windows so that he could enjoy the changing weather outside. Mom Cabot sat across the table from David. Jenn sat next to him by pure accident. Jim would sit to the side at the other end of the table as soon as he brought the meat in from the outdoor oven-smoker. The only point of contention emanating from Mother was her disapproval of the 'help' eating with the family. David squelched her conservative thinking by pointing out that without the help the table would be practically empty, and very dull, as Mom was about to learn.

Jenn spoke. "Mrs. Cabot, Dr. Fields always had wine with the evening meal. He—"

Annie interrupted loudly. "Humph. Hit ain't bad'nuf that jes' bout ever man up this holler air a drunk. Jenn, yew ort'a know that since ever dang one of your brothers, excep'un Bill, air addicted to drink."

"Annie, not a single one of my brothers would touch wine; you know that. You also know that the drink of all of our alcoholics is hard liquor, legal or otherwise. You know also know your bible; Jesus turned water into wine, didn't he? I know you take Paul's letters as preaching the Gospel of Jesus Christ and he told Timothy to 'Drink no longer water, but use a little wine for thy stomach's sake and thine own infirmities,' and that was straight out of your official King James Version, right?"

"Well" retorted Annie. "Drinkin' enythang with alke'hol in'it will lead to heavy drankin'. Hits lahk gittin' in'na tub of hot water. First yew pu'ch toe in and next thang yew know yew air in'it whole hawg. Yes, sir'ee bobtail. Drink'un leads gud pep'l to no gud. You take yer brother in law, Lula's husban'. He's the smartest man I ever seen. When he ain't drinkin', that is. One time he was all dressed up for a picnic in'a fancy new white suit, got drunk and sat down in a cow pile thankin'hit was a rock. 'nother time he drove his car in'a crick next to a bridge he was goin' to cross. Somebody as't him why he did hit, and he said 'they was two bridges and he tuck the wrong one.' So, you see, li'ker kin make a smart man into'a fool."

Everybody laughed, even Annie herself.

Chapter

Forty-Three

Dr. David Cabot was now a transitioned and genuine Mountaineer. He could not believe that almost three years had passed since that auspicious meeting with Jenn at the Bluefield airport. He still marveled at his position in the community and even more so about his relationship with Jenn. On several occasions, his memory flashed back to the first-sit down meal with Jenn at The La Saluda: 'Don't get any ideas soldier. It's this or Lynn's Drive-in, and I really don't like eating in a car parked beside a carload of teenagers'. For years he feared to ask her to share even a sandwich together for fear of being rejected. That had changed.

This evening they were invited to a formal Fourth of July dinner-dance at the Bluefield County Club. Jenn was tingly with joy and made no effort to hide her excitement. She had selected a Tanpell Sleeveless, floor-length mermaid gown of matte black satin with lace straps as her choice for the occasion. No one would ever believe the lovely garment was mail-ordered from Sears-Roebuck after Annie altered it to fit snugly to Jenn's perfect figure. The neckline was a bit revealing to suit David's mother, but for David, it was so perfect that he went to Alfred Land's Jewelry in Bluefield and purchased a double string of pearls as an enhancement.

The dinner had been marginal, and the fireworks display over the golf course was meager. But to David and Jenn, everything was perfect. Nothing could dampen their excursion into a near-fairyland experience. The dance following the fireworks had been pleasurable given the opportunity for David to hold Jenn close in public. The small band was excellent and specialized in simple versions of current popular songs. Jenn's favorite was 'Smoke gets in your eyes' mainly because David had taken her to see the remake of Roberta, (Lovely to Look At), with Kathryn Grayson singing the song herself instead of the usual practice of a beautiful actress with a lousy voice lip-syncing an unseen singer. The band was notable for its unusual makeup of WKOY radio personnel as well as the instrumentation of vibraphone, bass violin, and piano. David was particularly delighted by the absence of drums.

Midnight approached, and the band segued into 'Goodnight Ladies' signaling the end of the party. The crowd drifted to the exit and their automobiles for the drive home. Jenn and David followed suit with many a male glance at her glamorous dress. David was unaware of those admirers since he had only fleetingly looked at anything but her for the totality of the evening. For once he was driving the Packard and guided the fine car over Cherry Street Cutoff to Route 52 and the road home. Jenn had snuggled close to David as they passed The Ritz Curbway just across Easley Bridge doing a booming business with the loudspeaker flooding music over the randomly park cars nosed into the drive-in restaurant.

"Want something to eat? Perhaps a foot-long hot dog with all the trimming?" David teased.

"Hush your mouth. That would be too much sugar for a cent, after all of the hors-d'oeuvres I had at the dance." Jenn protested. "Now, I could go for a big thick juicy steak at the La Saluda," Jenn joked.

"No, you wouldn't if you heard Annie describe where his meat comes from."

"Doesn't matter if it's cooked like most people around here like it, unlike present company who eats steak almost uncooked." They laugh happily.

The radio had been playing quietly in the background, and Jenn suddenly reached for the volume knob and turned it up to hear Doris Day singing 'Sentimental Journey.' Except for the music, all was quiet.

As they approached Pinnacle Rock, Jenn suggested that they stop for a walk through the park. David complied by turning the big Packard into the deserted parking lot.

The park lights provided sufficient illumination, but still, David fussed over Jenn's progress up the stone steps ensuring that she did not trip on her gown. She could have managed quite well without his focused attention, but she leaned into him as if she needed the support. They sauntered through the moonscape of the park until they found a large tree guarding a rocky prominence protruding outward toward the valley below where individual efforts of single skyrockets unsuccessfully challenged the lightning-filled sky. He leaned against the tree, and she leaned into him, his hands grasping her around her waist, deliciously close to her lovely breasts. She lifted her hands to cover his and surreptitiously lifted them to cradle her precious breasts. They remained silent for long moments, absorbed by the valley beneath them, watching intermittent lightning flashes embroider lace doilies onto the green mountains below. Autumn would integrate the colors on the Maker's palate, like a child's finger painting, into a panorama of color unparalleled anywhere in the world, followed by winter displays of dazzling white that could paint the devil himself into a picture of purity. She ended the silence when as she lifted her eyes to his and queried, "A penny for your thoughts."

He pondered the intrusion of such a personal question, and for the first time, he revealed his inner self to her. "It has oft been said that home is where the heart is. You have my heart, so I must be home."

"Me too." She said.

Chapter

Forty-Four

Another glorious day ahead of him, Doctor jived down the back hall of the Clinic. Everything around him glimmered with new brightness. An irregularity in the wood wainscoting looked like a piece of Mondrian art; the old, obscure pictures on the wall shone with a new significance. Four men stood side-by-side posing for the camera: An army colonel, and three men, one fairly well dressed, but bedraggled, wearing a felt dress hat, one in coal-mining attire including a hard-hat, and a fourth, much younger than the other three, dressed in what looked like a lab coat. His curiosity piqued, he called out to Jenn to come and explain the origin of the photo and why it was on the wall of his practice. "Oh, that?" She sighed with a hint of respect. "That happened long before my time with Dr. Fields. He had just started his practice here and was asked by the army to go up on Blair Mountain to treat the wounded in a fight between what some sources claimed was around 10,000-armed coal miners and maybe 3,000 deputies and strikebreakers. It was all started by coal mine owners when

miners tried to unionize." Jenn paused and asked Doctor,
"Do we have time for this? It's a long story, and we have
patients coming before long." "No, time with you is value
time," he murmured. "Just give the edited version." "Okay,"
she purred giving him a furtive kiss on the cheek. "Jenn!"
He chided. "What are you thinking!"

"Heck, everybody but you already knows. Even your
Mom. She asked me the other day if our relationship is likely
to disrupt the Clinic."

"Don't tell me your response! Really, now. Get back to
the story."

"I'd rather drag you into your office and engage in a bit
of hanky-panky."

"Jenn! Shame on you!"

"Okay, if you're going to be a prude, I'll finish the dang
story. Many people think it started when the mine owners
sent agents to evict miners from their company houses. It
was raining at the time on a normal workday, and only the
women and children were home, but that didn't stop the
agents from throwing them and their belongings outside.
When the miners came home and saw what had happened,
they retaliated, and a gunfight started with several men on
each side killed. The whole incident became known as the
Matawan Massacre. You know where Matawan is, just over
the hill that way?"

"Yes, I recall."

"Well, the whole affair kept brewing until it finally
broke out into a wholesale war with machine guns, and even
a Gatlin gun. The US Army was finally sent in to break it
up, and most of the miners sneaked away and went home
after hiding their guns so that they could go back and get
them later. Times were scary for the miners; they even had

bombs dropped on them from airplanes, mostly filled with some chemical, maybe lye."

"And Dr. Fields was up there through the whole affair?"

"No, only a short time. When the army came, their medical people took care of both sides. Their medics were part of a peace-keeping effort and treated all wounded the same. They figured what's 'sauce for the goose is sauce for the gander' and didn't discriminate. Now, let's get to work. You have a couple of black lung patients, a woman with a boy she says his teacher thinks has something wrong with his eyes because he can't read and another woman that is about to bust with a baby and hasn't seen a doctor up until now. That's no big deal around here, but she says it hasn't been kicking like it used to."

"Let's see her first in the event we need to send her to Bluefield. Put her in room three; it's a bit more cheerful than the others."

"Yes, Doctor," replied Jenn, quickly returning to full professional mode. Doctor Cabot had gone to his reference book for some guidance when Nurse Jenn knocked, entered and said, "She's ready."

Doctor steeled himself for he knew what was coming. He tried to appear cheerful but failed when he saw an emaciated little woman before him that looked much older than the age he knew her to be. To avert his eyes even momentarily, he went straight to his writing table and feigned reading her chart. Finally, with great effort, he turned to her and asked;

"Are you in any pain, Mrs. Gates?"

"Ah don't thank frum the Baby, no."

Puzzled, Doctor asked, "Are you having other problems?

"Hit all started when mah hus'bun come home Sa'tee nahght drunk an' beat me'un two of air kids. Ah never seen him so mean drunk. He blamed me 'cause he had been fard frum his job. Ah tol' him what wif' all the machines comin' in, hit was bound ta' hap'n. Ah thank he kilt mah baby. The good lord knows ah don'need 'nother one. We can't feed the ones we got."

Doctor Cabot quickly stood from his chair, excused himself and left the room.

Jenn followed close behind and found him in the back hall in tears.

He turned to her and lamented, "I cannot believe that I am of the same species as the man who tortured that poor, pitiful woman. If there is a god why would he create such a monster? What did that poor woman do to deserve such treatment?"

Jenn tried to hug him, but he withdrew. "How can you love any man if that's what we become? How can you be sure that such behavior does not lie dormant in me? Such behavior can be possibly understood if its man against man in war, but to a poor, pitiful little woman that appears to be the soul of innocence?" He stood there against the wall for several minutes before he was able to say:

"I need to call the sheriff and have him take Mrs. Gates to the hospital in Bluefield. She needs more than we can provide here and that also serves notice to law enforcement regarding a crime of assault."

Jenn, realizing that the next step was hers, informed him that she had another patient waiting. He acknowledged her directions and walked slowly back to the exam rooms where he found a very prim, well-dressed woman sitting in the extra-room chair and an equally well-attired boy that looked to be about ten, leisurely ensconced on the exam table. The doctor glanced down at the chart to find a name and introduced himself.

"Good afternoon, Mrs. Peters and Calvin. I'm Dr. Cabot. How may I help you?" addressing his question to the apparent mother.

Mother was a real beauty. She wore quality clothing and wore it well. Her sitting posture was proper, and she spoke with a general American dialect, probably Ohio.

Instead, the boy responded. "They're all stupid."

"Calvin," his mother said calmly. "Talking like that don't help."

Dr. Cabot caught the grammatical error and almost jumped to an erroneous conclusion. Before he could respond Mom continued.

"The school says he can't hear. There's a woman that comes through here selling hearing aids who gave him a hearing test and told me he hears the tones on her hearing device and I should see a medical doctor to look at his ears in case he has wax in them. My husband stays busy and told me to get you to look at his ears, and if he needs more, we can go someplace where they have an ear specialist." She was visibly relieved.

The doctor opened a drawer and retrieved an otoscope. He turned to the boy and said, "Let's have a look at those shiny clean ears of yours."

The boy in rebellion reached up and pushed the instrument away. "Don't touch me!" he shouted.

"He don't like men," offered the mother.

"How so?" asked Doctor. "He allowed his hearing to be tested, didn't he?

"That was a woman," said mom.

"Ahaa, yes. You mentioned that. Let's see what we can do as a remedy."

He called Jenn, handed her the otoscope and said. "He doesn't like men. Will you give it a try?"

"Ah certainly will. Ah lost my dog. Maybe it's in here?"

The boy giggled and said, "No he isn't, but you can look anyhow." He sat perfectly still while she looked into his ears. He recoiled when she pumped the air bulb to see if the drums were compliant and reported the ears to be free of wax and the drums to be normal. She handed the otoscope back to David and, with a large smile, left the room.

Dr. Cabot went through the physical examination to the extent that the child would allow him. He checked the growth/weight vs. age charts. He read the school report that depended on academic performance and teacher–subjective behavioral assessment. Also, in the report was a report of an evaluation administered by the psychologist employed by the West Virginia Division of Maternal and Child Health Clinic headquartered in Charleston with a satellite Clinic held monthly at the Mercer County Health Department facilities on the Bluefield/Princeton Road. The psychologist had administered The Wechsler Intelligence Scale for Children (WISC), developed by David Wechsler in 1949 as an individually administered intelligence test (IQ) for children between the ages of 6 and 16. Doctor noted that the test reported results on two subtests organized into Verbal and Performance scales and provided scores for Verbal IQ, Performance IQ, and a Full-Scale IQ. Obvious to even a novice was the big gap between Calvin's two scores even though the Full-Scale IQ was rated as being above normal. The psychologist had written a narrative questioning the validity of the fairly new procedure that was now beginning to work its way into various programs that encounter underachievers formerly considered mentally deficient and routinely held back in school.

"Mrs. Peters, your son is healthy in all regards physically. The report from the psychologist covers a test with which I am unfamiliar. Psychology of that type is a developing field, and medical people like me are not versed in its attributes. So, here is what I suggest. I have a close friend who is about to complete his degree in a related field at the University of Virginia. I would like to take Calvin to their clinic so that we can all learn what is in the works for children like your son who has been falling through the cracks, so to speak, of the educational system of the past and today. What do you think?"

"I'm all for it, but I'll need to run it by my husband who will go along with whatever I want to do anyway. When would we go?"

"As soon as I can set it up both here and there. When you give me the go-ahead, I'll call UVA and set it up. Call me when you are ready, okay?"

"Thank you, Doctor, I feel better already. What do you think, Calvin?"

"Do they have hot dogs?" inquired Calvin focusing on something on the ceiling.

Forty-Five

Dr. Cabot was flipping through charts trying to decide whether to work on them or go for coffee. He was trying to make up his mind when Shirley stuck her head in the door and said, "They's a Mr. Jules to see you. Says he's a mortician from Welch. You wanna' talk with him?"

"I suppose. Probably about black lung. Show the gentleman in please Miss Shirley."

Shirley returned shortly with a small bald man who looked like he bore the weight of the world on his shoulders. He extended a hand to Dr. Cabot and introduced himself. Hello, Doctor, I am the owner and operator of the Welch-based Jules Mortuary. My compliments on what you have accomplished in our fair State since your arrival."

"Why, thank you, Mr. Jules. That is very kind of you. Is there something I can do for you?"

"No, Doctor. I have something that might be of interest to you." He removed an envelope from his coat pocket and handed it to Dr. Cabot, who immediately open it, looked inside and saw it was an object.

He spilled the object into his hand and exclaimed, "My heavens, it's a bullet!"

"Yes, Sir. I would guess by its size that it is a 22 short. Do you remember signing a death certificate for a man named Turner who committed suicide a while back?"

"Definitely, yes. It was a horrific scenario. Killed himself with a shotgun, I recall."

Jules looked at Doctor for a long moment and stated, "The severe damage is the result of a 12 Gage shotgun, but I don't believe that is what killed him. That bullet in your hand is what killed him. A 22 will most likely not exit the skull once it enters the space and that's why it was mixed in with the brain-salad caused by the shotgun. The shotgun was fired to make it look like suicide, I believe. However, that's just the opinion of a lowly undertaker; what do I know?"

Dr. Cabot quickly excused himself and found Jenn resupplying a treatment room. He quickly slammed the door and practically shouted, "Hoot Turner did not kill himself. He was murdered!"

Jenn immediately recognized the symptoms of a Recurrent Post Traumatic Event and began the process of talking him down. First, though, she broke an ampule of aromatic spirits of ammonia and waved it beneath his nostrils to shock him into some level of lucidity. The overpowering jolt of the 'smelling salts' had its desired effect. Although still shaken, Dr. Cabot dropped into a chair like a wet dishrag and sat quietly for several moments. Slowly, perhaps reluctantly, he raised his tear-filled eyes to Jenn and meekly said, "Thanks, I needed that," thus defusing his explosive response to the bullet and demonstrating the possibility that he was finally externalizing his post-traumatic symptomology.

The Clinic activity was busy and less than inspiring. Every day the same; black lung; more and more black lung. Today depression was hovering persuasively over his usual passion for his work. He could not clear his thoughts about Calvin Peters and autism. He had requested information from Radford College, and the topic was still in its infancy, mostly discussing the behaviors and language of the individual sufferer. In 1912 Dr. Eugene Bleuler used the term autistic as inclusive with schizophrenia. Dr. Leo Kanner in the late 1930's at Johns Hopkins University, used the term autism about a group of antisocial children. About the same time Hans Asperger, working with like-behaviors of those called autistic, was said to have *Asperger's syndrome*. Of course, the huge popularity of Freudian psychology suggested that children with autism suffered the absence of love and attention. So far, then, all that the literature told him was that the syndrome now had a name, so therefore it—was.

Dr. Cabot was mentally exhausted and decided to sneak up to the kitchen to see if Annie had the coffee on. She had some an uncanny ability always to have a fresh pot ready when he showed up in her domain. Bo trailed along behind with his usual big grin.

"Annie, I need a cup of coffee ree'ul ba'yod," he said mocking the local dialect while entering the kitchen.

"Fresh pot is ready, Your Grace," answered Annie returning the mockery.

"Annie, I just spent a most exhausting hour reading about our two young lads who cannot progress in the educational system."

"Th'ut mus'be an untol'ur'bu thang fer the Peters boy's ma an' pa,' and Jim too, Annie commiserated. "Mah l'il'un hain't smart an' ah tuk her out'n skul caus'ah was afreed that she wuz lef'out'n ever'thang. She di'n see hit but ah did. Hit's ruff on folks when chil'len hain't rahght. Yew knows wahy Jim quit school don'cha?"

"I have suspected it was mostly sociological," suggested Doctor Cabot.

"If'n that means cause of who he is, pro'bli that, too, but mostly cuz he wus book dumb but handi as a handl' on a bucket. You see that don'cha? His Pa saw hit and tuk him aut'n school an' put him ta'work a'fixin up old bicycles and sell'um fur a gud profit. If'n hit kin be fix't Jim kin dod hit. But he can't read a lick. Nosiree bobtail, not a lick."

"Annie, you ol' fox; you just opened my eyes to an unforgivable misapprehension on my part. I have been remiss in not seeing Jim as a failure of our educational system instead of a lack of familial guidance. Jim's dad took the correct action that allowed him to learn a useful trade. Jim has been a bastion of support of which I have been totally unaware. You knew it all along. You knew of Jim's value to this place. Why didn't you make me aware of his value?"

"Well, I recon'ed yew wuz smart nuf to see hit fer'u'self. He' hep'ed yew e'nuf times fer yew ta'see hit yer self."

Bo attentively followed the conversation and looked at Annie in full agreement since he had known Jim longer than anybody else.

"You are indeed correct, Miss Annie. Twice today I have been made aware of overlooked young boys with problems that might be neurological instead of intellectual doldrums. I must contact Wesley at UVA and discuss my concerns with him. My last conversation with him indicated that he had some ideas about language learning disabilities. An old professor of mine, as I recall, a Ph.D. instead of an MD, once told us that in any diagnosis, 'it's not so much what you see but what they say,' may have been prophetic."

Dr. Cabot had just given the operator the instructions to call the Speech and Hearing Center at the University of Virginia to locate Sonny Dotson. He was sitting at his desk, deep in thought, waiting when Jenn entered the room.

"A penny for your thoughts," she asked.

He looked up startled out of his reverie and blurted, "The last time you asked that question it almost evoked a proposal of marriage out of me," David replied.

They both laughed. The phone rang, and Jenn started to get up, but David put up his hand and in a 'wait' gesture and said, "Hold on. If this is the call, I'm waiting for I want you to hear it."

It was. The operator said "I have your party on the line sir. Go ahead."

"Hello, is this the speech and hearing program?"

"Yes, it is. Mary speakin'. May I help you?"

"This is Dr. David Cabot calling from Boston Knob, West Virginia and I am looking for a student from West Virginia that is enrolled there."

"We have two students from there in our program, Wesley, and Thelma."

"That would be Wesley."

"Hold on please, Doctor. He's here. I'll see if he is available."

David held the phone away from his ear and said to Jenn. "Your nephew, Sonny, has developed an interest in the use

of EEG in the study of how the brain processes sound. The last time I talked with him, he was using radio technology in the development of a special hearing test. I don't know the status of his research, but it occurred to me that we might try his ideas on Calvin. I'm convinced that he is not hearing...."
He heard the phone being picked up.

"Hello there, Doctor, where are you?"

"At home. Your Aunt Jenn is here with me. I am calling to inquire as to your research progress?"

"Perfect timing, Doctor. I have been discussing a new auditory stimulus for assessing the central auditory processing system with a psychiatrist over in the medical school. We have put together a pilot project and have been testing with some limited success. Why, what do you have in mind?"

"I have two patients that have piqued my curiosity because of the similarities in their clinical histories. Both appear to have normal hearing, but neither can read. One shows big differences in that new test called the WISC? Have you heard of it? The other is a whiz with his hands and, likewise, cannot read."

"We use the WISC here along with several other tests that measure language usage to correlate the two. Tell you what; if you can get the boys to us, we will be glad to include them in our research. It's a perfect time to visit Charlottesville. As mama always said about the fall and spring in Bluewell, 'I've never seen it so beautiful' and that's what I would say about the show Spring is putting on now. You'll want to take time to visit Monticello because 'Little Mountain' is outstanding this year. Let me know when you are coming and we will be ready. We would love to have you stay with us but we live in the old slave quarters on Fox Haven Farm, and we are crammed into our space as it is."

"Thank you, no. Your aunt, Jenn, will be along and we will stay close to the patient. The more we observe beforehand, the better informed we will be. I will write you the details. Thank you, and we will see you in Charlottesville." The doctor said and broke the connection.

As soon as the phone hit the cradle, Jenn asked, "Am I a part of 'we'?"

David smiled at her as he looked on his desk pad for a phone number. He dialed a number and waited for an answer.

"Mrs. Peters, this is Doctor Cabot. I just got off the phone with Charlottesville, and we are invited to be a part of their research any time that you are agreeable."

Mrs. Peters responded excitedly, "We are ready, and my husband has even offered us the use of the company airplane. It's a DC-3 and holds a bunch of people so we can all go and come as we please even if we have to make several trips."

David's curiosity about Mr. Peters had led him to delve into the man's source of income. He thought he had become familiar with most, if not all, of the wealth in the area since signs were on most things like mines, buildings, roads and even churches and schools. The name Peters was significant by its absence causing a bit of pause in Doctor's willingness to accept a gratuity of any kind from him. The mother's expensive apparel and her uncharacteristic dialect, yet not 'upper class' grammatically, was puzzling. He decided to have someone associated with the law look into it for him and decided to call William.

He called out to Jenn who was busy with a patient in the room next to him. "Jenn, when you are free will you please call my attorney for me?"

Sticking her head in David's office door, she said, "Your attorney? I didn't know you had an attorney?"

"Your brother, William, and you knew that! That's why I asked you to call him!"

"Oh, him?" laughed Jenn.

"Smart aleck," responded David.

Moments later Jenn called out, "Bill on line two, Sir."

"Smart aleck," David repeated not realizing he had already picked up the phone.

Bill said, "You interrupted my deeply involved legal activity just to call me a smart aleck?"

"I was speaking to your smart-mouth sister, and I have a serious matter to discuss with you."

"Ah have my lawyerly ears on so go ahead."

"Do you know a businessman named Peters?"

"Ah've heard the name but nothing specific comes to mind. Care to tell me why you are interested?"

"His son is a patient of mine for whom I have asked your nephew at UVA to arrange an evaluation. Wesley is engaged in some exciting new research at UVA. Mr. Peters has offered his plane for transporting us, along with the boy and his mother, to Charlottesville. I plan to take Jenn along since the boy relates to her."

"Oh, sure she does," teased Bill. "Ah am so very sure that's the only reason for Jenn going along."

"My heavens, William, why can't you two ever be serious?"

"Okay, seriously, I'll look into it and get back to you. Satisfied?"

"Most certainly, yes. I will await your call. I must go now as your clone is calling me to get to work."

Forty-Six

Annie and Harriet had become close friends although neither was fully free of distrust of the other's cultural background. They worked together in the kitchen where they spent many hours working and talking harmoniously. On one occasion they were duly engaged when a voice called through the screen of an open door, "Annie, air yew in thar?"

"Come on in, Ellie; door's open."

A youngish, rail-thin woman came in with a basket laden with eggs and butter. She gingerly set the wares on the counter and said, "Annie, this here is to settle air bill with Doctor. We ain't lik'ly ta have no cash money eny time soon, so maybe this'll hep until sech time as Tom git's uh'job. Hi'de'doo, Ms. Cabot. How'yew doin? They's a quilt n thar that maybe you can find a use fer. Ah been workin' on hit since Chris'mus and I done a pur'ty gud job if'n ah do say so mah self."

Mrs. Cabot, taking advantage of the use of the woman's name in Annie's initial greeting, was prepared to use a name when she offered, "We are so pleased to receive the fine produce, Ellie. Let me see that quilt. I have just the place for it in my quarters. Thank you for inquiring as to my well-being; you have paid your bill."

Mrs. Cabot delved into the basket of goodies and found unwashed, butter molded into a round shape with a flower bas-relief embossed on the top. She made sure that any product brought to the house in payment for medical services was accepted even when there was no need for them. At the bottom of the basket, folded carefully, was a lovely handmade quilt with exquisite, tiny stitches the likes of which she had never seen before. She abruptly took in a breath and exclaimed brightly, "Why this is the most beautiful bit of handwork I do believe I have ever seen! Is this your work, Ellie?"

"Yes, um," Ellie responded shyly.

Mrs. Cabot removed the quilt from the basket, shook it out to its full glory and spread it over the dining room table. She placed her hand against her cheeks, cooing her joyful satisfaction. She turned to the thin little woman and spontaneously pulled her into an embrace filled with explanatory jargon.

"Ah think she lahks hit," Annie ventured dully.

"Like it! It's the finest gift I have ever received in my entire life. I will treasure it forever!"

"Ah'm real glad," whispered Ellie. "Well, ah best be a'goin'. I left the kids by they self."

Ellie left hurriedly, and Harriet followed along with praise. When the screen door slammed, she turned to Annie and said, "I know money would help on a one-time basis, but I so wish that there is something that I could do that is more lasting."

"They is, and you jes threw hit over the table ovah thar." Annie offered.

"Really?" puzzled Harriet.

"Yep. Clear as day. Ellie cud sell all of them quilts she cud make but at a price so low hit wud do her no gud. City folks frum a'roun here com awantn' locals to make stuff fer'em but they 'spect them to mak'em fur less than yew cud git'em at Kresge's or Woolworth's if'n they had 'em. Why don'cha open a store whar all the handi'crafts here'abouts cud be sold at a fair price?"

"Annie, you are a genius!" sang Harriet!

The entrepreneurship was born. Annie and Harriet decided the first thing was to put a plan on paper so that they would enter the enterprise organized. First, they decided, a survey of the potential source of goods was needed. Annie cautioned Harriet that there would be suspicions about the process and that some method of assurances should be developed to get the flow of stock started.

Harriet had a ready solution. "I will pay for the first item from each new contributor placed in the store and then put that money into an individual account earmarked for that contributor only."

"Good idee," praised Annie. "That account book can be on display, so's that ever'body kin see just what they kin git if'n they do the same thing. Now, none of these folks have ever had a bank account, so we best allow them to draw from their accounts if'n they need hit fer food and sich."

"Okay," said Annie. "That takes care of pro'kur'munt. Let's look at fah'nances."

The next item on the business plan was financing. Harriet solved that problem post haste.

"That's my responsibility, move on. I'll start a list:"

"Next," said Harriet "is an outlet. As a perceived snob myself, I believe the best place for a market would be where the snobs go."

Annie quickly disagreed. "I think somewhar bu'tween the snobs and thartists would be best."

Mrs. Cabot, taking satisfaction in Annie's use of the word 'artist,' readily agreed. "Next item on our business plan is 'location, location, location' as the realtors are wont to say. I would venture to say that the combination of our experiences makes for a fine team."

"Yeah," said Annie. "Mah mama always did say that 'two heads'er better'n one even if one is uh sheep's head.'"

Chapter

Forty-Seven

Doctor Cabot was finishing up with a patient when Shirley, the receptionist, handed him a letter with the comment, "Th' mail jus' got here an' I thought yew would want this rah't away."

He thanked her and asked her to tell Jenn that he was going for a cup of coffee and for her to join him. He entered the kitchen, followed closely by Bo, to find Annie and Mom deep in conversation over supper preparation.

"I suppose there is no fresh coffee to be had amongst the founders of the mountain crafts executives?" He asked pleasantly.

"They'air, Dr. Smarty," Annie yelled back. "Hit jest finished perkin', and yew kin hep'ya'self, cause, as yew kin red'ly see we air busy."

"I will never impede progress," said David.

Jenn bounded into the room with her usual zeal and yelled, "Coffee hot?"

"Indeed, it is, and I have a cup ready for you since the kitchen help refuses to provide any consequential service.

I have a letter here from Wesley, about our trip, I suppose. Sit. We'll read it together."

Annie yelled, "Any excuse to sit clos'ta each other," and she and his Mom laughed with glee.

"Mind your own business," demanded David who then turned and whispered to Jenn, "She's right, you know?"

Jenn responded with a sneaked kiss and said, "Open the letter."

David pulled the letter from the envelope, placed it on the counter in front of them and began to read.

Annie and Mrs. Cabot stopped what they were doing and turned to listen.

> *Dear Dr. Cabot:*
>
> *I am very excited about your visit. I am really glad to hear that Aunt Jenn is coming. I don't recollect her ever going anywhere, vacation or otherwise. I think she will enjoy Charlottesville. She, of all of my relatives, I think, will appreciate my research since she will remember my difficulties in school. Ask her about the time I came home crying, during school hours, because the teacher had paddled my left hand with a ruler to force me to write with my right hand.*

Jenn interrupted and asked, "You remember that don't you Annie?"

"Ah shore do," replied Annie. "He wuz devs'tated an' his ma was mad as'uh wet hen."

"Don't interrupt," demanded David.

"Will if Ah want to," declared Jenn.

David resumed reading.

> *Coincidently, and serendipitously, handedness and brain dominance is part and parcel of my research springing from my clinical training in existing procedures of hearing science.*
>
> *A common question people ask me is how did I make the jump from architecture to audiology? At first blush, there appears to be a giant gap between architecture and audiology/speech/ language disorders. But the basic precept in all things new is discovery. In architecture, the task is to take a piece of raw land and design a unique edifice suited to the site. The comparison breaks down when considering the prolific information available to the budding architect via centuries of standing structures to emulate. An architect can copy something. Therefore, in architecture, the choices are, copy or create.*
>
> *In my new profession, there is little to copy and what is there, has been empirical. A few communication disorder models are available for deafness, language development, aphasia, and stuttering and speech production with neurological justification based on the invasive brain mapping that show stimulation of the right side of the brain would cause a response on the left side of the body. His book is required reading here. A second book on the required reading list is by group of Italian researchers did an experiment testing auditory*

perception to different speech signals going to each ear separately and found a way to test cortical hearing in temporal lobe tumors.

Now my reason for going into so much detail is that I have been developing a hearing test stimulus that shows different electroencephalographic (EEG) patterns for left and right-handed subjects in (EEG). The test results are positive but what is surprising in our preliminary data is that there are a disproportionate number of left-handers in our psychoneurological learning disabilities group that we have here in the UVA Speech and Hearing Clinic. Finally, our results correlate to the WISC.

We only need a week or so notice to reserve the EEG.

One other late item to report. I have been offered a position with the W. Va. Department of health. More on that when I see you.

Best regards to you and my love to Aunt Jenn.
Wes

David handed the letter to Jenn who proceeded to reread it.

"Wuz that letter in Ah'tal'yun? Ah didn't unner'stand a word of hit." Annie asked.

"No." interceded Mrs. Cabot. "It was a perfect letter that reminded me of the letters David's father used to write. Jenn, it sounds like your nephew is a very bright young man."

"That's what we all say, and he is making the transition in his education with apparent ease," interjected Dr. Cabot.

Annie spoke up again. "Air yew plan'n on havi'n him see Jim?"

"Most certainly," answered Doctor. "He is one of my reasons for the initial inquiry. He fit the subject requirements perfectly even to his left-handedness. We have plenty of room in the plane for him, and I'll pay for everything else. He will need some new clothes. We can do that here before we leave in case there is any need for tailoring."

Annie roared with laughter. "Now if'n that ain't too much sugar fer a cent? A tailor fer Jim? Hit's nuff yew agon'na git him some hep. He ain't got to be dress't up fer that. A'new par of over'hauls is all he needs."

"Annie, that boy has a fine sense of dignity. With minimal assistance, I believe he could go over to the county vocational school and successfully supplement his natural skills to the degree that he could open and manage a shop of his own. Of course, I am happy to have him here, but I do believe he would love his independence."

"He cud'nt git no more indee'pend'unt," mumbled Annie.

"Oh, and Annie, I failed to mention. We will need someone who has known Jim for most of his life to accompany us on the trip, and I suppose you will suffice."

Before Annie had time to react, David continued. "And of course, Jenn cannot possibly travel unchaperoned with an unattached male so that Mom will solve that problem. Now,

I think I have covered every contingency; sound satisfactory to you, Jenn?"

The chatter in the room drowned out her response for everyone but David. "I have never been anywhere further away than Bluefield. Did you know that? Bluefield! No more than thirty miles away! You asked me if going to Charlottesville with you and the whole damn town of Boston knob, including your mother, is satisfactory. Well. The answer is, No! HELL No, it-is-not! At first, when you told me that we were taking Mrs. Peters and Calvin, I was so excited. I thought we would be with them only during the hospital visit and we would have the rest of our time with each other. I imagined seeing the sights with you, eating out with you, maybe even going dancing with you, sleep…. Just you. Can't you get it through your thick skull that…."

David was speechless. He felt frozen to the floor. Finally, he took her in his arms, hugging her close and pleaded, "Jenn, forgive me. I am so…so…such a clod! I am so afraid of showing…offending…driving you away that I assume too much about how you might…may…Oh, dog bite it," not knowing anything else to say, he quit talking, lifted her chin and kissed her firmly, ignoring their audience, Annie, and Mom, who in unison called out, "Well it's about time!"

Mrs. Cabot excitedly exclaimed. "Okay, Annie this is what we are going to do. Do you think we can get everything together by next Sunday?"

"We shore kin," turning to Jenn and David she asked, "Do ya'll want a church weddin'?"

David practically shouted. "What a doggone minute. I did not ask Jenn to marry me."

"Ah hear'ed hit, didn' yew Harriet?"

"I most certainly did, and even if you did not, Annie and I say that was your intention. Jenn, do you want to vote?"

"Ah do. Don't those words sound good to you, David?"

"Yes, Jenn, they do. Let's make it legal: will you marry me?"

Forty-Eight

David sat on the balcony of his suite looking out over the woods. The sky above was an artist's brushing of puffy white clouds, with trimming of multiple flowering trees and bushes of many colors. Life was good. Can't see the forest for the trees? Who cares?

A voice called from below. "Penny for your thoughts," called William from below.

"Keep your penny. I am engaged to your sister because of that question," David answered with a happy laugh.

"So, I heard you proposed."

"I didn't. I was shanghaied, pure and simple, by a tribe of wild women. They are in there now plotting my doom. Come on up. I've got a thermos of Annie's coffee up here— good and hot."

Bill didn't bother to go into the house and use the steps. Instead, he climbed a trellis covered with vivid red roses, hopped onto the balcony and inquired, "Where's the coffee?" David pointing said, "in there."

"What's the good news?" Bill inquired.

"Really and truly, the exceptionally good news is that you are going to be my brother-in-law."

"That's good news?"

"As I have often heard hereabouts, does a bear poop in the woods?"

"Ain't the way I heard it," Bill said.

"I'm not vulgar like you," David said.

"Yeah, I forgot. You are of gentility," Bill said.

"You win, as always," David conceded. "What's new?"

"I have a dossier on your plane-man."

David responded with a querulous glance. "Dossier is it? Sounds sinister."

"I would say so. It appears that organized crime has been doing some probing in the area concerned with drugs, specifically marijuana."

"What does that have to do with Peters?" David inquired.

"The plane he has access to is registered with the FAA under a corporation operating out of Cincinnati that deals in a host of unexplained businesses. I dug as far as I could and found a connection between a couple of the board members of a mining company and real estate. That's about as far as I got that I can hang my hat on."

"So, you put two and two together and came up with a conspiracy, am I correct? David asked.

"Most likely," Bill replied.

There was a long period of silence while the two sat fraternally. Ultimately Bill spoke. "When's the wedding?" He inquired.

"Don't know. The female syndicate here hasn't informed me yet. All I know, I was told that I proposed and 'they' accepted. Other than that, I'm on standby."

"Better that way. Just go along; it'll work out."

"Indeed."

William took his leave abandoning David to his musing. Almost immediately after he left another voice called from below the balcony.

"Hey, Doctor, it's Sheriff Hare. Gotta minute ta talk? Bill said you're not doing anything."

"Why of course, Sheriff. Go on in through the sunroom, and I'll meet you in the kitchen for coffee and a viable substitute for a donut."

Doctor descended the steps just as the Sheriff entered the sunroom. They performed the ritual handshake, and greetings and Doctor gestured toward the kitchen.

"Annie," he said. "We have a visitor from the law enforcement community whom I would venture to say is already among your acquaintances?"

Annie looked up from the oven in which she was looking and gleefully declared. "Little Sonny Hare. Course ah know him, ah remember th' day his wuz born. His ma is salt'a th'earth people and a gud quilter' too. Coffees' hot and ah got goodies comin' out'a the oven. Sit'cha self-down and ah'll git'em fur ya," she ordered as she retrieved the coffee pot and cups.

Dr. Cabot inquired tentatively. "Is every boy around here named Sonny/."

"Pert near," said Annie. "Any Mom aron' cud go ta'th door an' yell 'Sonny, supper's ready' and ever' kid in the neighborhood wud com runnin'. Not only that, they'd be welcome at th'table too."

"That's' right," added the sheriff. "There was five of us named Sonny within yellin' distance of all of our houses. One of those Sonny's got a new name one time when he went in one of the poorest families' house while they were eatin.' Sonny said, 'Ah see ya'll air finally down'ta nothin' but jelly'un bread.' After that, his name, for that family anyhow, was 'jelly bread' later shortened to 'Jelly' that stuck with him forever."

Everybody joined in a healthy laugh, and Sheriff turned to Doctor and asked, "Got a minute?"

Both sat down at the table and no one spoke until Annie had poured coffee and placed a platter of oatmeal cookies in front of them leaving them with the comment, "Now ah've got work'ta do. Ya'll go'ahead and enjoy."

Sheriff broke the ice by speaking first. "Doctor, it ain't no coincidence my showing up about the same time as Bill. He is your lawyer, ain't he? Never mind, none'a my business actu'ly. What is mah business is why he was lookin' into the business of a man named Peters for you?"

Doctor Cabot bristled momentarily but decided to answer a question with a question. "That question would suggest that Mr. Peters is a concern of yours."

Sheriff looked short of a response. He ducked his head and scratched his temple, finally, he said, "We ain't sure what he does, and we're lookin' into 'it."

"Are you suggesting that he might be engaged in shady endeavors?" asked Doctor Cabot.

"Well…. yeah, you could say that. Okay. Here goes. Tit for tat. Let's draw a profile of this man. He shows up and all of a sudden, my officers see an increase in unusual activity such as the number of out-of-state license plates. We are beginnin' to see an increase in prescription drugs for pain, and we're seein' more amphetamine and barbiturate usage. At the same time, Peters shows up with no visible means of support. Am I crying wolf? We are wondering, so why are you?"

"My dear sheriff..." Doctor bristled as his first inclination was to tell the officer that it was not of his affair but decided cooperation would serve his own interest. Mr. Peters' son is a patient of mine. Possible answers to the nature of his disorder are lacking here in our medical community, and I have referred him to the University of Virginia. His visit there avails me of a continuing education opportunity, and I am making plans to be at Charlottesville to observe the evaluation. Mr. Peters has access to a sizeable aircraft in which he intends to transport his son and the son's mother to the UVA Hospital for evaluation. Since there will be excess seating in the plane, Mr. Peters has generously offered me and anyone I wish to accompany me, to ride along. Now, since the receipt of gifts and accommodations in most cases is considered unethical, and particularly so if those favors may be benefits of ill-gotten gains, I simply had my attorney check into the source of that offered gift to cover my ethical butt, as William so colorfully put it." The doctor concluded with a look of determination and closed the discussion.

"Ah sure understand, and I won't bother you on that topic again. Ah do advise you to get to Charlottesville some other way since we have doubts about what might be on that plane besides passengers."

For the first-time realization hit. Dr. Cabot's boorishness diminished as he realized that the sheriff was concerned about him. "Thank you, Sheriff. Why didn't you come out and warn me rather than beat about the bush?"

"We sheriffs have ethics too, you know. Ah had to let you give me a reason to warn you without unethically revealin' something about Mr. Peters. What if he's innocent; maybe he is and maybe he ain't. Maybe we'll never know."

Sheriff Hare sat quietly for a very long time with his elbows resting on his knees, just looking at nothing on the floor. Slowly he sat up straight and looked over Doctor's shoulder focusing on nothing behind him.

"Doctor Cabot, I gotta' another problem that you might help me solve.

"We found a young man drowned in Bluestone Lake on the West Virginia side where the lake follows the West Virginia line for about two miles in Mercer County, and that puts it in my jurisdiction. We ain't got no reason to believe it's anything but accidental."

Dr. Cabot interrupted Hare's questioning, "I don't see where this concerns me?"

"Oh, Ah think it does," the sheriff responded emphatically.

"He had no identification on him. All we got is this wad of dirty paper found in his shirt pocket. Can you tell us anything about it?" handing the 'evidence' to Doctor Cabot.

The doctor took the paper and unfolded it carefully. The paper had been torn leaving only part of a hand-written message: *"en contactant Captian Cabot à Bluefield."*

Doctor Cabot examined the filthy piece of paper and read it again. Puzzled he said, "It's in French translated loosely as 'by contacting Captian Cabot in Bluefield.' Means nothing to me," he said.

"But that last name is either yours or the same as yours. Could it be you?"

"As I just said. Means nothing to me. Sorry. Besides, I was a Major. Yet, in the back of my mind.......? No, nothing. If I make any sense of it, I'll give you a call," finalizing the conversation. Dr. Cabot saw the sheriff to the door and bade his goodbyes. He returned to the kitchen and suddenly remembered the bullet and called out, "Sheriff, wait a minute. I have something for you."

The Sheriff returned to the kitchen and stood waiting while Doctor hasty retreated to his office in the Clinic. He dug into the top desk drawer where he probably had tossed the bullet on the day the mortician had given it to him. Readily recovering the questionable missile, he hastily returned to the kitchen and the Sheriff, who was discussing gardening with Annie.

He handed the bullet to Sheriff Hare with the explanation, "A local man, name of Turner, reportedly committed suicide up in Butt Hollow a few months back. I signed his death certificate listing 'suicide' as the cause of death. That bullet suggests otherwise. Mr. Jules, the Welch Mortician who prepared Mr. Turner for burial, found this mixed with the double ought buckshot falling from the deceased's skull. He took it to the McDowell County sheriff and told him to give it to Mercer County officials, so he felt no obligation to do anything with it. He was traveling by here one day and gave it to me thinking I would know what to do with it. I, at this moment, present you with conceivable evidence to a murder, thus discharging myself of the weight of legal responsibility."

Sheriff Hare laughed at Doctor's declaration and responded, "You could well be right. Now, finding the gun that fired the bullet is all we have to do. Ya'll take care now, ya hear?" waving as he departed.

Doctor found his cup and went for a coffee refill. "Annie," he said, "I think I have painted myself into the proverbial corner. I am now engaged to be married, a potential participant in criminal activity, getting ready to embark on a research mission in autism, and probably a recruit in a new mountain artist gift outlet. Can I handle all of that and practice medicine too?"

"Aw boy, don't blow up ever'day thangs in'ta problems. They're too small to be seen on a gallopin' horse."

"You are probably correct Annie. Why should I burden you with my perceived problems?"

"Time'll tell; time'll tell," Annie prophesized.

Chapter

Forty-Nine

Dr. Cabot was settled into the protective cocoon of the kitchen with a fresh cup of morning coffee' just placed in front of him by Annie, and the 'on your porch before breakfast' newspaper—The Bluefield Daily Telegraph—when Jenn barged into the room with a dour look on her face.

With little fanfare and no hesitation, she rudely declared, "The weddin' is off!"

Annie reacted first: "What in tarnation you rantin' uh'bout girl? Even if'n hit's th truth that ain't no way of goin' bout uh'tellin' hit!"

"Ahm sorry Miss Annie," she apologized. "The mother of that boy we scheduled at The University of Virginia just called and canceled everything."

Dr. Cabot, having been dumbly monitoring the exchange up that point, finally reacted. "Did she give a reason?"

"Something about her husband 'putting a stop to it."

"Well, that concerns me about the boy, but it is the father's decision to make…in Annie's words, it's a fly in the ointment but is only a brief hindrance as far as the wedding is concerned. We will have it right here." Doctor said unenthusiastically. "It will be even better since we can invite more people and have a gargantuan party."

"Glory be," exclaimed Annie. "That's what ah hoped fur in the first place. Jenny, me and yore Ma will put on the best weddin' this here part'a th'woods has ever done see'd. We'll git yore brother's band to play th'music. Won't that be good, Jenn?"

Jenn was not listening. Her mind was on Jim. He had been reluctant at first to be a part of the Charlottesville 'study,' but as the time for the trip became shorter, he was, in his words, rarin' t'go.' Finally, she turned to leave and distractedly said, "I'll see you when you're ready to see patients."

Dr. Cabot took longer than usual at the breakfast table dreading facing Nurse Jenn and her bitter-tongue of anger which she would take out on him, as usual. Finally, with a big sigh, he rose from the table, thanked Annie for another fine supply of buckwheat pancakes and dragged himself to the Clinic with faithful Bo, in a similar apparent state of mind, following closely on his heels.

Jenn's strong feeling that she had let Jim down with the Charlottesville cancellation continued to plague her even though that evaluation would have offered nothing toward career training. She had considered several possibilities, but the one she was actively pursuing was Bluefield State

College was introducing two-year certificate programs as well as specially scheduled single semester job training courses. However, Jim's academic preparation, as well as his questionable intellectual level, probably precluded any academic choice.

Jenn's search led her to the State Unemployment Office where she found recently introduced Federal employment and training programs where the Area Redevelopment Act provided subsidized training to workers in depressed areas. Further, The Economic Opportunity Act created an array of new employment evaluation and job training programs, including Job Corps. She found Welch to be a hub of those opportunities, and a decision was made, pending Jim's acceptance, of course. She was pleased to find that for the trade schooling there were no educational prerequisites. However, the applicant needed to pass an *age-level verbal-skills test of understanding* she took to mean that the student needed to have the ability to follow normal verbal instructions. That, Jim, could do easily.

Chapter

Fifty

One cold and blustery day, somewhere north of Morgantown, West Virginia near the Township of Connellsville, Pennsylvania, a history-changing meeting in the annals of organized crime took place—particularly in the southern Appalachian Mountains—since the purpose of the enclave was to discuss territorial rights of the rapidly changing crime market. Moonshine was losing its luster as the illegal mood-altering drugs extended their cruel tentacles into chronic poverty where hope remained. Marijuana was becoming an ideal cash crop since it was a native plant of the mountains, often growing wild amongst the rhododendron, dogwood, chinquapins, ginseng, and trillium. Change was on the march, and organized crime was right instep.

The delegates of the meeting were a heterogeneous representation of locales and peoples quite different from any other organization with similar goals. A newcomer to the alliance sat reverently aside of the assemblage studiously acquiring an image for himself. What he saw were demigods of crime attired in the 'robes' of power purchased from the best shops but lacking 'taste' in their sleaziness. He took note of this, and since he was doing forced labor, he decided he would stay with off-the-rack garments to reduce identification. His work environment was among simple folks who scoffed at people who 'put on airs' and generally were distrustful of 'outsiders.' He had observed the vehicles in which the other participants had arrived, and he decided that he would stick to his plain ol' Studebaker. He thought this meeting was doing a good job of teaching him what he should not be. He had arrived at this meeting in a 'company' plane, and he decided that its use placed him too much in the public eye and that, too, was detrimental to his ability to gain the trust of the independent people with whom he must develop an involuntary working relationship.

He was first and foremost, an accountant. He had studied his market and found a changing Southern culture; Appalachian moonshiners were following the market and switching to marijuana. The 'Feds' were finding more marijuana patches than moonshine stills. In one location agents found only 90 stills, down from 1,200, while running into 20 patches of marijuana ironically planted in rows with corn. His research showed that moonshine was a local product generally transported by 'runners' in modified automobiles. Marijuana, on the other hand, was a national market even finding acceptance as a medicinal product. As the demand for weed grew, so did the demand for a more potent product leading to the 'Mexican connection' providing stronger stuff to mix with the poorer quality mountain-grown marijuana. His job was to Investigate this more marketable product for the 'mob.' But, he had a problem; most of his potential growers were from fundamental Christian backgrounds where moonshining was considered government meddling having nothing to do with religion. Drugs? A whole different ballgame.

Fifty-One

The Field Mansion was abuzz with excited activity as the board of directors, and craft providers of the Community Arts Cooperative celebrated the acquisition of a rent-free building visible from Route 52 in Simmons that was once a company store. They decided to call their new store The Mountain Crafts Company Store. The location was near perfect since the boundaries of Bramwell, Freeman and Simmons were fuzzy at best. Route 52 heading north, dropped down the mountainside from Pinnacle rock and confronted the Bluestone at the mountain's foot. The road to Bramwell cut sharply and uphill with its modern high school appearing to the left just a short drive west. Freeman and Simmons sat a stone's throw further up on the banks of the Bluestone River. The community of Bluewell was four miles south, halfway between Bramwell and Bluefield. Speculation by some suggested that Bluewell got its name by taking the first part of Bluefield and the second part of Bramwell as a credit for being a 'half-way' point between the two.

Doctor, Jenn, and Bill sat on the balcony of the living room hidden by quilts. Down below there were Antimacassars, doilies, afghans, hot pads, lace-edged towels, trivets, coal-carved statuettes, wooden toys, stools, chairs, birdhouses, yard-art of all kinds and much, much more. All lovingly created for the new store. The balcony sitters were ignored by Annie, Mom and the gaggle of ecstatic folk artist thoroughly enjoying their role as creators of the art scattered about the large living room.

Bill spoke: "Jenn, did you know that the graves of our grandparents on Papa's side of the family are just east of Simmons?"

"What? No, I didn't. Wonder how come I didn't? How is it that you knew, and I didn't?"

"The reason, I guess, is that before I went into the army, I used to take Papa over there to clear the graves. Sonny took over when I was drafted until he went into the air force and by then Papa wasn't able to do it anymore. Sonny told me he tried to find the place once by himself, but the location eluded him. I guess they're still there. I drove over there myself a time or two, but it's just too grown over with weeds and trees along there to get even an idea where it might be. Earth to earth, I suppose. Their burial there is a mystery to me. The only tie that I know of about the area is that Aunt Nan lived out that way."

David perked up and said. "Hey Jenn, that's where you took me to see your aunt across the swinging bridge, isn't it? I'll always remember chasing you down the railroad tracks…." he exclaimed before he realized what he was saying and turned a vivid red in embarrassment.

Bill, never one to miss an opportunity to tease David, latched on to the comment by declaring, "Oh, so Simmons Road is now lover's lane?"

Jenn joined in gleefully, "He finally got up enough gumption to realize that I was more than an office nurse to him. That's where I got my first real kiss from Dr. proper."

David jumped up from his chair and headed for the kitchen gruffly pronouncing, "I was chasing you because of your abominable behavior on that dangling footpath. You scared the wits out of me by willfully swaying that thing so dangerously. I…. Oh, I cannot win with the two of you against me. I need a cup of coffee." He left with laughter striking him in the back. As he entered the kitchen, he caught a glimpse of a police car pulling into the back entrance of the house. He walked back through the sunroom to meet Sheriff Hare at the door who entered and helped himself to coffee.

"Doctor" the sheriff began, "I need your help. It's no small request and ah'd not blame you if you told me that I've become plum' addled. Ah want to deputize you."

The room fell silent. Doctor was speechless. He finally leaned forward and opened his hands in a questioning gesture. "You…want to deputize…Me?" he inquired incredulously. "Why, in heavens name?"

Sheriff inhaled deeply, leaned back in his chair and huffed out his breath before saying: "It's a long story."

"I am intently listening," exclaimed Doctor.

"I'll start by askin' you if you recall the piece of paper I showed you that had 'En contactant le Capitaine Cabot à Bluefield' written on it? Pardon my French."

"Don't be ridiculous, Of course, I do. Go on." Doctor testily responded.

"Well, first of all, we found that item on the young man found drowned in Bluestone dam. Or at least we thought he had drowned in the dam. An autopsy showed he had drowned in chlorinated water, not water from the lake."

Dr. Cabot tried to interrupt. "I do not see —"

"Just listen to me...please. You and your family are in danger if you don't follow along with me and maybe if you do. Organized crime, Ah don't mean a few moonshiners from a bunch of relatives, Ah'm talking about Chicago, Pittsburg, and places like that where the nasty stuff goes on; you know what Ah mean since you're a big city boy. Are you with me so far?" the Sheriff inquired.

"Yes, but..."

"Ah ain't finished," the sheriff continued. "The potential is such that the Governor issued an executive order creatin' a secret unit of the State Police sent out of State to study with mob crime specialists who have been dealin' with it for many years. Part of that was because West Virginia has only had to deal with locals, mostly in the liquor business, and partly because honesty in the local police departments ain't the best when it comes to moonshinin'. Any effort to try to change the way we do business as cops will meet with the hillbilly stubbornness that is a part of us; change is a tough row to hoe in these parts. So, while we're runnin' around makin' and peddlin' moonshine, the savvy outsiders see a growing market for far more evil things such as drugs. We hear a lot about the popularity of marijuana but here in the mountains, it ain't anything new. Heck, people here have been using it for asthma for years. You don't need to go to no crime boss to buy it; it grows everywhere around here, but it likes the side of roads makin' it easy to pick. It ain't considered no worse than Cubeb that helps people with asthma, and people wonder why all the hullabaloo over a dang 'ditch weed.'"

Sheriff stopped to catch his breath and Doctor interjected a comment. "We briefly studied the benefits of Cubeb in medical school. It never really caught on."

Hare ignored him and continued. The problem now is that they're startin' to bring in the strong stuff and breedin' it with the prolific natural stuff here creatin' a whole new very valuable product. The people doin' this ain't locals but major crime syndicates lacking the morals of the true mountaineer. Nobody wants that, least of all my people."

"I still don't see my role in any of this," said Doctor Cabot.

"Ah'm getting' to that," the sheriff continued. "Ah contacted the sheriffs of Giles and Bland Counties, both very long-time, dependable and ethical friends of mine from way back. I met with them in Bluefield 'cause it's kinda a central location for one thing, and another is Ah don't feel secure using the phone anymore. I told them about the water in our mystery man's lungs and it maybe not bein' an accident. Neither was surprised because of strange behavior in their jurisdictions. Now I told them about the note we found and that I planned to start an investigation about its source. Ah didn't give them details about the content of the note or hints as to how Ah was goin' to go about it but they agreed that we should not involve any local authorities in any investigation. We are going' to work together in documentin' unusual doin's in our three counties. We discussed the geographical importance of our counties—and the jurisdictional restrictions caused by state lines— because of the many roads going in all directions without passing' through any big cities and the number of airports we have available. We have set up our own Tri-county Crime Task Force and...that brings me to you. First, you already have skin in the game and second what better person to freely mingle with all sorts of people but a doctor."

"I sup'ose ya'll hav'uh plan for me?" Doctor whined pretending defeat, well aware that he might as well 'go with the flow.'

"Most certainly, my dear fellow. We have considered your options and have drafted the following scenario, whuther you lah'k hit er not," Sheriff Hare shot back in kind.

Fifty-Two

The DC-3 followed a straight approach over the curvaceous New River into the New River Valley Airport (NRVA) at Dublin, Virginia. The plane had departed Joseph A Hardy Airport at Connellsville, Pennsylvania earlier in the day with no flight plan and three passengers aboard. The DC-3 landed smoothly, taxied to the gate area and did a one-eighty before coming to a stop. The steps momentarily dropped disgorging one passenger who quickly passed through the small empty terminal to a waiting car that did not stop for the passenger to enter.

The driver spoke first. "How did it go."

"Ridiculous," replied the passenger. "They're still a bunch of Capone wannabees. Thank goodness we're pretty much on our down here and that's the way I like it. Take the back-way home."

The 'back-way' avoided major roads. The NRVA was on RT 100 north of Dublin. Going north to Poplar Hill and west on the Wilderness road led to RT 52 to Bluefield and north the coal fields beyond or south to his farm home.

By staying on RT 100 to Pearisburg, one could also avoid major roads in getting to the coals fields. Another reason for using the NRVA had to do with an Executive Order issued by the governor of West Virginia. A secret—short-lived secret as it turned out—recently established tactical strike force (TSF) made up of selected state troopers to combat the illegal manufacture, sale, transportation, and use of narcotics was now in place. The TSF also collected and disseminated intelligence on organized crime activity throughout the State. All airports in West Virginia were under surveillance including Bluefield and Beckley.

Consequently, the mobs were reducing the size of their aircraft to smaller planes that could land on any flat field surreptitiously; hence reduced payloads occurred, but that was just a price of doing business. Peters was happy with this since this reduced the number of mob-provided soldiers. He was living on a rented farm in Bland County, Virginia just south of Rocky Gap where he maintained a grass runway kept in tip-top shape as a part of his lawn thus provided a resource if there was a need for a plane.

Chapter

Fifty-Three

It was mid-October. The foliage had been spectacular. The doctor business was booming so much so that Doctor Cabot was becoming bored with general practice as his only activity. Every day the same people with the same problems highlighted by men dying, hopelessly, with black lung. He longed for some variety; maybe some surgery? After all, he was a trained surgeon with extraordinary experience in Korea at the MASH unit. He had been encouraged repeatedly by fellow members of the Mercer County Medical Association to accept the proffered privileges at both Bluefield hospitals. Finally, he capitulated and was now spending one day a week in surgery that, as it happened, was good for him and his practice. He was wool-gathering at his desk after a very busy day of black lung, sore throats, a broken arm and other routine cuts and bruises when Jenn briskly entered his office without knocking as she was wont to do and to which he was not, in the least, annoyed. She plopped herself in the chair beside his desk and addressed him in a very business-like manner.

"I have a serious question for you." She said.

"I know" he pleaded. "I am so sorry about the wedding …."

"Nah, not that," she interrupted. "I got you hooked so Ah'm not worried about that.

It'll happen soon enough. What Ah'm wondering about is the large amount of money someone is spending to get the Company Store up and runnin.' Your Mom had agreed to provide the funds for a modest start, but this gung-ho investment from an unknown source is too good to believe. Annie, your Mom and a host of excited mountain folks are hustling to stock a restored large building into a first-class retail outlet. It has 'place to go' written all over it after the article in the Telegraph was picked up by the Associated Press. Oh, Ah'm happy as a lark about it. People from all around are comin' in and payin' outlandish prices for whatever is available no matter the quality. Oh, Ah'm not saying that any of the work is shoddy but, let's face it, some are better than others and some of it, well, really, is just junk…no, not junk…frivolous? Haven't you wondered?"

David could not resist laughing as he responded. "I have indeed puzzled over the situation. I have even entertained the possibility of money laundering but quickly dismissed that as a big city activity."

"Money laundering?" Jenn questioned. "What's that?"

"Hum. Let me see how I can explain it. Okay, try this. Organized crime in big cities generate a large amount of ill-gotten cash, say in drugs or illegal liquor. That money is not spendable because it has no legal source of record. So, the crooks 'buy' legal businesses and put the ill-gotten gains in the cash register, counting it as part of the day's profits and, then legally, putting it in the bank. Dirty money into clean money—hence laundered money. Got it?"

"Yeah, Ah got it." Said Jenn. "But how could money be laundered through a non-profit like the Company Store since the crook doesn't get any of the passed through cash?"

"Maybe it buys goodwill," opined David.

Fifty-Four

Doctor Cabot sat at his desk with his head resting in the cradle of his hands and his elbows tripoded on the desk, when that most beautiful voice in his world requested a "penny for your thoughts." He raised his head to look at her and felt that familiar never-ending heart-leap reserved for her. He soaked in her loveliness for more than a brief moment before responding to her question. Then he spoke.

"I cannot get that note out of my mind."

"What note?"

"You know; the one the sheriff continues to nag me about; the one found on the drowned young man? Out of the blue, awake or asleep, there appears a brief glimpse of a scene-past, but the instant I try to focus, it's gone. The more I think about it the note is personal; it is addressed only to me, and I should recognize it. Several times in the past three or four weeks an image of a time or place briefly appeared but, like a butterfly, flitted away. The vague, fuzzy edges of the apparition are, I don't know, maybe from a suppressed memory?"

"It'll come," suggested Jenny as she edged around the desk to give him a quick kiss on top of his balding head, "But, I came in here with something else on my mind."

"That tone of voice and faraway look generally portends a disruption of my stolid existence, am I correct? May I assume that the delay in our nuptials is bearing on your mind?"

"Nuptials? What? Heck no. Why do you always a think Ah'm in a such a big rush to marry you? Heck, I ain't even sure I like you enough to call you a friend, much less a husband, Yuck," she jokingly declared.

"Well, as your rejected fiancé I am properly scorned, and I fall before you humbly seeking a restoration of your good graces," he pleaded.

"Aw hush up. I came in with a serious concern, and you have turned the conversation into a Burns and Allen comedy bit. Now listen to me, will you?"

David realized her seriousness, got up, encased her in his arms, gave her a more than an adequate kiss, and pleaded. "Forgive me, my love. Let's go get a cup of coffee, and I promise you my total and undivided attention."

In the kitchen they found the usual unexplained, perpetually fresh, pot of coffee and equally predictable 'hot-out-of-the-oven' treats. This time, miniature popovers. Instead of sitting at the kitchen counter, as usual, David led the way to the living room.

After the were situated David softly said, "Go."

"My upbringin' was with church-goin' parents, as you already know, and I have missed that in my life. It's mostly my fault since I have been afraid to say anything about church knowin' that your religious experience was in a fancy big city 'proper' church where the preacher was called 'priest' at church and 'father' everywhere else. I remember the time you went to church here with Bill and how you the service irritated you. Now, I can't give an appraisal of a liturgical church because I never been to one. Here in the mountains, misunderstanding of the Catholic Church is such that my understanding of anything liturgical is tainted; you understand?"

David started to speak. "Jenn...."

"No, wait a minute. Let me finish. Ah'm not done yet."

"Okay, let me warm my coffee, and you will still have my full attention, and, if the truth be known, my understanding. Be right back my most precious one," David said as he kissed Jenn gently on the mouth on his way out.

David went in search of his mother. He found her and Annie working on the Company Store inventory. Why he sought his mother he did not know; probably in the back of his mind, she could provide something that he could say to Jenn? He intended to ask her how to approach the apparent...gap?... between different religious backgrounds, but he found that he did not know what question to ask. Both women looked at him expectantly. He stared back and finally said, "Never mind," and turned to leave.

His mother was the first to speak. "David, wait. You are concerned. Tell us what it is. You will be addressing the top brains of the court of mediocre advice in this household."

Annie piped up with her input by offering, "You bet'chem Red Ryder. Gud ad 'vice and hit's cheap. Have we ever led you astray?"

"Mom, Miss Annie, this is no laughing matter. Jenn has confronted me with the desire to get involved in...well... going to church. What do I tell her? We grew up in such differing philosophical settings that I do not see a middle ground."

Annie took the challenge first. "Tel'me, my lad. What's the purpose of religion anyway?"

David mulled the question for a brief period and hesitantly responded, "salvation?" vaguely recalling something from his Episcopal catechism as a boy.

"Rah't cha'air," exclaimed Annie as his mom nodded enthusiastically.

"And salvation is'uh heap lahk butter" Annie reasoned. "Yew git butter frum milk frum all kinda cows, black, white, brown, Holstein, Jersey, but hit don't matter none, cuz hit's still butter after hit's churned. Most rele'juns air 'bout the same in that respect. Oh, some air fancy with the preacher wearin' robes and big hats, readin' out of big ol bibles, held up by'uh little boy wearin ' a nightgown, with the congega'shun bouncin' up and down, sayin' things lahk 'and also with you,' while simpl'r ones jest git down to redin' the bible, preachin' 'uh'bout hit and sayin' a prayer in thar' own words about somethin' goin' on local, lahk the need fur rain, or askin' God to take ker of a sol'chur boys, cause we air always in'a war sum place or 'nother. Anyhow, what's important is they're all gittin' to the same point, mostly about Jesus, ain't they?"

Mom, nodding her head vigorously, put the exclamation point on Annie's soliloquy by adding, "Amen, as they say in your church, Annie."

David marveled at the bond that had matured between the two since his Mom had moved into the Fields Mansion.

"But Annie," pleaded David, "what am I to do? I am an intellectual snob; you know that all too well; Early childhood experience shaped both of our religious attitudes.

Intellectually, the choice of religion and consequentially the church one attends is not a matter of self-determination but rather a part of the historical heritage. Mine was high church. Now, I have considerable doubt about the relevance of the church altogether, liturgical or otherwise, and their declaration of faith stated in 'creeds' that are contrary to my intellect that stands in the face of new knowledge that most churches seem to ignore in favor of 'tradition' based on archaic protocols. I must admit that I lean towards the simplicity of Jenn's teachings since they do leave room for critical thinking outside the parameters of the rigidity of the liturgy."

"Unfort'nate," Annie offered, "they all seem ta'have some petty ah'dees 'bout which'ns rah't and which'ns wrong, lah'k sprank'lin or 'e'murshun, but all that stuff kin be ignored if'n hit's jus' not turn't into an issue. The important thang is if'n Jesus Christ is the central focus all th'time. If'n He ain,t then do what Jesus told His disciples, and Ah'm not just talkin' about the twelve original one's, but us too, He told them, in Mathew 10-14 to 'shake the dust off'n your feet and move on.'"

"Mom...Miss Annie...the two of you comprise an unbeatable team. Thank you. I know what to do now," said David as he rushed out of the room to continue his conversation with Jenn.

He found her, more composed, sitting primly on the sofa patting her eyes with a dainty lace handkerchief. He sat beside her, gently taking her hand in his and spoke.

"Jenn, I have been a dunce; no not just a dunce, but an arrogant dunce. What I know about religion will not fill a thimble. I went to church on Sunday Morning with my parents because it was the proper thing to do in Boston.

I was required to remain silent, and motionless through a dreary, mind-numbing, monotonous ritual that never deviated except for the addition of equally boring liturgical-season changes that lengthened the torture I endured. I suffered through the catechism..."

Jenn interrupted him in mid-sentence stating, "I know that catechism is a class that Catholic Children because We rode buses to Junior High School with Italian kids. I have always wondered what it was."

"During the Protestant Reformation," David began, "you know what that was?" He inquired of Jenn.

"Well yes, Ah'm not that ignorant." protested Jenn. "If Ah didn't learn it in Sunday school or bible class in junior high, I read about it in romance novels that we passed around during nurse's training. People were becoming unhappy with how management of the Catholic Church and several theologians took them to task. The dissenters were excommunicated, just in case you don't know, that means thrown out..."

"I know what it means, Miss Smarty Pants," David laughed. "Wait a minute." He backtracked. "Did you say bible class in school?"

"Ah did, and it was fun. It was a required course unless you were exempt for religious reasons such as being a Jew. There was an itinerant teacher that did nothin' else. She used a flannel board as a visual aid to illustrate the stories. In particular Ah remember the lessons on the reformation not associated with the major people like Luther but by what she called 'The Radical Reformation' that were called Anabaptist and Mennonites and...maybe Quakers?... She said that their attitudes were the foundation of most of the fundamental American churches. That' about all I know about it."

"That, my dearest, is an amazingly detailed summary of something of which I know little. Admitting that, I have an idea for an exploratory plan. Both of us have science-based professions. We never make a diagnosis without a case history and basic physical, do we?"

"Yeess...?" replied Jenn hesitantly. "Go on."

"Well then, it appears to me that you are longing for a church affiliation and you think I am too snobbish to approve of what's available locally."

"Now hol' on jus' a dog'gone minute mister better'en-anybody-else. Don't you go puttin' words in mah mouth!" Jenn, reverting to her hill-country dialect in her anger.

"Whoa, whoa," rejoined David. "No offense intended; just stating a fact. Didn't I admit that I am a snob."

"Well, yes but you did infer that local churches are... well...unacceptable...?"

"I implied no such thing, but that could be true if we took an objective look at all of the possibilities? A diagnosis, as it were?"

"Ah accept your apology."

"I did not apologize."

"Yes, you did. And I accepted it. Move on."

David laughed heartily and said, "I love you, you stubborn, beautiful Hillbilly."

"Ah ain't no hillbilly."

"Yes, you are."

"No, ah ain't, but ah accept your compliment about bein' beautiful. I am ain't Ah?" as Jenn leaned into David seductively. "Wanna' fool around?"

"This ain't workin'" David laughingly surrendered. "We *will* solve the church problem. Jes' yew wait'un see."

"Yeah, but right now I am not focusing on church, can'cha tell?"

Chapter

Fifty-Five

Dr. Cabot was surprised, after a very tiring day in the Clinic, to find Sheriff Hare sitting at the kitchen table having coffee with Jim. He said nothing as he moved to Annie's perpetually-fresh coffee pot and poured himself a steaming mug of the world's best. He was preparing himself for what he knew was coming.

"Jim, have you been properly catering to our Chief County Law Enforcement Officer?"

"If'un yew mean am Ah bein' nice to the sheriff, then, yes sir."

"And Sheriff, have you been heeding to the sage advice of one of my most true and trusted advisors?"

"Ah have, and he tells me things are relatively stable here'bouts. But he also confides in me that there are new people workin' the area in shady-like activities. You know anything about that?"

"Not at all. I am much too engaged in the practice of primeval medicine here in Utopia. What goes on amongst the proletariat is of minimal consequence when compared to the carnage created in the name of industrial progress by the absentee coal barons," Doctor Cabot lamented.

"Doctor David, ah do d'clare that you air the mos' confoundin' talker Ah ever did see. What the heck did yew jus' say?" Jim inquired.

Sheriff Hare laughed and said, "Jim, he's just bein' sarcastic."

"That don't hep none," pouted Jim.

"Okay, Sheriff, you are most certainly not here for congenial banter, what's on your agenda? Asked Doctor.

"What I have to say is a bit sensitive…"

"Hey, I ken tak'uh hint," mumbled Jim jumping to his feet. "Buh'sides, Ah got chores ta'do. Ya'll 'scuse me?" Jim said over his shoulder as he stomped out of the room.

From the kitchen came the voice of compassion. Annie called out, "Jim, fresh cookies jus' out'a'th'oven. Come fill up before you go out."

"There's one of the finest women you'll find anywhere. Her sense of passion is a model for us all. Known her all my life and she just gits—well, better if that's possible," observed the Sheriff.

"She is my advisor, moral guide, solace, Jester…I don't know how I would have managed, or continue to do so, in my life's transition here without her guidance. Now, continue with your purpose for being here," Doctor requested.

"There are some rumblings' detected around the tri-county alliance that I mentioned to you. Nothing new. One noteworthy observation was a couple of practically touch'n go landings of a DC-3 at the New River Valley Airport. Only one time was anybody seen gettin' on or off, but they only have one guy there most of the time. You could probably load or unload an elephant, and he wouldn't see it. Neither time did the DC-3 request landing information or permission. Also, over in Giles County, a kid keepin' track of license plates told a deputy that he had seen several cars, or one car several times, from Ohio on back roads. It could be nothin', but it sorta fits the scheme of things."

Sheriff Hare paused for a long spell causing Doctor to intensify the focus of his attention for the first time. Doctor asked, "Am I to anticipate the dropping-of-a-second- shoe?"

"Well...maybe...something like that." stuttered Sheriff Hare. "The dispatcher of the Bluefield Police Department got an anonymous call a while back asking if they had a Captain Cabot on their force. When the dispatcher said 'no' the caller hung up."

A cold chill ran up the Doctor's spine. Now they— whoever 'they' were— had his full attention.

"Sheriff Hare," declared Doctor, "I do believe that it is in my best interest to become one of your deputies. Please proceed with the swearing-in ceremony. All I ask is that I remain anonymous and that I am not required to carry a weapon."

"Ah believe I can assure that your best interest will be guaranteed," said the Sheriff. "We should have a couple of witnesses, but considering the need for confidentiality, we'll go find another route.

The Sheriff instructed Doctor to hold up his right hand and repeat the usual affirmation after which the Sheriff welcomed him to his department.

"Here is your credentials jacket. Inside is a badge and a picture ID. Carry these with you always and display them only when necessary, and not then, if you can bluff your way out of it. You are a special investigator that does not require you to be in hazardous situations resulting in an arrest. Never enter a threating situation where you might be in jeopardy. Your firearm is strictly for protection of yourself and your loved ones. Are these instructions clear?" asked the Sheriff.

"Wait a moment, my dear man. Clarify, if you will, the morsel about a 'firearm?' I believe you gave me your assurance that I would not be required to bear arms?"

"Ah made no such assurance. Ah believe what Ah said was that 'Ah can assure you that your best interest will be guaranteed' and that is what Ah will do. And besides, the law requires that all my deputies be armed. End of argument. Now to what you can do to help out. First, the people around you are the drivers of our community. Miss Annie and your Mom, for example, are the heart and soul of the new Company Store and therefore in a position to notice unusual cash flow. A business like that is a fine pass-through for illegal money."

"Perhaps it is more than coincidence that you mention money laundering. Just a few days ago I used the Company Store as an example of a business conducive to exploitation by organizations seeking sources for legalizing ill-gotten gains. Jenn was puzzling over why an anonymous donor would dispense such extravagance upon such an unlikely endeavor," said Doctor.

"You're right on target, and for that reason, I think that we should maybe hold a small conference with your enclave?" Sheriff suggested.

"Indubitably," said Doctor. "We can meet at the Clinic, but you will need to be the organizer and moderator. If it comes from me, they will most certainly dismiss any concerns as the mental aberrations of a big city fear monger."

"Outstanding," Sheriff said rising to leave. "Oh, by the way. We found the gun that fits the bullet. It's a Beretta 950 Minx that fires .22 Shorts like the bullet you gave me. It was on a dead guy found over near the new Interstate construction. There was no ID of any kind on him. He had on expensive clothes, but the labels were cut out. It looks like the gun was left on him intentionally. Nothin', you need to be thinkin' about. Welcome to law enforcement."

Chapter

Fifty-Six

Dr. Cabot was reading the morning newspaper when an announcement caught his eye:

Church to present Handel's Messiah

The combined choirs of Christ Episcopal, First Presbyterian, and Immanuel Lutheran Churches, accompanied by The Bluefield Symphony Orchestra along with the entire music department of Bluefield College and the Beaver High School Acapella Choir, will present Handel's Messiah in a concert at Westminster Church on December fourth. There is no charge for the concert, but reservations will due to limited seating will be required. Tickets are available at the offices of any of the participant organizations. Live remote broadcasts with be provided by WKOY radio to the Granada Theatre, where the high-quality

sound is available, as well as the regular
radio audience.

Dr. Cabot grabbed the phone and asked the long-
distance operator for the Westminster Presbyterian Church
in Bluefield. He waited for the call to go through only
the hear the operator inform him that that number did
not answer. He asked her to try Christ Episcopal and got
the same answer. Becoming disheartened, he requested her
to try the Immanuel Lutheran Church. He waited several
moments when the operator informed him, "I have your
party on the line. Go ahead."

"Hello, to whom am I speaking: Doctor inquired.

"This is Pastor Linebarger," came the replay.

"Oh, thank Heaven," Doctor said. "Pastor this is Doctor
Cabot, in Boston Knob, down toward Welch. I just read an
article in The Telegraph about the upcoming presentation
of the Messiah..."

"Well, Hello, Doctor. I know who you are. The Cole
family belongs to this church, and one of them shared your
experience with the moonshiners. I hope you got over it."
Pastor inquired.

"How profoundly embarrassing," exclaimed Doctor,
"Basing my reputation on that event is less than inspiring."

"Your reputation is intact, I assure you. To add to that
assurance, you are welcome to join our homebrew group
where we make the best beer agoin' from a 'blest' recipe
developed at the Southern Lutheran Seminary. Oh, excuse
me. You called. What can I help you with?"

"About the Messiah; I am seeking reservations for
the live presentation. Are you in a position to assist me in
obtaining four seats?"

"I am. Give me a second or two while I find the reservation sheet. Hold on...here it is. Four seats, down front?"

"No, thank you. I would prefer the balcony for a more panoramic view as well as the blending provided by the distance from the performers."

"There you are then. Four seats, front row balcony are... now...yours. Give me your address, and I will mail you the confirmation, or would you rather pick them up? I've got an even better idea. Why don't you visit us at church some Sunday? We would be delighted to have you. Please do."

"That is a splendid idea," David opined. "We will see you there."

David received a cool reception for his plan to attend the Lutheran Church. However, Jenn reluctantly did agree to go, "just this once." David had considered inviting his Mother to accompany them, but he decided that her presence would reinforce Jenn's anxiety about being in a strange environment.

They were greeted at the Narthex by a jolly fellow wearing a name tag with 'Dave' scribbled thereon who, personally, escorted them to a pew about four from the front. Jenn's angst increased somewhat since she wanted to sit at the very back of the room. (Truth be told, so did he.). Several well-dressed gentlemen stopped by and introduced themselves, including Mr. Cole whom David had met at the West Virginian.

The service appeared to be beginning as a small choir dressed in black robes entered the choir 'loft', followed by the preacher, wearing the traditional white cassock and stole, grinning broadly, stepped up to the Lectern.

"Good morning. It's nice to see all of you. We do have visitors in the congregation today. Dr. and Mrs. David Cabot from Boston Knob are here with us today. Make the welcome. Please stand for the Confession."

Pastor: "In the name of the Father, Son, and Holy Spirit."

People: "Amen."

Next, the Pastor reads a couple of prayers and continues to the confession of the people who then read: "We confess that we are in bondage to sin…, etc., etc. followed by one of two possible Absolutions the one used causing Jenn to catch her breath and overtly declare "Whoa!" Her reaction was to the portion that reads, "…As a called and ordained minister of the Church of Christ, and by his authority, I, therefore, declare to you the entire forgiveness of your sins." The service progressed following the traditional Order of Worship used for many years by any number liturgical churches.

After the confession, Jenn sat rigid as a post throughout the balance of the service and was ready to dash for the exit following the completion of the closing hymn. She acknowledged the Pastors welcome and handshake with a weak smile and rushed out of the building. David lingered uncomfortably to exchange pleasantries at the door and move as quickly as was polite to assuage Jenn's acrimony. He didn't even wait to get his tickets to the concert.

Neither spoke until the car was cruising down Bluefield Avenue heading for home. Ultimately, David said, "May I assume that you were not impressed with the service?"

"Ha!" declared Jenn.

"Okay. Thank you for going today. I will never ask you to attend a liturgical service again. I love you too much to see you so unhappy."

Jenn sat quietly for a lengthy period and then suddenly, scooted across to snuggle up against David, and cooed, "You notice that the preacher called us Dr. and Mrs.? You know what that means, don't you?"

"It's hard to tell what wanton thoughts you might be entertaining."

"It means if you are reaaally sorry, there are ways you can make it up to me."

"Okay, the Dairy Queen is just down the street. I'll buy anything you want."

She popped him one on his shoulder and declared, "You know good and well what I mean and they don't serve it at the Dairy Queen!"

Fifty-Seven

Mrs. Cabot and Annie were busy in the kitchen chattering away about their many joint activities when the house phone rang. Mrs. Cabot answered it, paused a bit and exclaimed excitedly, "Everything?" as she looked incredulously at Annie.

"What is hit? Somethun' wrong? Queried Annie.

"Mrs. Poe down at the store says that a man is there and wants to buy everything in the store. He has the cash to pay a flat price for the entire inventory. What do we do?" pleaded Mrs. Cabot.

Tell'um ta'hold on. Ah'll get Doctor. He'll know wha'ta do. Jes' hold on. Be right back."

Annie dashed down the back steps to the Clinic and bumped into Jenn in the hallway. "Jenn, we have th' makin's of a disaster, down at the store. Some man is a'wantin' to buy ever'thang. What do we do?"

"Whoa," said Jenn. "Everything?"

"Ever' thang; they're holden' the phone 'til we tell'm what ta'do," Annie said.

"Ah'll get David; he can tell you the best thing to do."

Doctor Cabot was finishing up with another black lung patient when Jenn knocked on the examination room door and said, "We have a nonmedical problem and need you, stat."

"Alright, I'll be in my office shortly," Doctor acknowledge her intrusion and calmly finished up with his patient.

When he entered his office, Jenn and Annie were anxiously waiting for him, and Jenn spoke first. "The Store is on the telephone, and some man wants to buy everything. What do they do."

With his usual calm manner, as if he were examining a patient, Doctor inquired, "Does he have cash?"

"We don' know," answered Annie. "Come on up star's and tel'us wa'ta'do and don' give us none'uh yor smart mouth."

"Right. On my way," He said.

As Annie hurried ahead to the kitchen Jenn said, "David, wait a minute. Do you think this is what you were talkin' about some time ago? You remember…? Money laundering? It sure sounds fishy to me. Somebody coming into a no-profit store and offering to buy everything?"

"I believe you have correctly assessed the situation, my love. The timing of the execution, however, is surprising occurring much sooner than I would have anticipated. I think it best that you become the spokeswoman for the telephone portion of this transaction. If this is what it appears to be we need to keep the relationship active for legal purposes. We are not so much interested in the income as we are of documenting the exchange of funds. So, here is what you do. Tell them that to simplify the purchase, the

Store will accept a single payment, in cash, of five thousand dollars. If that is agreeable with them, then have the Store attendant tell them that she is not authorized to accept a payment that large and that an officer of the Non-profit will be there shortly to complete the transition. You will need to remain here to tend the Clinic until I return."

They arrived in the kitchen to find Mrs. Cabot apprehensively clutching the phone to her breast. Jenn took the phone from her and asked Mrs. Poe to give it to the potential buyer and to stay within earshot so she could hear that end of the conversation.

Jenn inquired, "Who am I speaking to?" she asked.

"Name's Wilson. Are you the one that can take care of my offer?" inquired a surprisingly cultured voice.

"Not directly, no. Ah'm the temporary secretary of the non-profit, citizen-run, Company Store. You have offered to purchase the entire inventory of the store?"

"Yes ma'am. We have ready-buyers from up-scale retailers ready to market your crafts. We are offering wholesale value for your inventory."

"Fine," Jenn replied. "I have our Association President on his way, and he will be there directly to handle the deal. By the way, how do you anticipate payment?"

"Sounds good to me, and we will be paying with cash," replied Wilson.

"Gotcha," whispered Deputy Investigator Doctor Cabot.

Fifty-Eight

The traditional Stone Clan, Thanksgiving Day gathering, featured a panorama of Heavenly proportions providing undeniable evidence of a Supreme presence. It had snowed. Oh, how it had snowed, the depth of which could almost cover the sins of man. The ugliness of strip mining, of clear-cut timbering, the filling of deep valleys with lovely mountaintops to make roads; no artist could capture it, and no poet could describe it.

Bill had called and insisted that he provide David and Jenn with transportation since he had put chains on his pick-up truck tires that, in this type of snow, barely slowed it down.

"I'll swing by and get Jenn and pick you up on the way back," offered Bill.

"Come straight here. Jenn's here."

"Oh, the snowstorm get to her?"

"Yes and no, she is residing here now—" before David could finish the sentence, Bill chimed in with glee.

"Without the benefit of wedlock?"

"You, my dear brother-in-law-to-be, are a scandalous reprobate. For your information, the Simmons-shanty that your Uncle Henry left you, in which she has been 'living,' partially collapsed under last night's heavy snow. I have been trying to get her to move into the suite next to Mom for a while now. I suppose decorum does imply a more imminent wedding date to mollify people who reason as you do."

"Aw, come on down from your high-horse. Common-law marriage has been a way of life around here; it keeps you from marchin' down the aisle." Bill retorted.

"The consummate lawyer who must have the last word. Come and get us before that herd of vultures you call relatives devour the victuals."

"Vultures don't herd; they flock."

David hung up the phone as a definitive statement. He abated his annoyance somewhat by informing Jenn of her younger brother's impropriety; that would teach him a lesson he would not soon forget.

Bill, soaked with melancholy, took a slight detour to the gathering and guided his truck to the-top-of-the-hill where in previous years they would have descended to the old homeplace. It was gone, buried under over one hundred feet of fill dirt, yielding to a wider, straighter, quicker road to the coal fields. He recalled sitting in the 'front' room of the cozy old house and listening to his father reflect on the convenience of the new road based on a survey stake just twenty feet or so outside the window. Bill was glad 'Papa" had not lived to see that that stake represented a point far above the roof of the home he had, single-handedly, built many years before and where he and 'Mama' had borne thirteen children and raised them on thirteen acres of hillside land. Thank goodness, the snow-covered this as

well. He turned his attention to Jenn and saw the glimmer
of a tear on her cheek. She too was probably thanking God
for the beautiful blanket of snow obliterating the scene of
the present, but not the memories of the past.

The partakers of the festivities had, of necessity, parked
their cars at a good distance away and walked to the house,
the footsteps of the previous arrivals leaving a meager path
to be followed and the smoke from the chimney, providing
a friendly beacon of welcome.

The gathering reflected the progressive dwindling of
numbers, a result of migration and death. Three sisters
and four of their offspring were there. The Boston Knob
contingent made a noisy entrance, offering warm greetings.
The huge solid oak round table, dominated by a large
turkey—complements the pharmacy where Sister Lula
worked since Wesley's retirement—a home-cured ham from
the smokehouse, green beans, peaches, homemade chow-
chow from the garden, candied yams, homemade rolls and
topped off with—*fresh strawberry cobbler*! When queried about
the source of the fresh strawberries, Lula simply replied,
"Seek, and ye shall find."

Fifty-Nine

The Clinic had been typically busy this cloudy and dreary day. People prefer not to get sick on nice days. While trying not to be impersonal, Doctor often found himself preoccupied with matters not associated with the task at hand. It was one of those days precipitated by a letter that had arrived in the morning mail from Sheriff Hare.

The letter was short and to the point: "Thank you for the very valuable report. Follow-up belongs to people with more resources. Are you planning to attend the Medical Meeting at White Sulphur Springs next week? Important that you do. Please advise." It was not signed.

The referenced report was the sale of the Company Store inventory that had been hand-carried to the Sheriff by Jim along with the untouched cash involved in the transaction. The shouts of protest from the Store's management—Mom and Annie—still rang in his ears but he had convinced them to allow him to hold on to the money and not to disperse it to the membership of the co-op for a while. He had appeased them by dipping into his savings that they quickly distributed to the co-op to the great pleasure of all. David knew that the funds delivered to the Sheriff would be returned once they were fingerprinted and traced, if possible. He would be hounded unmercifully and with regularity until the full amount was handed over to the Co-op board of directors.

He was not unhappy with the idea of spending a couple of days at The Greenbriar. He immediately contacted the hotel and reserved two rooms in anticipation of inviting Jenn to go along as a special treat. He held a slight uneasiness about her fears of 'what people might think,' but discharged those his fears when Jenn squealed with excitement and declared, "Ah don't have a thing to wear!" A trip to Bluefield solved that problem.

To get to the Greenbriar, they had to go through Bluefield. They took U.S. 460 to Rich Creek where they picked up U.S .219 most of the way. The road was surprisingly straight and level except for a few miles along the Seneca Trails. Farming appeared to be a dominant activity even in the hillier areas. At Union, the land took on the characteristics of the Shenandoah Valley of Virginia with lush farms as far as the eye could see in every direction.

They drove into White Sulphur Springs on US 60 and found their destination easily. David guided the big Packard onto the tree-lined Village Run Road and followed its winding route to where the opulent elegance of the Georgian structure jumped abruptly into view with its commanding gabled façade lovingly supported by four very smart Doric columns.

Jenn's eyes became the legendary saucers as they approached the resort. "Oh, my," she repeated numerous times as they left the car with the parking attendant. She oo'd and ah'ed as they entered one of the several lobbies. The one they had entered was resplendent with a large green leaf design and gold wallpaper and draperies of art nuevo patterns. The size of the room dwarfed a grand piano standing to one side of a room They registered and were escorted to their rooms by a uniformed bellboy who opened the door to Jenn's room first to find that her bags were their already.

"It's beautiful and lovely and gorgeous and...and... swell...oh, thank you, David, for this trip. I love it...and you," she bubbled.

The room broke all the rules for color coordination. The carpet was a checkered royal blue, and the walls papered with a green floral on a beige background. A pseudo canopy of lagoon blue and olive green with red trim served as a headboard between massive four posters. The bed skirt was also lagoon blue, and the folded-down bedspread was a bright red and green floral pattern. An armchair and luggage racks were a mix of olive and turquoise, the chair a floral pattern and the racks stripped. A large fireplace was ablaze with wood enough to last awhile. The bellhop informed them that the wood would be replenished as needed if the do-not-disturb card was not on the door. He then turned to David and said, "I'll show you to your room, sir. It's right across the hall."

By the time they reached the dining room the novelty of the opulence was satiated. It too was lovely with a large chandelier dangling from the center of a huge bas-relief circle. The walls were in tangerine orange. The windows were big and arched. The floor was highly polished hardwood.

Jenn and David had dressed for dinner, not so much to meet the dress code, but for each other. Jenn wore a simple black short sleeve, knee length, stretch cocktail dress with a scooped neckline that fit perfectly. Accessories consisted of a single strand of pearls and red medium high-heel shoes. David chose an off-the-rack tailor-fitted Hart Schaffner & Marx grey worsted wool suit. They made a striking couple and stood out amongst the large crowd of well-dressed couples.

They were seated, after a short wait for a table in the crowded dining room by an attractive young woman and followed by a swarm of waiters bearing miscellaneous items and menus. Jenn viewed the menu and pitifully moaned: "Oh, David Ah don't know what any of this is. Chicken liver what...? Pattie? And Tiger Shrimp? Salmon Gravlax? Sounds like a laxative! Don't they have any just plain food like fried chicken or roast beef? And look at those prices. What is Free Range Chicken anyhow?"

"Free Range means not raised in cages; they supposedly run free. To what degree, I don't know. Perhaps still in very crowded conditions." answered David.

"Well heck, that's the only chickens we ever had at home. They were shut up in the shed at night but run loose all-day long. Why don't they write the menu in English? What's all of this; French? Oh, well, new experience. Here goes. Ah'll have the Chicken Liver Pattie for the First Course, Cream of Five Chicken Soup for the Second Course and the Mint English Pea Ravioli for the Main Course. Ah'll have ice tea with m'ah meal and coffee with dessert."

David chose the Salmon Gravlax, Romaine Salad, and the Prime Filet Mignon. In so doing it gave Jenn an opportunity to sample other menu choices. The room was abuzz with conversation. A grand piano fought pitifully to be heard but lost to the cacophony. Jenn and David ate silently except for the on-running critique about the food by Jenn.

"This smashed-up liver tastes just as bad as the liver puddin' Mama used to make every year at hog-kill'n time. She made it like so many things, chit'lens and crack'lins so as not to waste any part of the hog. You know they could make a mint out of pig knuckles with the people here since they seem to like the leavins' of a hog killing. Pigs' feet would go over big, and that onion soup with ramps and shallots was nothing but a thin onion broth with little green onions and slices of just another onion in it. Ramps and Shallots, my big toe; just fancy words for little green onions and full-grown onions." David smiled affectionately and shared tidbits from his plate to kindle further amusing analysis of the cuisine. He did not reveal his own opinions that, curiously, agreed.

David signed the check, and they left the restaurant to the tune of Jenn's continuous indictment of the food with such opinions as, "if the desert had been a teaspoon smaller there wouldn't have been any," and "the coffee cups were so tiny they wouldn't hold a robin's egg." They sashayed along the plush corridors to the Ball Room where the conventioneers were gathering for an official ball.

Jenn excused herself to 'go powder her nose.' Doctor meandered through the wandering crowd unconsciously looking for familiar faces. He was mildly startled when a well-dressed man touched his arm and inquired, "Dr. Cabot?"

Dr. Cabot answered in the affirmative as he searched the inquirer for recognition—that did not occur. The man responded by presenting official credentials for Doctor's perusal.

"I'm Captain Blake, Commander of the Governor's Taskforce on Organized Crime. May I see your ID please?"

Flummoxed at the request Doctor hesitated several seconds before remembering that, he too, had a badge. He reached into his inside coat pocket and, with an authoritative gesture, flipped open his badge and photo ID. He was pleased with himself for remembering to heed the Sheriff's instruction to carry his badge and a gun always. However, he still refused to carry a weapon.

"Thank you, sir. I'll be brief. The money used to buy the inventory of the Company Store was not traceable, but it did yield several fingerprints, most not on record. One identifiable print did pop up for a Tom Duggan, U.S. Army. He was discharged in 1953 sometime around the end of the Korean War.

"Tom Duggan, hmm…" pondered Doctor. "Duggan… Duggan…somewhere in the back of my mind…no, not there. Not familiar with the name."

"Also, we looked closer at the water in the unknown drowning victim's lungs and concluded that it was probably from a swimming pool based on the amount of chlorine present. The note that allegedly had your name on it? It had no chlorine on it, so it was put there after the drowning and before the body went into the reservoir. An interesting error on that note is that the rank of captain preceded the name Cabot. You were a major, weren't you?"

"Yes," replied Doctor, "During my entire tenure as active military."

"Well, may mean nothing. One more thing and I'll let you go. Our agents were surveilling a gathering of suspected crime bosses up in Connellsville, Pennsylvania. Three of those attendees were observed there departing Joseph A Hardy Airport on a DC-3. One of those persons of interest is from Maybeury, last name of Toth. Our new request for you is to learn all you can about him, very cautiously understand. We will be in touch. Thank you for your help, Doctor, Detective? Few people would step up as you have." He then melted into the assemblage of people leaving David just as Jenn emerged from the ladies' room, approached him and said, "The evenin's young. Let's do somethin'. The only time Ah have had champagne was at that New Years' Eve dance at the Country club, and I liked it. Since this is kind'uh a celebration let's get some."

"Alright, that sounds wonderful to me, shall we go to the bar?"

Jenn quickly responded, "Let's have a bottle delivered to my room so we can sit by the fire where there's not a bunch of people. We could even watch television if we get bored," she giggled.

"Whoa, sounds kind of risqué but it would be most pleasant having you as my very own for a change. I will order up a platter of munchies too. Let's make an evening of it," David added.

Jenn returned his response with a broad smile and said, "Dress is informal she giggled. See you later," ending with a lingering kiss.

Each returned to their rooms with a new sense of eagerness. David went to his suitcase a retrieve a new pair of lounge pajamas that he had purchased so long ago that it occurred to him that that might be out of style. Did pajamas of any kind go out of style he considered? Probably not. No matter. These are new and shiny. Too shiny? Sleazy?

Inappropriate? Assuming? Suggestive? Well, what did it matter? She said to dress informally, didn't she? Maybe she meant jeans and a tee shirt. Perhaps I am too forward; I don't have any ulterior motives. Well, to heck with it. He put on his new pajamas and viewed himself approvingly in the mirror. He had been so bold as to shower, shave and brush his teeth telling himself that that was just a courtesy one accomplish for an evening out with a lady friend for any occasion.

Appropriately prepared and Satisfied, he retrieved the bouquet of roses he had delivered from the flower shop downstairs and proceeded to her room. He knocked softly.

The door opened immediately to present an image that astonished David into speechlessness. Standing angelically in front of him was the most beautiful woman he had ever seen, absolutely, without a doubt. Jenn was wearing an all-white gown that fit her shape from her shoulders to her ankles. The v-neckline dipped to her waist and was carefully, but revealingly, filled in with exquisite lace that also graced the rest of the neckline. A long-sleeved robe of the same fabric and trim at the wrist with the same lace, fell from her shoulders to the floor, leaving a full view of the gown and the magnificent body it attempted to encase. She wore a modicum of makeup and bright red lipstick. She smiled at him and said. "My, but you do look handsome in your loungers. How did you know I would be wearing white?"

It occurred to him that he was unaware of the color of his white pajamas. "We do make a pair, don't we?" He continued to stand in the hall.

"You with me? Don't just stand there, enter!" She ordered.

He entered the room; she closed the door, he handed her the bouquet of roses, and replied, "Do you realize that is one of the first utterances you made to me when we first met?"

"What?"

"You said, 'You with me?' I was so mesmerized that I could not speak and you said, 'You with me?' Then you said, 'Don't just stand there, come on.' I followed you like a puppy."

"Well, then; Come on in. The goodies are here, including me, and the Champagne is cooling on ice.

He laughed, took her hand and led her to the very large, soft sofa.

They checked out late the next morning after a really fine breakfast. At the front desk when Doctor asked for the bill, he was told that it had been taken care of and all he had to do was sign a voucher placed in front of him. The issuer of the voucher was the Governor's office. He hastily placed his arm between Jenn and the voucher to block her view. He glanced her way to see her giving him a puzzled look. An inquisition was inevitable.

Sixty

The trip home was uneventful except there was an increase in touchiness between the two. Jenn chattered endlessly about their experience at one of the world's premier resorts showing how unimpressed she was. She concluded that if that is what high society was, then she would prefer being a lowly hillbilly. "Lots more fun," she opined. She was particularly put-off by the food as being "too uppity." She prattled on and on to Annie and Mrs. Cabot and Shirley at the Clinic about how beautiful everything was and how fine the restaurant was, and how pretty the food looked. David decided that she did have a good time and her criticism of the adventure was to hide naivete from him. His suspicions were confirmed the following morning as he entered the kitchen to the chatter of three women preparing breakfast. He stopped at the door and eavesdropped as Jenn regaled the other ladies about the opulence of the Greenbrier.

"There was a big bowl of fruit of all kinds, and fresh flowers in the room when we checked in. The colors didn't match at all. They mixed greens and blues and olive and stripes and florals. Things we would never do. The bathroom had all kinds of soap, lotions, shampoo; everything anybody would want or need. And towels! Must'a been six or seven different sizes and enough of them that you could dry every part of your body on one and still had clean ones left over."

"Sounds a bit too fancy fer me," opined Annie. "How much did all'a that cost?"

"Ah think each room was about uh'hundred and fifty dollars."

"What? Uh'hunner'und'fifty fer one room? Ya'll shoud'a stayed in the same room. What'a waste."

There was a noticeable pause in Jenn's reply. "We aren't married, Annie. That wouldn't have been proper."

Annie stopped what she was doing and looked at Jenn curiously. "Proper m'ah foot. You air purty clos'ta bein' married. Close enough."

Mom, feeling a need to support Jenn interjected, "Now Annie, she's right. It would have been improper for them to share a be... room. Was the food good Jenny?"

"It was pretty and strange. Everything had a fancy name, and there wasn't much of it. And it was expensive! A couple uh teaspoons of liver puddin' cost nine dollars. A bowl of onion soup was twelve dollars. David's steak was thirty dollars."

"Thirty dollars fer a piece'uh meat? Yew cud buy the whole dang cow fer that," protested Annie.

David decided it was time to make his entrance. He rounded the corner, and the room fell silent, but not for long. He became the focus of the interrogation that delved into every aspect of the trip.

The Clinic was buzzing with activity as they caught up from the absence. Black Lung prevailed, as usual, allergies running a close second. He was listening to the familiar sounds of a defective lung when Shirley called down the hall that there was an emergency coming in. Doctor apologetically excused himself and rushed to the waiting room where a man on a stretcher was just being brought in by the rescue squad. Completely covering his face and hands were wet dressings. One of the EMTs expertly summarized what treatment they had employed before and during transportation. Dr. Cabot lifted the gauze; the damage was extensive on the face, but the eyes seemed to be unaffected. "What happened?" Doctor inquired.

"A Battery explosion," replied the EMT.

"A battery explosion?"

"Yes. Damage appears to be mostly caused by battery acid, the EMT said.

Battery Acid…battery acid? "BATTERY ACID…! I know who the note writer is, C'est le cuisinier! It's the cook!" Doctor practically shouted to the puzzlement of all of those around him.

"Forgive me," pleaded Doctor Cabot. "another time, another place. Let's get this man on his way so that treatment can commence."

Jenn, who had witnessed the whole episode, did not remove her eyes from David until he replaced the bandage on the damaged face. She then whispered, "What note?"

"Tell you in a moment." He then turned to the EMTs and said, "Excellent work. There's nothing more than I can do that you have not already done. Now he needs a hospital. Please transport him."

"Which hospital? Welch or Bluefield?" asked the EMT.

"The closest. Your choice," Doctor replied. He then turned to Jenn and said, "Come with me."

They went to David's office where Jenn took the chair behind the Doctor's desk, and he sat in the side chair.

"Explain," she demanded.

"On the day I finally was transported out of Korea, I was gathering wool in the sunshine of the MASH compound. I had been left by the unwritten rule of 'first one in the first one out' to attend to a couple of wounded boys until proper transport became available. The helicopter that had finally extricated them made a return trip, it turned out, to get me. While I waited, a young sergeant came out of the mess tent…"

"Mess tent. What's that?" Jenn interrupted.

"Dining hall of sorts. To continue. He exited the tent and approached me with a big smile on his face. He was carrying a pot of coffee and a mug. He asked me if I wanted a cup of 'this battery acid'. I don't remember his name. We chatted on for a while, partly in French. His name escapes me, try as I will, but I well remember the French because he had cooking experience with an old Mess Sergeant who had been a French Chef before he was drafted and made an army cook. In our conversation, I revealed to him that I was heading to West Virginia and he said he was from Rocky Gap, Virginia. While we were chatting my transportation away from that miserable MASH experience arrived."

Jenn, her frustration growing, said. "So, his calling coffee 'battery acid' and the mention of 'battery acid' today triggered a significant memory to…of…what?"

"That is not the end of the story," David continued. "The sheriff recently sought my advice regarding a drowning in Bluestone Dam Lake. A note was found in the victim's pocket. It was in French and said, *'En contactant le Capitaine*

Cabot à Bluefield that translates loosely as 'contact Capt. Cabot of Bluefield'. The sheriff thinks that that is me."

"Holy Moley, David! Does he think you know something about the dead guy?"

"No, not specifically but he is concerned with the possible incursion of organized crime, here in this local, associated with the popularity of marijuana nationwide and the suitability of West Virginia as a product source. He is asking people who might encounter strangers to be vigilant. That is the reason he called me," he fibbed.

"Humm," pondered Jenn. "Do you suppose that the cash deal at the Company Store might have something to do with it? That deal was in cash; did you suspect anything illegal in that deal? Sounds crooked to me. That man comin' in with all that cash and buyin' a whole lot of stuff. Of course, he got his money's worth, and he can readily sell it for a whole lot more than he paid for it to rich folks in a city. Right?"

Chapter

Sixty-One

Annie was in a cheery mood when Doctor entered the kitchen. It was a bright sunny day with a blanket of light snow providing a canvas for the sun to draw intricate shadow patterns with bare-tree branches.

"Good morning, Miss Annie. How are you and your family today?" inquired Doctor.

"Ever'bodi's fine. My Hubby's black lung aint'gittin' no better as you well know. Ah don't thank he kin last much longer. One day at'a time as the ol' sayin' goes. My girl is beginnin' ta'read a little bit. She's got a new teacher that seems to understan' retards a little more."

"Annie, what did I tell you about calling you sweet daughter a 'retard'? It is more proper to refer to them as 'special' or 'exceptional' children."

"She's special alright, but she is still a retard in school, hit don't matter what the proper name might be. The big problem with children like her is they ain't no jobs they kin do. She's uh willin' worker, but nobody'll har her. She's still school age and not allowed to work no job but hast'a go to school by law. We been talkin' about seein' if'n the health department could set up a program where non-profits like the Company Store kin har' them under some sorta special exception, but so fur we ain't hear'd nothin.'"

"That is a commendable suggestion and bears looking into. I will take it on as a project. Meantime are you ready for the big day at the Messiah Concert? I am rather excited about it."

"Me too. I jes' don't know what to expect. Air they any preachin.'"

Doctor answered seriously. "No preaching."

"Whada'bout an invitation? Will thar be any?"

"Invitation? I'm not sure what you mean. We have our seats reserved. The invitation for the recital was a note in the Telegraph."

"Naw, Ah mean, will somebody git up and try to git us to jin their church after everthang else is done?

Doctor Cabot had to smile at such a thought. "No ma'am. The invitation occurs after regular services in non-liturgical churches such as the Baptists."

"That's gud, cause I git's tired of that after ever sermon cause most of the people air already saved. Corse, they's always a backslider er two sittin' out thar that could stand a bit of renewal of the spirit given' the 'mount of drunkenness in air part uh th' woods. Will they take up a collection? Should I take some money with me?"

"My dear Annie, you go you and Mom and enjoy yourselves. No one is going to expect you to do anything but experience the joy of the music. It is a most special musical accomplishment. It has been a Christmas tradition for many years bringing the true miracle of the Season into focus."

"Ah jes' hope hit ain't too hi falutin' fer me. Ah ain't had no music trainin' ceptin' fer a couple of sangin' conventions at the church when ah was a girl."

"You do not need training to appreciate the classics or any music for that matter. What is a singing convention?" Doctor inquired.

"Hit's whar a music teacher come's around to schools and churches and teaches folks how to read music. We larned square notes. Unfortunate, none of the new song books uses them eny more."

"Square notes? I don't think I am familiar with that method."

"Yes, you do; Do-re-mi-fa-so-la-ti-do; ever' note has hit's own shape. 'do' is a triangle layin' on hit's long side, 're' is shaped like a water dipper, 'mi' is a lopsided squar,' 'fa' is a flat circle, 'la' is a rectangle; all of them have tails on–um. Unner'stan?"

"Yes, strangely, I do. They are more frequently referred to as 'shaped' notes."

"well, hit don't matter none since ah don't sang enythang excepti' by mem'ry now enyhow. Ah still lahk the ol' songs. This new stuff ah don' lahk a'tal."

The rest of the family began to assemble in search of breakfast. Jenn and Mom stepped in to help Annie in preparing a hearty meal since they would not eat again until supper because of the recital that was to begin at 2:30 in the afternoon.

They arrived at the host church a few minutes before the event was to begin and found their perfect seats on the center balcony. This location placed them slightly above eye level with the last row of the choir loft. The choir loft was not adequate to contain the combined choirs, but the church had been creative in spilling the participants into the areas on both sides of the communion rails. The small orchestra was grouped strategically around the organ to compliment the antiphonic capabilities of the fine old treasured instrument, the main reason for the selection of the recital's venue. The organists had been with the church for about thirty years and were quite accomplished adding appreciably to the eminence of the performance.

Annie was as fidgety as a wind chime. The presentation was limited to about one hour, focusing on what has been named the 'Christmas Portion' of the Messiah with the first thirty minutes including several solos. During that time, Annie acted if she was about to bolt. The solos, particularly the soprano, seemed to increase her agitation. But when the Hallelujah Course was begun, with organ and orchestra at about fifty minutes into the concert, she perked up and sat in a near state of rapture to the fading echo led to silence. The congregants sat in respectful solitude until the lights were gradually turned up. Then, an unexplainable event occurred; the normal burst of applause did not occur. In near total verbal silence, the church emptied; only whispered conversation was evident.

They reached the car, parked on the street close to the church before anyone spoke. It was Annie who finally chirped, "Well, ah ain't never seen nothin' like 'at before in my whole life. Is that what them lur'cal churches do when the service is over?" she asked.

Mrs. Cabot answered her. "No, Annie. That was very unusual. It was if we were awe-struck. I can say that I have never heard the Hallelujah Chorus rendered with such a combination of tenderness and vitality. Having part of it acapella made all the difference in the world. I think the sweetness of their performance created a holy solitude that followed. In my experience, the Hallelujah Chorus meets with enthusiastic applause."

"I fully agree with your assessment mother," David interjected. "That was the Beaver High School Acapella Choir made up of volunteer students directed by Miss Liz Sheldon, according to the program."

"Well, whoever they were they were special. If only we had a church choir half as good as them somewhere nearby, I would be there every Sunday."

"I think I would be inclined to join you," declared David.

Chapter

Sixty-Two

Celebrating the new year was a big occasion at the Field Mansion hosted by Mrs. Cabot. She was at her graceful Boston Matron's best and the party was a monumental success. Particularly noteworthy were the members of the Company Store Association made up of the volunteers and arts and crafts contributors. It was a strange mixture of peoples brought on by a successful community collaboration. People who previously seldom mixed socially, or otherwise, joined together in celebration of a new year and a new fellowship.

Annie circulated continuously to be certain no one was feeling neglected. Platters of ham biscuits, fried chicken livers, corn muffins slathered with a black-eyed pea chutney and pickled peaches predominated the non-dessert table. The dessert table was a masterpiece of sweets including a layered cake, cookies, brownies, and cobblers. Non-alcoholic eggnog, apple cider, bottled soft drinks, coffee and hot chocolate, sat available on another table. Jenn and David wandered politely through the happy party-goers until the party begins to fizzle out, directly associated with the reduction of food and, accompanying appetites somewhere around ten o'clock. Jenn went to her suite to settle in for the night, and David went to his office for a nightcap of brandy. Doctor could not clear his mind of the 'Mystery of the Drowned Man' and his role as a reluctant investigator. He had before him a list of occurrences, facts, assumptions. The one single 'piece of evidence,' that seemed to be his alone to pursue was the note that appeared to be from a Tom Duggan of Rocky Gap, Virginia who's fingerprints on the Company Store money further muddled the mystery. He sat broodingly for several minutes pondering a strategy that would appear to be a casual visit to Rocky Gap. An obvious ploy would be to have Jenn with him, and they could be looking for antiques but in January? Probably not a good idea.

Bo became impatient that his adopted master was not coming to bed. Try as he would to convert, 'that dog,' as Annie referred to him, Bo was fully in charge of Doctor's Clinic off-time. So, like a good master, Doctor changed into his night clothes and pulled back the covers on his side of the bed. Bo was already lying crosswise underneath the pillows on his side of the bed. "Goodnight Bo. I don't suppose you have any ideas as to how I might proceed into Bland County without suspicion, do you?" Bo just groaned and passed a whopper of a stinker, silently of course.

After airing out the room with January night-air, Doctor appreciatively crawled under the cover waiting for Bo to change to his final night time sleeping position; sprawled lengthwise as close to his master as he could get. His warmth was as steady as an electric blanket and had become a source of solace in a strange sort of way. The doctor had just reached the twilight stage of sleep when he remembered—or dreamed—a story Bill told him about Sonny's Dog, with the paradoxical name, Petunia. He was a big solid black Gordon Setter who got his name from sleeping in Lula's flower bed.

Petunia loved to travel. He would hitch rides in or on any conveyance that would stop long enough to mount. On one occasion, he rode all the way to town on the sloping trunk of Wesley's 1946 Studebaker Coupe. Most of his chauffeurs would bring him back home on a return trip or call for him to be picked up. His coup-de-grace was a trip to Bland, Virginia on top of a load of hay. He had to stay there for two weeks until the truck came back through Bluewell. Dr. Cabot spoke out of his reverie and said to himself, "That is what I will do. I'll go in search of Petunia. Everybody would appreciate that, particularly in such cold weather."

The next morning Doctor Cabot woke with a realization that he did not have a plan. Looking for a dog, indeed! Any child would see through such a transparent ploy. Circumventing the truth leads to doubt and suspicion.

Sunday rolled around with light snow falling—again, being part of the approximate sixty-two inches annual average. Bill had invaded the premises for one of his frequent forays seeking gossip and other extraneous news. The family was congregating for Sunday Dinner of roast beef, mashed potatoes, home canned green beans, hot rolls with fresh butter, miscellaneous jams, jellies and pickles and dessert of apple pie. Bill was his usual irreverent self. He endeared himself with his sister with the query, "Are ya'll still cohabitating?"

Jenn took the bait and physically attacked him with a spoonful of mashed potatoes that she was preparing for the table. He ducked but not before she struck the bridge of his nose with a robust whack splattering his face with hot potatoes, following the blow with the question, "Why can't you be civil just once? You always try your very best to humiliate me in front of people."

Bill stood looking at her with surprise on his face— underneath a layer of potatoes— and David commenced laughing joyously. Jenn then saw the expression on Bill's face and followed suit with the whole family finally joining in. Bill had his comeuppance and sheepishly said, "Guess I kinda' touched a sore spot, huh?"

Jenn removed her apron and gently wipe Bill's face. "Just be grateful Ah was dippin' up the tater's and not the gravy 'cause the gravy is boilin' hot," she said laughing. "Now go to the bathroom and clear off the rest before I whoop you." Bill meekly complied mumbling something about how big sisters were always picking on their little brothers.

There were extra places set at the table this night. Annie's daughter and Jim were sort of guests of honor since they both had birthdays this month. Jim's birthday was unknown, so Annie had designated his birthday to coincide with that of her daughter since they appeared to her to be about the same age when Jim appeared at their doorstep— having no home and too young to relate his story— to be taken in by Dr. Fields. Annie had originally resisted Doctor Cabot's efforts to meet her daughter, Margie, but he persisted, and she finally complied. When he had first come to West Virginia Annie had told him she had a 'Mon'goid

Idjit' daughter and he did not challenge the name since that was the common referent for the genetic defect at the time. He had since learned that Down Syndrome—after English physician, who first classified the syndrome as a separate form of mental disability in 1862—and he had counseled Annie accordingly.

Jim came in through the back door with a hearty greeting for everybody. Annie called out, "A'fore yew take off yer boots, go git Margie, will you Jim." I compliance, he went next door to escort Margie to the birthday party and took off his snow-covered boots and left them in the mud-room.

"Margie was a surprise to Doctor Cabot. She was Definity a Trisomy 21—an extra copy of chromosome 21 in every cell— the most common form of Down syndrome, with a prevailing symptom of obesity. Margie was stocky, but not overweight, indicating extraordinary parenting. She entered the room with a princess-like bearing and introduced herself to everyone in the room, including those whom she already knew, with, "Hello, Ah am Margie and Ah kin write mah name. Jim is mah best frin' an' yew kin be too."

Annie sat Margie and Jim next to her in her usual 'jump seat.' Everyone in the new extended family had yielded to the placement of Annie as the reining Matriarch, at the dinner table, at least. Without preamble, she said, "Ever'body bow yer heads fer a blessing." she continued. "Dear Lord Jesus, bless these here birthday children and thank you fer makin' them so special to us. Bless this here house and all in't. Amen."

A hearty "Amen" was added by everyone.

Bill, the gregarious one, started the table conversation with a question aimed at no one in particular. "Tell me how the concert went. The Messiah. Did it go well?"

Mrs. Cabot responded first with an exuberant, "I have heard it many times, and I would say it was among the best renditions I have ever experienced. Wouldn't you agree David?"

"Yes, Mom; well done indeed, I thought..."

Annie interrupted. "Well, Ah wish't ya'll would es'plain the whole thang ta'me. Hit didn't make a bit'a sence excepten' that part ya'll called the Hallaluh course. The firs' part seem'duh be a man bellerin' lahk a bull an' uh woman skreemin' her head off an' lookin' lahk she wuz agoin' to jump offen the platform that she'wuz'a'rockin'back'n forth on. Why don't they jus' stand an sang normal instead of screamin' so loud. An' some uh'those people playin' instru'munts keep jumpin' roun' and jerkin' lak they had the heebie jeebies. Fer uh'while thar Ah thought Ah was at'uh holy roller meetin' with all that shout'un and jerk'un goin' on."

Jenn broke in to defuse Annie by suggesting, "Ah thought we were here for a birthday party. Let's eat so we can cut the cake, and I believe that there's a present or two to be opened?"

The rest of the party time was ruled by Margie who took over as hostess and did a rather commendable job of it. She and Jim blew out the candles and shared the task of cutting and distributing the cake. There was ice cream too.

Chapter

Sixty- Three

Winter was the quintessence of frustration. Snow provided a unique beauty for a short spell only to be painted black by the mines and trains. Folks were longing for Spring, and the Jonquils were sending up probes. The forsythia was sneaking peeps with yellow buds of promise. Crime too was emerging from Winter hibernation as witnessed by a reminder from Sheriff Hare. The doctor decided that he would wait for the Dogwood, Redbud, Rhododendron and other colorful Spring glorifiers to make an appearance before he set out in search of his former MASH contact. For now, he would bide his time. One of his favorite pastimes during lulls in the Clinic was to browse the bookshelf bearing the book selections and personal notes of Dr. Fields. He was currently engrossed in a thick loose-leaf notebook of handwritten personal historical interviews collected from the first days of Dr. Fields' practice in Boston Knob. Most were passed down by word-of-mouth through families and, often, in the family bibles.

A particularly noteworthy interview of an Irish immigrant transported to the new country planted the idea the Irish were 'white slaves, ' outnumbering black slaves and enduring worse treatment at the hands of their masters. Dr. Fields, being a scientist, sought the truth of that claim and found that, like impoverished people of Ireland, Scotland and many other nationalities, were forcibly exiled to America in the 17th and 18th centuries as indentured servants. He found that a small number were placed into indentured servitude during the period of the English Civil Wars, but that was a unique case. He also found that indentured servants often lived and worked under less than suitable conditions and were sometimes treated cruelly. Furthermore, unlike Black Slaves, white indentured servants had legal rights and were not considered property. Indentured servitude played a strong role in the survival and growth of the original thirteen colonies. Many settlers were brought to America because they could not afford the travel from Europe and contract to work off their passage, room, and board over a period of two to seven years. About half of the immigrants who came to the New World during the colonial period came as indentured servants.

At this point, Dr. Fields departed from the third person to the first person expressing his view on the concept of indentured servitude.

"In the Science of General Semantics, an axiom declares that 'the word is not the thing.' Alfred Korzybski published a book called Science and Sanity: An Introduction to Non-Aristotelian Systems. In that book, he presented the hypothesis that language, while a powerful communication advancement for humanity, is still flawed in that it is a major abstract tool. First, words are arbitrary symbols assigned to indicate an object, but might also represent something else, even another object. When the object is 'real' like a chair, confusion can be averted. But when there is no object, and the word is applied to a 'feeling' or 'situation,' then the resultant intended concept is fuzzy."

"Thousands of Irish people delivered, against their will, into indentured service is a fact. When a person is forced, against his/her will, to work for another without the option to leave, the question is whether they are fulfilling the role of a slave. The labor they are doing is slave–like and refusing to call it slavery is pedantry. Any form of forced labor can be called slavery. But what do we gain by doing so, besides blurring historical distinctions? As I become acquainted with the people of the area, I see people who were born into slavery by their dependency on coal. Yes, they can quit, but what can they do? They probably went into the mines with their fathers rather than going to school. They never have any cash, only script issued by the mine owners redeemable only at the company store. They are inextricability, Slaves: Slaves to their heritage, Slaves to the Coal mines, Slaves to the Company store and Slaves to a certain, slow, painful death by Black Lung. Slaves they were born and Slaves they will die leaving their progeny to the same fate."

Here his essay ended leaving Doctor Cabot deeply depressed.

A light tap on the door failed to rouse him from his reverie. Jenn pushed the door open and informed him, "You have patients...my goodness! What's wrong with you? You look like you just saw a ghost!"

"I believe I just did, Jenn. Have you read any of Dr. Field's essays in his diaries? I just finished reading one that presented a scenario so disheartening that I fleetingly realized the fruitlessness on my endeavors here for the future. I am not practicing medicine; I am a subordinate of the Grim Reaper, preparing men, women, and children for their death brought on by a centuries-old system of indentured servitude...NO...call it what it is...slavery."

Jenn gently closed the door and went to David. She took his head in her hands and gently pressed him to her breast saying, "My dear sweet man, you need a break from this. I have a great idea. Let's get married and take a long honeymoon? It's about time you know. We can go anyplace you want to. How does that sound? We can have a nice wedding right here in the house and invite lots of people. You kind'a liked Pastor Linebarger from the Lutheran Church in Bluefield so you could ask him to perform the ceremony. I would rather not go away from here because of the travel problems for locals. It would be fun to take a train all around the country where we could stop anywhere we want to and stay over—"

"Whoa, slow down. I am not contemplating an escape. I might entertain a change of venue someday. Right now, I need to reacquaint myself with a former unseen reality that was obvious to Dr. Fields but has escaped my awareness. What he implies in his thesis is intriguing but by no means a rationale for alarm. Depressing? Yes. Cause for immediate action? No. Now, as pleasing as my resting place is at the moment, kindly release me so that we can return to work."

Jenn had released her hold on him and sat down looking at him with concern. "Are you mad at me about something?" she asked.

"Of course not. I could never be angry with you. That essay by Dr. Fields just initiated some concern about my professional future. Is this what I want to do for the rest of my life? With your life? Look at our social life. We have none! In the length of time, we have been here together we have been to the Greenbriar for one night and the Country Club once. That's' no life for...well...for a beautiful, talented woman like you. You merit better. While my skills are still sharp, I should be in surgery every day, not checking off the days of dying Black Lung victims. And you, you have excellent nursing skills and manners. Look at how you spend your days. What a waste of talent!"

"Then Ah tell you what you should do. Go find the openings for surgeons anywhere in the United States... anywhere...and contact them stating your interest in their position. We, or you, can look at any offers you get and if you find something that looks good, and you are sure you like the area, and the people better than you do here, we will move there. Okay?"

Sixty-Four

As had become an adventitious custom, Bill showed up for Sunday dinner at the Field Mansion. However, there was a noticeable difference in his countenance. He was polite but subdued; the usual banter was absent. He gave Jenn a peck on the cheek accompanied by a quiet "Love you, Sis." He did not tease Annie. Jenn reckoned he was not himself and maybe not feeling well. But, she dispelled that thought since he would not have come for his usual Sunday visit if he were sick. Without Bill's stimulus, conversation lagged, and the meal came to a silent end. The women excused themselves to tend to the after-dinner chores, leaving Bill and David at the table with coffee.

David spoke first. "Okay, my dear friend, what's in yer craw As Annie would say? You have been moping around ever since you got here. Are you ill?"

"No, I'm not sick! I have a legal problem that I think you can help me with, but I don't know how to approach you with it. Will you hear me out without interruption until I can tell you about it?"

"Since you asked so nicely, you have my full, undivided attention until you announce the completion of your dialogue," answered David seriously but with a smile.

"I got roped in a very old, long-standing black lung case not too long ago. I thought it was going to be a hearing before the Coal Mine Health and Safety Act that usually ends with some form of compensation for the black lung victim, but I was shanghaied into a full-blown lawsuit against a very high-powered legal group with offices all over the country and with very deep-pockets footing the bill. It's just me against them." Bill paused to collect his thoughts.

"Continue, you have my full attention. Your conundrum is intriguing so far."

"Conundrum is an understatement. Choosing whether to have coffee or tea this morning was a conundrum; what I am talking about is a full-blown disaster. How would you like to be the only doctor at a mine disaster with only a tongue blade? Please don't minimize my problem!" Bill practically shouted.

"I shall remain silent," Doctor whispered.

"Thank you. Please forgive my rudeness. To continue. Under the workers' compensation law, unforeseen difficulties cropped up involving claims for occupational diseases primarily involving the cause of the disabling or death of a worker, or even whether or not the disease was even present or the identification of the disease itself. Until recently, the compensation of industrial injuries or diseases was under state control. That too, recently changed when the feds passed legislation to provide compensation for black lung. The Feds surmised that coal mining is different than any other kind of work because of the nature of risks involved. Also, its isolation, both geographically and culturally, caused a unique, singular society untouched by the 'outside' world. Neither the union nor mine owners showed concern for safety, occupational health or educational dysfunction of the worker's children."

Bill paused and suggested that they warm up their coffee. Dr. Cabot agreed that was a fine idea. The arrived in the kitchen to find it empty except for the perpetual fresh pot of coffee with a pitcher of thick cream waiting. They replenished their cups and chose to go to the living room with its stuffed furniture instead of back to the dining room table. They settled in.

"Continue," requested Doctor Cabot.

"Okay. From now on you can interrupt anytime you want since this part is almost all related to medical. I will not reveal the name of the plaintiff to be rigidly ethical for both of our sakes. By the way, the patient is from Beckley. He might have worked in the mines near here, but I don't know that. Bares looking into he concluded. Several years before he had applied for benefits for symptoms he was experiencing the same as many and his peers. It started, as usual, with shortness of breath followed by the coughing up of a black mucus. At this point, he finally applied for federal benefits and a U.S. Department of Labor certified doctor gave a diagnosis the most lethal form of black lung, complicated pneumoconiosis. The government ordered his employer, a large coal company, to begin paying him monthly benefits, but, as is almost always the case, the company appealed. The patient now found himself in a world of administrative law judges who must parse through mountains of medical evidence, legal arguments, strange rules, company lawyers who were experts in circumnavigation and procrastination and company doctors who seemed to diagnose almost anything but black lung."

"Just a moment, please Bill. Are you intimating that physicians have been making fraudulent diagnoses? Really! That is preposterous! There must be hundreds of physicians involved in the diagnosis and treatment of lung diseases and chance alone would prevent most false claims on either side."

"True, but the big law firms have selected doctors who are in their pockets, and they manipulate the situations to guide the claimant through the system to get a favorable diagnosis for their purposes. You will see an example of that as I continue with the story."

"I will be paying rapt attention," Doctor Cabot said haughtily.

"Okay, the first day of court, I'm told, a bevy of lawyers huddled around the defendants' table with more behind them in the gallery. The patient was there by himself; I guess you would say he was representing himself. He couldn't find a lawyer, and that was before he talked me into representing him. Failing to find counsel is common. Possible claimants' attorneys have avoided the federal black lung system en masse. Time and money favor the coal companies because they have the funds to hire all kinds of experts and drag things out until the cows come home. Even worse, if a claimant can find a lawyer, he's legally barred from charging fees, so he must gamble on winnin' an unwinnable verdict."

"Question. Do I understand you correctly that a lawyer for the plaintiff cannot charge for his services?"

"You heard me right."

"Hardly equitable. What is the justification for such a rule?"

"Don't know for sure but some politician must have thought he was defending the plaintiff from exploitation by any ambulance-chasing, legal beagle. Strangely enough, that rule applies to only coal-mining disability cases."

"Puzzling, to be sure. Okay, continue. You left with the patient at a table by himself with no legal representation. What could he possibly say?"

"All he could do was to read the report from the examination paid for by the Labor Department with a diagnosis of pneumoconiosis, and that's what he did. After that, it was the coal company's lawyers turn, and they bombarded the court with exhibits, medical reports, depositions, names and credentials of doctors who had reviewed the evidence."

"What was missing from the record is what's important. Back some time ago, a suspicious mass was removed from the plaintiff's lung and sent to the hospital's pathologist—same hospital mind you—to rule out cancer, and that is exactly—and only—what he did. He didn't mention anything related to black lung, or even that the patient was a miner."

"Sloppy work, indeed," commented Doctor.

"True. But my case is strengthened by an anonymous phone call from someone who said he had evidence that the coal company lawyers had obtained the pathologists' slides and sent them to two of their pathologists whose opinions typically supported the firm's case. This time though, they were snookered. Both pathologists did the ethical thing and said the mass was probably a result of black lung. While this would normally be a final blow to most lawyers, the mining firm's lawyers did not give up. Instead, they withheld the reports of their own consulting physicians thus leaving only the incomplete hospital pathologist's report and its singular diagnosis of 'inflammatory pseudotumor.' The informant told me he would only tell what he knew to just one person...only one person."

"So, what do you want me to do? It appears you may be inexorability defeated unless your anonymous benefactor provides a solution. There is nothing I can do about that."

"Not so," retorted Bill, because YOU are the only person the anonymous caller will talk to."

Sixty-Five

Spring was singing its theme song. Beauty was everywhere, unabated. Birds sang; frogs chirped; trees shouted with pink, white and red blossoms. David recalled a greeting offered by the pastor at one of the services he and Jenn had attended: "This is a day the Lord has made." At the time he heard the phrase he thought it was trite, but today it was a glorious expression to be shouted to the hilltops. He decided it was a day to explore Bland County and the likelihood of magnificently adorned mountains a multitude of blooming plants and trees. Fortuitously, he had an intern assigned to him from Welch Hospital, so he determined he was quite capable of attending today's caseload. So, he called Jenn and declared, "We are going for an outing. Go, prepare yourself accordingly," he teased.

"Well, that could mean anything. Do you mean my little black nightgown or clogs and blue jeans?"

"Do not tempt your lord and master, evil woman. Hiking clothes are the dress of the day."

"For real? Where are we going?"

"Rocky Gap, Virginia. We might try to find an antique shop or an eatery. Or maybe an old army buddy. Who knows?"

Jenn's demeanor changed from jovial to serious in a flash. "You are going to try to find the writer of that mysterious note, aren't you?"

"That might be a side consideration, yes. But mostly I plan to spend the day watching you in your tight blue jeans. I could not handle that glorious sight without the distraction of the Spring foliage."

"You are so full of bull hockey, but Ah will try my best to outshine Springtime just for you."

David loaded up the Jeep with a basket of goodies and a thermos of hot coffee prepared by the loving hands of his mother. Mrs. Cabot had fully integrated into the Appalachian lifestyle to the degree that her son often wondered if she was the same woman. She had shed the two-piece suits with the frilly blouse that had been her uniform while living in Boston. She now wore loose-fitting flowery house dresses, comfortable flat leather oxfords with men's white socks. Except for their hair, from the back, you could not tell Mrs. Cabot from Annie.

Jenn came bouncing out of the kitchen door wearing a M★A★S★H tee shirt, sneakers and...tight jeans. David might be a Harvard gentleman, but his mouth dropped into a lascivious stare, quickly morphed into a sheepish grin, neither unnoticed by an impish Jenn. After looking her up and down, he inquired, "Where did you get the t-shirt?"

"Ah ordered if off the TV show. Did I get it too small?"

"Too small?" Silence. "Too small? Uh...no. It's... magnificent," he blurted.

"You said tight and Ah aims to please. Kind of brings out the lecher in you, don't it?" Jenn teased.

"I am not given to lecherousness," David protested.

"Well, if'n you ain't yew orta be 'cause yew air a'lookin' at one sexy woe'mun," Jenn teased in the native mountain dialect.

"Get in the Jeep before I turn you over my knee."

"Promise?" Jenn mocked.

"Now cut that out!" David yelled, mimicking George Burns of radio fame.

The drive down—a definite contradiction since it was mostly uphill—was inspiring, especially Pinnacle Rock where they had stopped for a brief stroll down memory lane. Its base was embroidered as with white lace by dogwood trees. The carefully placed color of rhododendron, redbud, the tantalizing aroma of honeysuckle and the raucous songs of the many birds combined to create a multidimensional mosaic on the senses. They strolled along the path resplendent with tulips, crocus, daffodils, even dandelions heading to the spot where they had had their first kiss those eons ago. They relived the moment, but with far more fervor, and resumed their trek to the Wolf Creek Valley via the East River Mountains.

Route 52 twisted and turned through South Bluefield where 'money' still occupied millionaire homes built during the hey-day of King Coal. They were particularly lovely now, ablaze with Springtime foliage. David guided the Jeep up Bland Road to where it dead ends on Cumberland road, then a right turn to where Maryland Avenue ends on

Washington Street. A 270-degree switch-back from west to east starts the long upward climb on Route 52 to the top of East River Mountain where they parked the Jeep at the overlook and took in the splendor of the view of the valley below enhanced by an abundance of Spring color.

The descent from the summit was far more curvaceous with many twists and turns to cause the drive to be extraordinarily time-consuming. Unlike the ascent, the descent revealed more colorful foliage appreciatively with few distant views. At the foot of the mountain—now on the Virginia side—they were surprised to encounter a massive construction project that turned out to be the beginnings of a tunnel through the mountain. A short stretch of dirt road ended at the town of Rocky Gap situated on Wolf Creek.

They found a small diner across the street from the high school. "Does this look like a decent place to you?" asked David.

"They have a daily blue plate special and, in my experience, they are nearly always good since they are mostly homecooked the old fashion way," opined Jenn.

"The blue-plate special it is then," David complied as he nosed the Jeep into the small parking lot.

The temperature was pleasant, and the entrance to the eatery was blocked only by a screen door. David held the door for Jenn, and she led the way. A middle-aged woman wearing a lace-trimmed apron greeted them and smilingly led them to one of six tables all covered with spanking white ornate, tablecloths. David decided to use the "shot-in-the-dark" direct approach, and as they were being seated, he inquired. "Does Tom Duggan still work here?"

"Mercy sakes alive! He ain't worked here since before he left for the war in Korea. He's my cousin, you know?"

"He was in my outfit in Korea, and I remember him saying that he was from here. Do you know where he is now?"

"Last Ah heard, he had gone up north somewhere to go to school and is now workin' for the gov'ment in some capacity. What kin Ah get ya'll to eat?"

Jenn said, "We'll both have the blue-plate special. You want ice tea, Hon?" She inquired of David, and he agreed with her choice, noticing the use of the term of endearment for the first time.

"Lemon?"

"Yes, for both of us."

"Be right back. You kin warsh your hands through that door over there," the waitress pointed.

It wasn't five minutes later that the waitress returned with two large platters featuring a large slab of meatloaf and a mound of hand-mashed potatoes, both smothered with brown gravy, and a side of green beans. They heartily polished-off their plates and sopped up the remainder with home-made light rolls. They reluctantly declined apple pie and asked for the check. The waitress placed the check on the table and commented, "I asked my Mom about Tom, and she said he had been seen recently down at the old Jennings Place over at The Gap."

"The Gap? Where is that?"

Gesturing, she indicated a direction and accompanied it with, "Down the road about eight miles. It's got a big fancy sign.

David looked at the check and remarked, "I can't believe we got all of that food for such a pittance." He then placed a tip equal to the total bill and still thought he had gotten a major bargain.

"So, I guess that we are going to visit The Jennings Place," said Jenn. It was not a question.

"We will take a quick look. Nothing more. It's probably a wild-goose-chase anyway."

"You wanna bet?"

"I will take that bet. What are you putting up?"

"A roll in the hay." She said sassily.

"I don't have anything of equal value to match that bet. Tell you what, I'll let you set our wedding date and we will not deviate from your selection. Fair enough?"

"You got a deal. That's the only way Ah'll get that roll in'a hay from you. Then she said quite seriously, "You mean that about the weddin' date?"

"Yes," he answered.

Just then the sign for the farm came into view. They passed under the arch created by the sign and followed a well-kept dirt road through the lovely plush, green grassland. The house just down the road was a two-story Salt Box with a large, inviting front porch. The road ended at the yard that doubled as a parking lot since there was a lone late model station wagon sitting in front of the house. Doctor parked beside the station wagon and started for the house. A man with a shovel came around the house and asked Doctor if he could be of help.

"Yes," answered Doctor. "Is the owner available?"

"You mean the real owner? He ain't here but th' lady who's a'rentin' it is. Jes' go'head and knock on the door. She'll answer."

David started for the porch, and Jenn jumped from the Jeep and caught up with him just as he reached the door. He knocked and called out. "Anybody home?"

A voice from within said, "Just a minute. I'll be right there."

They waited as footfalls came closer to the door. The screen door opened and there in front of them was Mrs. Peters, Calvin's Mom. No one spoke. A dead silence prevailed.

Mrs. Peters, finally recognizing her visitors, quickly pushed the screen door open with a big smile and equally large greeting, "Dr. Cabot, Miss Stone, what a wonderful surprise. Come in, come in, please. I cannot believe this. I'm sorry Tod is not here. He will be so sorry he missed you."

She led them to a comfortable sitting room furnished in early American and bade them to sit.

"Thank you," Jenn and Doctor said in unison. "This is a lovely room," Jenn added.

"May I get you some refreshments? Coffee? Tea? A beer maybe? I am so thrilled to see you. Calvin is doing better here in the country with horses and cows. He has his own dog! An English Setter! They love each other so much. Oh, please forgive my rudeness. Why are you here? Do you have some news for me about Calvin and maybe testing? Tod didn't explain why he canceled the Charlottesville trip, something to do with his work and, also, the company got rid the plane. Is it possible to still get the evaluation?"

"Yes, it is," Doctor replied as Jenn shot a look in his direction.

"It is not too late. We were apprehensive about losing contact with you after your abrupt cancellation. Finding you today was fortuitous. We were looking for a young man that

I had served within a MASH Unit in Korea who lived in Rocky Gap when he entered the service. I have anticipated seeking him out on several occasions but always encountered an interruption. Upon awakening this morning to such a glorious day, we decided what better occasion could present itself for a foray across the mountain?"

"What is the soldier's name? inquired Mrs. Peters.

"Tom Duggan."

"Oh, we know him. They are working on a case together."

"Case together?" Jenn inquired.

"Yes, they both work for the Government."

"Well now, this is another fine mess you've got us in, Stanley," opined Jenn. "Reminds me of being in a dairy barn lot. No matter how careful you are you're gonna' step in cow..."

"Do not say it!"

"Ah was gonna' say 'doo.' You got your mind in the gutter."

"To the contrary, the situation is well in hand and going precisely as I had anticipated."

"Bull..."

"Do...not...say...it!"

"There you go again. Ah was going to say 'hockey.' You never learn, do you?" Jenn said, laughing at him.

"Enough. Please get serious; we have important matters to consider."

"Like what?"

"Our wedding principally. Then..."

"Whoa. You mean real soon?"

"Yes."

"Well, glory be. Ah thought you would never ask. Are you goin' to plan it, or are you leaving it up to me?' Jenn inquired cattily.

David laughed at her and replied, "Neither of us will get the honor. As you are aware, Mom and Annie are just waiting for us to set the date to activate their strategy."

"No joke," Jenn said. "What are you going to do about the Peters' thing? You left her with the expectation of receiving help for her boy. You're not giving her more false hope, are you?"

"The answer is unequivocal, NO! Bill told me just last week that your nephew is still at UVA for an extra semester to take a couple of qualifying courses to prepare himself for his new job with the State better, and to finalize the Autism study, that, by the way, is turning out to be of major significance. He will be glad to schedule us, you'll see," David said, pleadingly.

"Okay, Ah'll yield to your dubious wisdom. Let's head for home, so I can get the girls started on a weddin' before you back out again," replied Jenn.

"There you go again. Manipulating the facts to suit your perception of a situation. I did not back out as you say. Unforeseen Circumstances intervened of which you are well aware."

"You backed out. Admit it."

"Aww...Bull hockey" fussed David.

Sixty-Six

The hint suggesting that his prime suspect in organized crime activity may be an employee of the Federal Government prompted Doctor Cabot to seek the counsel of the Sheriff, who suggested they meet at Doctor's office around five the next day.

"I will have 'The Girls' set another plate at the supper table, and I will not take no for an answer."

"See you tomorr'a then," responded the sheriff.

It was almost six o'clock, and Shirley was closing up shop. It had been a heavy day. Jenn had left about half-hour ago leaving Doctor Cabot to turn off the lights and lock the file cabinets. He had previously thought the security of the building was adequate until about a month ago his files were pilfered. One high-profile black lung patient record was taken or misplaced. Since then all black lung cases were placed in a new steel vault with a sophisticated combination lock. It was probably not coincidental that the file disappearance occurred around the same time Bill spoke to David requesting his possible testimony in an ongoing black lung case.

Dr. Cabot completed his assigned chores and went to join the womenfolk. He found them so deep in discussion of wedding plans they didn't even notice his arrival.

He cleared his throat and announced his presence by declaring, "I am an integral part of these nuptials, are you not aware?"

"Only minimally," Mom declared. "Supper is on the stove. Help yourself."

He did as he was told—with pleasure—since that was the first time in his life that his mother had given him such a command and he knew it was because she was part of the same 'whole' as he. She felt secure with her new family— categorically secure.

Sheriff Hare pulled up and parked in back of the house at precisely five P.M. As usual Clinic was still going strong, so he went straight to the kitchen in search of Miss Annie. He found the 'Bobbsey Twins'—his new name for Mom and Annie—joyfully engaged in cooking and conversation.

"It smells plumb heavenly in here," Sheriff declared.

"Well it orta, cause two ang'uls air'a doin' th' cookin'," Annie declared in her loudest voice. "Come on in an' set'ch self-down. Supper's almost ready and we'r a'waitin' the Clinic crew. Yew want coffee?"

"Now Miss Annie, when did you ever know an officer of the law to refuse coffee? Please and thank you ma'am."

Yur'welcome. If'n you ain't seen the mornin' paper hit's over thar on the table."

Sheriff had just settled down when the noise of Jenn and David ascending the back steps to the kitchen reached them. They seemed to be engaged in a friendly argument, and as they bounded through the kitchen door, she pushed him along in front of her yelling, "Tell them. Go ahead, tell them, "you chicken poop, mealy-mouthed, back-slidin' weaseling quitter."

"I said nothing that deserved such verbal abuse…"

"Shut up and tell'um before Ah get physical, then you'll know what abuse is. Tell'um, NOW!"

"Okay, okay. I simply suggested, suggested mind you, that maybe circumstances dictated the need to postpone the wedding for a week or two."

"Week 'er two? You just said downstairs until the first of th' year. That's uh week er two?"

Mom finally stepped forward and suggested calm. "David," she said, "I have never spanked you before in your life, but if what Jenn is saying is factual, then I am about to break a record. There is no way on God's green earth that you are going to…weasel, is that the word, Jenn? Out of the plans that we have all been slaving over for…how long? Now you get ready for supper. We have a guest in case you do not recall?"

"I was teasing, Mom. Gee whiz, you women certainly are serious over a minimalist ceremony…" and that opened a floodgate of feminist angst.

David made a rapid exit yelling and laughing over his shoulder tauntingly.

Table-talk was light and followed a line of mostly fluff. The Ladies baited David with wedding suggestions that he pointedly ignored as he and the sheriff were politely waiting to get to their appointed conversation. Dessert was a deep-dish peach pie with the choice of the cream, plain or whipped, along with the requisite coffee. Sheriff polished off two large servings with about a quart of cream on each. Doctor abstained electing only for Annie's special blend of wild-picked chicory and Chase and Sanborn coffee. The sheriff took the last sip of coffee from his mug and suggested, "Doctor, let's refill our coffee cups and go into the library. I believe you have something for me?"

Grateful that Sheriff had taken the initiative, Doctor stood up and said, "Let's. Pardon us ladies," and meandered to the library via the coffee pot, followed by Sheriff Hare.

They sat in Queen Anne armchairs with an ornate baroque table between them for what seemed like an eternity. Finally, Sheriff broke the silence; "Ah believe you have some new information?"

"I do." Silence, as Doctor pondered.

"Well?" inquired the Sheriff.

"We found Tom Duggan."

"Really? Where?"

"Big Gap, Virginia. He was recently seen on the Peters farm by a lady who owns a restaurant in Rocky Gap where Duggan worked before he was drafted into the Korean War. We went—"

"Who's We?"

"Jenn and I."

"Does she know the whole story?"

"No. Mrs. Peters thinks that I was looking up an old army buddy."

"Are you sure?"

"No, I am not...sure. We went to the Peters Farm, and there we were met at the door by Mrs. Peters whose son is a patient of mine. She was excited to see us and invited us in for refreshments. I asked her if she knew Duggan and she gleefully answered in the affirmative stating that her husband and Tom were 'working a case together' for the Federal Government."

"You gotta be pullin' my leg. That ain't possible."

"Just stating the facts Sheriff. That is exactly what she told us."

"Now ain't that a fine kettle of fish? Workin' for the government. Well, let's consider that she is tellin' the truth as she knows it and that they are working for the Feds, which agency? And if they are coming into Mercer County, which I suspect they would be, then why haven't they contacted my office?"

"Perhaps, in line with your concerns for the possible involvement of law agencies in the area, they do not trust you either?" asked Doctor.

"Rite'cha are. Good detective thinkin'. Now with that in mind, consider the anonymous note found in the drowin' victim's pocket, and the evidence it was placed there after he was drowned, and before he was dumped in the Bluestone, then somebody is tryin' to get a message—to you? No, not you, but through you? Did he use a dead body as a messenger? It must be Duggan! He's around and knows from the past that you might be in the area, so he chose Bluefield as a likely place. So, did he, or his agency, move the body into Mercer County?"

"A real long shot, don't you think?"

"Not if you consider that along with the fact that Duggan's fingerprints wuz on the money found used to make the Company Store purchase. That had to be a real goof or— on purpose and Ah'm uh' bettin' it was deliberate.

"That is most illogical. There is no way that such an isolated, incidental clue would find its way to me."

"Wrong. We are being watched. They–whoever they are—are tracking just about every move you make which means 'they' know that you are collaboratin' with me. Now if the good guys are tracking each other, then who are the bad guys? We have been assuming Peters to be tied in with the mob somehow when he just might be undercover. Is Duggan teasing you into contacting' him? If he is, he sure ain't givin' you much with which to work. Your finding him was pure luck even though that's what you were after. And Peters; what was his motive for getting' you on a plane to Charlottesville? Why did he change his mind? We know that the plane registration is for a suspected mob associate. Did he get wise to Peters? Are we bein' suckered inta' somethin'? Questions, questions. That's all we have. The big one, though, is what do we do now?"

"I think I have already addressed that concern," Said Doctor Cabot.

"How? What have you done.?"

"At the bequest of Mrs. Peters, I intend to reschedule the evaluation of her son at UVA. Jenn's nephew is involved in a research project directed at identifying unique neural correlates in auditory processing deficits, and I cleared the way for her son to for that evaluation. One of the caveats of that opportunity is that each parent must stand for a personal interview."

"What if one of them is not the real parent?"

"No matter. The history is more for parenting than being a parent."

"Well, Ah suppose that makes sense to you; it don't to me."

"Another reason for the interview is to see if Peters even shows up. He seems to have disappeared or made himself quite scarce for some time now. Where is he? Maybe this will bring him to the fore so that we can begin to extrapolate some tangibles related to our enigma. Are we chasing our collective tails? Are we engaged in activity related to the Governor's edict? It appears to me that Mr. Peters is a critical player in those details."

"Doc" puzzled the sheriff, "You plumb lost me there. Just be careful, and lawful, in anything you do, and I am behind you all the way."

Chapter

Sixty-Seven

Jim had been in school for several weeks now and tonight was family conference time planned to coincide with a first progress report. Miss Annie had fixed all his favorite dishes—Jell-O—and Margie was playing hostess—she had made the Jell-O. Everyone was excited, even Doctor who had ordered in a specially decorated cake for the occasion—with Annie's approval, of course.

The table set ready, and the family began to assemble. Jenn noticed an extra place setting and inquired whom it was for, and Annie said, "Fer your brother, Bill. He has uh way of showin' up fer spe'ul uh'casions."

They were preparing to be seated when Jim said boldly, "I wish't ever'body wud hol' hands so Ah kin say a blessin' if'n ya'll don't mind, cuz ya'll are my family an' Ah want to tell God how much Ah 'preciate that."

Hands joined with no hesitation. Jim began. "Lord fer u'long time Ah thought yew din't care 'bout me. Now Ah know better. Thank yew. Amen."

A pin dropping would have sounded like thunder. No one spoke. The spell was broken by Bill who stormed through the kitchen door with a hearty cheer, "Hear there's a celebration for our schoolboy here tonight. Wouldn't miss it for the world."

Doctor whispered, "Annie you ol' con artist. You knew he was coming all along." Annie just grinned and ordered, "Ya'll start eatin'now."

Bill was the first to ask Jim for details of his studies. "What's the first thing you learned of importance, Jim?"

"Well ah guess ah'd hav'ta say Ah ain't supposed to say ain't," said Jim laughing.

"You're joking aren't you, Jim?"

"Ah am, and, yew notice Ah put the D on there? Ah am real proud to say that we are learn'n to talk in'tell'gee'bul? So's we can ku'mu'nu…talk so we can unner'stan' each other. Air teacher says if'n we don't larn to talk rite, he will have trouble teachi' us. He says Ah.m doin' good."

"He is correct, Jim, and I for one, think you are doing marvelously," said Doctor.

"Hear, hear," said Jenn and Bill enthusiastically

Margie said, "Eat'ch Jell-O, Jim. Ah made it."

Joyful laughter followed. As the party appeared to be ending, Bill turned to David and asked, "Got a minute for me? Ah've got information on the trial. Ah'm scheduled to present my case next week, and Ah'm puttin' you on first. Are you ready?"

"I most assuredly am. I don't think there is an iota of doubt that you will win with the irrefutable evidence revealed to me by your anonymous tipster. Let's go to the library where we can talk."

Chapter

Sixty-Eight

The Bailiff called the court to ordered by announcing the arrival of the Judge.

"All rise. this court is now in session, the honorable Judge Fred Green presiding."

The Judge lumbered to the dais and fell into his chair and mumbled, "Be seated."

He then turned to the jury and asked them if they were ready. He saw nodded heads and heard whispered yeses. The judge then said, "well then, let's get back to it." The Judge turned to Bill and inquired," Mr. Stone, Ah believe it's your turn. Are you ready?"

Bill, the lone companion of the Plaintiff, was seated with him at one table. Bill glanced over to the defense table where enough occupants sat to field a basketball team with reserves aplenty.

Bill then faced the Judge and said, "Ah am your honor. Ah'd like to call as my first witness, Dr. David Cabot."

"Objection, your honor," called the Defense. "Dr. Cabot could not possibly have any pertinent information regarding the case since he arrived into the community long after this claim was filed."

"Mr. Stone?" the Judge questioned.

"To the contrary, Dr. Cabot is in possession of vital information supporting the Plaintiff's position."

"Objection overruled. Continue Mr. Stone."

Dr. Cabot came forward from the gallery and turned toward the Bailiff.

"Please state your name for the court."

"Dr. David Cabot"

"Please raise your right hand."

"Do you solemnly swear that the testimony you are about to give is the truth, the whole truth and nothing but the truth, so help you, God?"

"I do."

"Please be seated."

The jury was obviously acquainted with the Doctor and smiled at him as he passed them on his way to the witness chair.

Bill rose from his table and asked, "Dr. Cabot, do you have any experience with black lung."

"Yes, I do. I have a practice in Boston Knob where over fifty percent of my caseload is men dying from black lung."

Several jury members nodded their heads in agreement.

"The Defense violently responded, "Objection, Your honor, prejudicial."

"Sustained."

"Fact," retorted Doctor.

"Doctor, your standin' in the community don't allow you to sass me. Now act rahght."

Bill accepted the free point and asked the next question. "Please continue, Doctor."

"Black lung disease can be surreptitious. Early on, it may be specifically asymptomatic often mistakenly considered to be the result of smoking or other medical problems like heart disease or asthma both of which can be comorbid with black lung. Too often simple black lung develops into progressive massive fibrosis before a diagnosis, usually after about ten or twenty years of exposure. However, due to more careful diagnosis, we are finding that miners are now dying at a much younger age."

"Objection. Calls for a conclusion not in evidence."

"Overruled."

"Additionally, the cases of progressive massive fibrosis appear to be growing exponentially—"

"Objection."

"Overruled."

"— as reported by the National Institutes of Health."

"Thank you, Doctor. Now let's move on to the diagnosis and treatment of progressive massive fibrosis. How is it diagnosed?"

"We usually see the coal miner first experiencing breathing problems or chronic coughing. However, the preponderance of coal miners ignores all signs of black lung until its insidiousness becomes irreversible—"

"Objection. Calls for a con—"

"Overruled."

"—repeat, irreversible. I do not believe it is ignorance of the disease that causes coal miners to not seek early detection, but rather the inevitability of the results… 'Objection'

…the miner is locked into …'OBJECTION'…a lifestyle where he is doomed to die no matter… 'OBJECTION, YOUR HONOR, OBJECTION. Immaterial, Lacks Foundation!'

"Sustained. Doctor, you will save your editorializin' for the newspapers."

Bill grabbed onto the presented opportunity by asking, "Doctor, what percentage of progressive massive fibrosis sufferers die of the disease?"

"Objection."

"Overruled."

"Really no one can say. There is no cure, so if a miner acquires it, he will die, most likely, because of it. Too often the miner is aware that he has black lung but cannot afford to quit work, so death by the disease is a foregone conclusion. If they had the opportunity to leave the mine once the disease is suspicioned and diagnosed, then progression is stopped and even sometimes reversed."

"Now Doctor, so far your testimony has been regarding generalities. Let me ask you this. Do you recognize the plaintive?"

"No, I do not."

"Have you seen him before today?"

"I don't know. His name appears in my appointment book and a chart with a number assigned to that name, but we did not find his chart in my records. Recently we had a break-in, and the files were..."

"Objection."

"...pilfered."

"Move to strike. Irrelevant."

"Sustained. The jury will ignore the reference to a break-in."

Bill continued. "So, what you are saying the Plaintiff has no records in your Clinic?"

"No, I did not say that. I said no such chart was found in my records."

"Oh? There are other records?"

"Yes, in the stored files of my predecessor at the Boston Knob Medical Clinic, Dr. Stan Fields.

"Objection. Those records are inadmissible for lack of evidence as to their origin and verifiability. Anyone could have put anything they wanted to in those unsecured files."

"Sustained. Git at it another way, counselor," ordered the judge.

"Tell me, Doctor, where are those files?" Bill innocently asked.

"They are in a secure vault at the Bank and have been ever since the death of Dr. Fields."

Have you seen those files?"

"No. I have not."

"Then how do you know the Plaintiff's charts are in those files?" Bill inquired.

"Two reasons. First, the Plaintiff told me he had been a patient of Dr. Fields, and second, in Dr. Fields's papers was a report on his research on black lung. He had carefully documented every black lung patient he had been following for twenty years and placed them in the bank vault several months before his death."

"Objection, Your Honor. This is the rankest form of hearsay."

"We'll see about that. Ah think that we need ta'be doin' a bit of vault divin'. Court will adjourn and meet at the Bank at nine in the morning."

Bill and David lagged behind and left the courtroom later to avoid good-will wishers. David lounged in a chair, and Bill sat on a table. They were silent for long seconds. Finally, Bill mused, "Ah sure hope you are right about the records in the bank vault. If they are as detailed as you expect, this trial should be over in the morning."

"I am confident it will be. I never met Dr. Fields, but I feel that I have known him for many years. Two different men could have written the documentation he left behind. His clinical notes were simplistic if not naive. He probably wrote them in the same language he used to explain his findings to his patients. On the other hand, when he was writing in his journal, he used precise, articulate and scientific language suitable for the most sophisticated medical journal. I expect to find his black lung notes to fit that protocol. I do not doubt the existence of those records nor do I doubt the release they will offer to your client and others caught in this dishonest trap set by the mine operators and their collaborators."

"I do so hope you are right," Bill whispered.

Morning came, and the Bank was swarming. The word had spread and newsmen as far away as Charleston were on hand. The Judge had ordered the presence of Sheriff Hare and two of his deputies as crowd control and to assure the security of the contents of the vault. The vault was, in fact, a file cabinet-sized safe-deposit box, the rent through automatic withdrawal from Fields Trust Fund. Limited space demanded the reduction in the size of the defense contingent to one, Bill, the jury, the Judge and Sheriff Hare. The bank president did the honors of removing the box and carrying it to a table placed in the center of the lobby that was not yet open for business. The bank president inserted his key into the box and turned to the Judge with the question, "Who has the other key?"

Silence. Nobody moved. Then, from the back of the room, a voice called out, "I think Ah do."

The entire room turned as if on a puppet's string to see Jenn holding an unopened envelope toward Sheriff Hare. He took it and passed it to the Judge who checked to see that the seal had not been broken and tore off the end. He tilted the envelope into his hand, and the key fell out. The judge then handed the key to the Bank President who inserted it into the other slot of the box, turned both keys and the box, stuffed with medical charts, opened. Without a word, the Judge went to the alphabetically ordered files to that of the plaintiff. He extracted the fat folder and dumped its contents on the table for all to see. There were x-rays, lab reports, clinical notes and before and after pictures of the Plaintiff. The Judge turned to Bill and said, "Mr. Stone, Ah will entertain a motion for a directed verdict."

Chapter

Sixty-Nine

The court decision was received with the same stoic acceptance as just about every other event in the Mountains: "So what? We won't git nothin' out of hit." As Dr. Cabot considered these events, he concluded that, to a very large extent, such an attitude was justified. For over a century the coal miner had been at the mercy of scoundrels of one kind or another. If it wasn't the operators with their company stores, or, it was the Union with their agendas not necessarily aimed at helping the man under the mountain. Multiple agencies set out with altruistic goals that often created an unwieldy maze of laws, rules, procedures, etc. that too often worked at cross purposes to lead the applicant to an administrative dead-end. Hence, if a claimant had even a slight chance of obtaining any compensation for the disease, early detection was necessary to allow time for the resistive application process while, at the same time, continued exposure—out of the necessity to earn a living—was further complicating the disease. Ostensibly, under new federal laws, any miner diagnosed with black lung should be assigned a different job to be removed from the offending environment. Claims could be filed under some new federal regulations, but total disability was required. Surviving spouses and children of miners who died from black lung were also entitled to monthly benefits.

Unfortunately, it was often an uphill battle to qualify for benefits under either the Federal program or State workers' compensation. The mining industry fought these claims vigorously, leading to lengthy legal battles. The laws favored the miner; the enforcement favored the operator.

Dr. Cabot had been researching the beginnings of a campaign to have coal miner's pneumoconiosis (black lung) established as a compensated disability that began in the West Virginia coalfields in the 1960s. He noted that, as the amount of coal mined increased, so did the number of miners with the disease. That black lung was generally ignored, appalled the doctor. His medical colleagues contended that 'miner's asthma' was a normal condition for mine workers and posed no serious problems with claims that the disease did not show on x-rays. It was a fairly common perception that malingering was rampant causing cynicism toward all claims, even the legitimate ones.

Dr. Cabot's newspaper presented articles about the President, of the United Mine Workers Association (UMWA), pushing for black lung recognition at a time when an explosion at a Consolidation Coal Company mine occurred taking the lives of over one hundred men. A national television audience heard defenders of the company suggest that disasters were an accepted risk in mining. He was pleased to read that social unrest was thriving, and the miner's situation was leading 'Poverty War' volunteers to become engaged in multiple civil protests, encouraging the formation of the Black Lung Association to guide a compensation bill through the state legislature. Events in West Virginia made black lung a national issue as Congress passed the Coal Mine Health and Safety Act of 1969. The new law placed strict standards on dust levels and provided federally financed compensation for affected miners, and their widows and children. However, the number of conditions, exceptions, alternatives, substitutes and a multitude of cross-agency conflictions made the application process near impossible. But, that was the easy part; before the application could be submitted a doctor's report was required. Since the coal companies employed most of the doctors, a diagnosis was not always forthcoming. This attitude was incomprehensible to Dr. Cabot who maintained that he was an advocate for his sick patients and the conscience of malingerers. He would tolerate no shenanigans, and he became an expert in spotting them in the Army Medical Corps.

Seventy

David was luxuriating with his feet propped up on an open file drawer with Bo's cushion serving as padding. Bo did not need it as he was comfortably ensconced upon Doctor's lap receiving an ear rub. They were both approaching Level one REM Sleep when Jenn bounced into the room with the inquiry, "What are you two hound-dogs doin? Ya'll are sleepin! Aren't you?"

Neither dog nor man made any effort to move. Jenn moved in front of them and plopped down on David's lap, after that, both dog and man applied affectionate kisses to her protesting face.

"Yuck! Stop that. Ah don't know which of you is the worst. Now cut that out!"

Bo decided he had had enough and jumped to the floor and David pulled Jenn closer and said, "Let's set a wedding day, right this instant."

Jenn, showing no reaction replied, "You got a deal." But right now, you have a visitor; we will discuss those plans tonight at the supper table, rest assured."

Dr. Cabot sent Bo upstairs to Annie, and he straightened his desk to receive whomever Jenn had called a 'visitor' instead of a 'patient.' Shortly the door opened, and Shirley presented an expensively dressed gentleman with the introduction, "Mr. Peters to see you, Doctor.

Dr. Cabot stood slowly— to appear neutral—and extended a welcoming hand. He gestured to a chair and said, "Mr. Peters, what can I do for you?"

Peters, seating himself replied in a cultured voice, "It is finally good to meet you face-to-face after all of this time, Doctor. We have much to talk about."

"Oh, and what would that be?"

"Don't play coy with me, Doctor. I am not one of your hillbilly coal miners to whom you can play doctor superior."

Doctor bristled and responded with an equivalent tone. "And you, Mr. Peters, are not communicating with one of your...cronies."

"I am truly sorry, Doctor. I deserved that. Let's start over."

"Agreed. You go first."

"I came into this community with less than altruistic purposes. You may have heard that I had a connection with...the mob, and that is partially true. Because of my wife, I found myself beholden to...the mob. She is unaware of that obligation and that she and her son are in danger if I fail to fulfill my obligation to them. My job has been to assess this area as a staging point for a tri-state crime syndicate involved in cigarette smuggling, drugs—primarily the growth and transporting of marijuana—and the mass production of illegal liquor. I have been slacking on the performance of my duties—intentionally—and we are in danger of reprisals from my employers..."

provide you with a cup of coffee and something to eat and I will have a confidential conversation with the Sheriff. He is a stalwart, honest man whom I have grown to respect and he, I'm sure, will properly advise you. If he says you need to be arrested, I shall comply with your request. I will surrender you and my badge simultaneously. Satisfactory?"

"Yes sir, Officer."

Chapter

Seventy-One

Doctor Cabot placed a call to Sheriff Hare post haste. The Sheriff's office answered after a short wait for a connection. He informed the secretary that the call was a bit urgent and she said that the Sheriff was out in the County somewhere. Dr. Cabot requested that a radio call go to the sheriff with the following message: "Officer needs assistance, Code 2, Deputy Cabot." Minutes later Shirley informed Doctor that the Sheriff was five minutes out, Code 3. "Lights and siren, hot dog!" responded Doctor. He was beginning to enjoy himself as the Mercer County Crime Wave appeared to be waning.

Sheriff rolled into the Clinic parking lot with lights and siren orchestrating a symphony of urgency. He was in the door before the last note faded into pianissimo. Shirley pointed to the back of the facility and said, "He's waitin' fer you back 'air."

Doctor heard the commotion as well as the whining of the siren and met the Sheriff in the hallway. "Come on into my office. I have noteworthy news for you. I believe I have unraveled all of our mysteries as being in a single ball of yarn."

"Your message sounded hopeful. What do you have for me?"

"I have the solution to the mystery in custody upstairs drinking coffee with Annie."

"What? In custody? Who...in custody? You don't have arrest powers! I told you, you wouldn't have too. Didn't I?"

"Yes, that is what you said. But you did not say I could not, correct?"

"Okay, forget that. Tell me what you have."

"Sit down, and I will lead you through the solution. Here is a tablet and a pencil if you want to diagram it as we go along. First, you had a mysteriously drowned boy, young man really, in The Bluestone Lake. Next, he was found to have chlorinated water in his lungs rather than the lake water. He had a cryptic note in his pocket, in French that directs the finder to a 'Capt. Cabot in Bluefield'. I remembered a word that led me to recall an incident in Korea where, and by whom, that unique word was used, and it provided a clue as to the possible writer of the note found on the drowning victim. You found a fingerprint on the note belonging to a Tom Duggan. He had served in same MASH Unit as I. Duggan's prints were on the money used to buy the inventory of the store our ladies have established to sell their artwork. Now, my informant can put all of this together for you. Let's go see him."

Sheriff Hare followed Doctor Cabot up the private stairs to the kitchen. Just they reached the top Doctor stopped and whispered to the sheriff, "Wait, they appear to be having an intense conversation. Annie has a way of gleaning information from reluctant sources. Let's see what they are talking about."

Annie was talking. "Then why'did'cha tell folks ya'll wuz mair'ed if'n yew ain't?' she inquired.

"Because she is the source of my conundrum," answered Mr. Peters.

"Wh'tha heck air a conum'brum?" asked Miss Annie.

"Problem, puzzle? I found her and her little boy huddled in the entryway of my office one morning on my way to work. I confronted her more with aggravation than anything else since she was blocking my door. Then she looked up at me; her face was a mess. She had been beaten. The child just had a blank look on his face and never spoke. There is a doctor in our building, and I asked him to take a cursory look at them to see if they needed to go to an emergency room, and he found her to be free of any more than bruises. Whoever had beaten her knew what they were doing. He said that the boy appeared to be severely retarded."

"Ah got'uh retarded dotter, so Ah know all'uh'bout that. She is uh Mongol'un idjit. Doctor Cabot says Ah ort to call her a Down Sym'drom. Wha'cha do with them?"

"I am an accountant, so I don't need a big office, so there was no room to bring them in there. So, I took them to my apartment. I'm single, so I have plenty of room for them. I really did not have the time to search for a home for abused women. I did call the police and the welfare department there in Cincinnati, and they told me there was little they could do unless the woman would come forward and file a complaint, which Angie would not do, Thus, forcing me into the role of caretaker for them."

"Did'cha mind doin' that?" asked Annie.

"Not at all. We were doing quite well until one day I came home from work and found a rough looking man there and Angie had been worked-over again. She made the mistake of going back to where she had been working to pick up her belongings when she encountered the man who claimed she was indebted to him and owed him a lot of money to be 'worked off' at his establishment. He asked Angie what her 'new man' did that he could afford her and she told him that I was an accountant. The man brightened and said I could work off Angie's debt by providing services for a company in which he was the part owner that turned out to be a crime syndicate looking into moving into Appalachia. At first, all they wanted me to do, they said, was go in and see if moving into the state could be profitable, and if the people were conducive to mob control. I did that, and that's where I am now."

Dr. Cabot decided he had heard enough and he and the Sheriff entered the room. He addressed Annie. "Well Miss Annie, how are you doing with my guest?"

Annie spotted the Sheriff and greeted him. "Howdy, Sonny. Yew doin' al'rite?"

"Fine Miss Annie. Me and the Doctor want to talk with Mr. Peters here. You can stay if you want'a but it would probably be borin' for you."

"Ah got work'ta do anyhow. Ya'll go right ahead. I'll be over in the kitchen if'n yew need me."

"Thank you, Miss Annie, for entertaining Mr. Peters for me. I am sure you did a commendable job."

He then turned to the sheriff and said, "In the interest of time I am going to provide an abridged version of what Mr. Peters elucidated for me earlier that prompted my call to you, Sheriff. Is that amenable to the both of you?"

Both indicated the affirmative.

"Okay. Here is the way I perceive the scenario developing.

"One: Tom Duggan had given the note to Peters to give to me, reason unknown. Peters put the note in his coat pocket. He was wearing that same coat when they found the drowning victim. Peters covered the dead man's body, out of pity or respect, with his jacket. He left the scene without retrieving his coat. Someone put that coat on the victim, perhaps to clear the possible crime scene, before he was thrown into the lake, most likely by someone with the syndicate that moved the body, but not Peters, because he was with Duggan. At the scene of the actual drowning, the motel manager handed over the victim's bag to Duggan who opened it, checked its contents, closed it and gave it to Peters leaving his fingerprints on the money used as payment for the crafts store's inventory.

Two: Sheriff's Office extracted the body from the lake, found the note bearing the title and name 'Capt. Cabot', and location, Bluefield; this appears to be more than coincidence. Why it was in French remains a puzzle. An autopsy revealed that water in the man's lungs was not lake water but chlorinated, confirming that the victim had died somewhere else. I surmised that the reason for the note had to do with Duggan's concern for Peters' predicament thinking that I might be in Bluefield practicing and could help him with a solution.

Three: Sheriff questioned why I had my lawyer investigating Peters and informed me that his office was also curious. This brought about my involvement in the mystery causing me to search my memory for the identity of the note writer. As often happens, a unrelated event prompted the recollection of an exchange I had experienced with a Sargent Duggan on my final day at the MASH Unit in Korea and completed the circle of evidence except for his position as a Federal Agent. This knowledge came when Jenn and I were directed to the residence of Peters over the mountain in Virginia by a restaurateur. She is a relative of Duggan before his military service. She said that her mother thought she had seen him at a home nearby. Upon visiting that home, we were greeted at the door by Mrs. Peters who informed us that Duggan and her husband were both Federal Agents.

Four brings us up to where we are right at this moment. Do you have anything to add Mr. Peters? Sheriff? Questions?" tossing the initiative to the Sheriff allowing him to broach the overheard conversation between Annie and Peters.

Sheriff Hare pondered the question for several seconds and appeared hesitant when he spoke. "Mr. Peters, Doctor and I overheard a portion of your conversation with Miss Annie. Sorry about eavesdroppin' but right now we are beyond bein' polite about this whole mess. You seemed very honest with her. Were you?"

"Yes sir, I was, and I'll expand on that statement if you want."

"Later. You said you are single. Is that correct?"

"Yes."

"And you had never seen the woman and child before you found them at your door?"

There was a long pause before Peters answered. "Well... no, that's not exactly true. I had seen her at the lounge where she worked a time or two."

"So, she had not randomly selected your doorway?"

"No. She had been there before."

"Is there a reason you are unwillin' to tell us about your relationship? Were ya'll close? Datin'? What?"

"I had met her at the lounge where she worked. We talked a little. Her bosses kept a close eye on her. They didn't want her getting too close to the customers."

Sheriff Hare paused thoughtfully before asking, "Were you just another customer?"

Peters looked first at The Sheriff and then at the Doctor. He covered his face with his hands and leaned back in his chair and whispered, "No, I am not just another customer. It's complicated."

That's' what ya'll always say when you are backed in ta 'a corner. The best I can tell, so far, you ain't done nothin' that will buy you any real hard jail time. Why don't you quit beatin' about th'bush and tell us the whole story? Just what in the tarnation are you doin' in our part of the country? It's obvious you ain't here handin' out Watchtower Tracts or sellin' Fuller Brushes. You are knee deep in this mob stuff, ain't'cha?"

Doctor Cabot interrupted saying, "Sheriff, I think that is what he has been trying to undo for the past couple of years. If he was enthusiastic about his assignment, I think we would have seen major criminal activity occurring. I think he is frightened because of his lackadaisical efforts towards gaining a criminal foothold hereabouts. Am I not correct Mr. Peters?"

"Maybe, maybe not." Interjected the Sheriff. "Nobody stays that clean that long and lives to tell about it. That business down at that motel was a hit gone wrong wasn't it?" Sheriff aimed at Peters. "You were the target of unhappy mob action. Somehow you escaped without a scratch, and that young man took the brunt of that action. Why did Duggan give you that bag of money? If he's a Fed why did he allow more criminal activity? As far as Ah am concerned you are just another slick Yankee comin' down here to take advantage of us poor ignorant hillbillies."

"Aren't you a bit harsh?" asked Doctor Cabot.

"Heck no. Think about it. Would the head guy of a big-time mob turn over, even a minor questionably legal job, to an unseasoned outsider? There's more to it than that. What do they hold over you that is an iron-clad guarantee? There's gotta' be something more than you have told us. If you don't open up with the truth, Ah'm gonna turn you over to the State Police and let things take its course, mainly cause this ain't no local matter. On the other hand, we can make it a local matter if you explain, in full, how you got in this mess. Maybe we can straighten it out, real quiet like, among ourselves if you will open up."

Peters sat silently looking at the floor for several moments. Finally, he spoke. "I do have an accounting practice in Cincinnati. My office, if you can call it that, was in the same block as the nightclub that was the…uh… headquarters of a southern Ohio Don. They gambled there, and I got into them for big bucks with no way out. They had a use for me as a legitimate accountant, and I thought that would work off the obligation. Instead it got worse. As a part of my 'job' I got in deeper and deeper to where I was as trusted as any member of crime organization can be, I suppose."

"How did the woman become enmeshed in the situation?" asked Doctor.

"Pretty much like I described it to Miss Annie. That part was true."

"She worked at the nightclub?" Asked Sheriff.

"Yes. She was...is...very pretty, and she worked as a barmaid and sometimes sang. She had studied music at the University of Cincinnati. She was very good. Wanted to go on Broadway. Having that idiot baby ended that dream, so she worked in nightclubs to make a living. Watching out for her was the only good thing I have ever done. What's going to happen to her now?"

"Not my problem," uncharacteristically mumbled the sheriff. "What I need now is for you to quit beatin' 'bout the' bush and tell me just what the heck you been doin' here in my county for the past two years. Whatever it is it ain't been legal. Just how illegal it's been is to be determined. We can probably convict you of somethin' local so you can serve your time in my jail if you just come clean. The doctor seems to be on your side. How about justifyin' his faith in you?"

Peters paused for a long time and finally sighed deeply and started. "Mainly I have been trying to set up marijuana farms and coordinating with the Mexican growers to grow a hybrid plant that has the hardiness of the West Virginia natural growing plant with the potency of the Mexican less hardy plant. There is an abundance of growing areas on the periphery of abandoned strip mines that looked like a possibility for the unobtrusive growing area and also, abandoned mines that were thought by the Mob to be good places to make meth. I used several ways to explore both options and sent my recommendations to the Boss. He took it from there."

"Did any money change hands beside the Craft Store purchase?" Asked the Sheriff.

"No. All I did was find the sites and explore them."

"Did you have permission or were you accompanied by the owner or owners or an approved agent of the same?"

"No."

The Sheriff sat thoughtfully for a very long time. He stood and walked around the room. He then declared that he had to speak with the County DA before he could decide. He asked Doctor Cabot to accompany him as he left the room to make a phone call. The Sheriff had a plan that he wanted to propose to Miss Annie and the Doctor. The three engaged is a very serious discussion and came to a suitable agreement after which the plan was presented to Peters by the Sheriff: "Okay, here's what we're gonna' do. The DA is goin' to indict you on two charges: First, criminal trespass with intent to commit a crime and Second, Criminal activity with intent. You plead guilty to these charges, and the DA will reduce the charges to Misdemeanors with one-year in the County Jail. If you have any assets, they will be liquidated and used to provide for the rehabilitation of Mrs. Peters. You will also be sentenced to 2080 hours of community service, to be served concurrently with the jail time at the discretion of the County that can use an accountant. Are you Agreeable to this?"

"What about Angie and her boy? I can't just abandon them."

"You have no choice. As they say 'you did the crime, you gotta' serve the time.' But Doctor thought about that. "Miss Annie to going to take on Angie as an apprentice paid for out of your impounded funds. The child will be home-schooled by a therapist for one year giving Angie time to get her life together. She is free to stay, but not obligated, for up to a year. At that time, you will be without a criminal record to take over if the two of you want."

"I don't deserve it," responded Peters.

"Indubitably," said Doctor.

Seventy-Two

Dr. Cabot had badgered Jenn's brother into sitting with Tod Peters to satisfy possible doubts concerning his rights. Bill had agreed. The two were seated at the defense table. The District Attorney sat at a table by himself and Dr. Cabot, and Sheriff Hare sat in the gallery behind the rail.

The Judge came through the door from his chambers and said, "remain seated. Mr. DA, what have you for me today?"

"Your honor we have Mr. Tod Peters who chooses to plead guilty. He is being charged with Criminal Trespass and the intent to introduce hybrid Cannabis into the State. Since the laws on Cannabis are grossly unclear in most states, we agreed to drop the Criminal intent charge and agree to a Misdemeanor charge on all counts. We suggest one year in the county jail and 1080 hours of community service."

"How do you plead, Mr. Peters?"

"Guilty, your Honor."

"Counsel, you discussed these conditions with your client?"

"Yes, your honor."

"Mr. Peters, do you understand that by pleading guilty you lose the right to a jury trial?"

"Yes, your Honor."

"Do you give up that right?"

"Yes, your Honor."

"Do you understand that you are waiving your privilege against self-incrimination?"

"Yes, sir."

"Were you in any way forced into accepting this settlement?"

"No, your Honor."

"Are you pleading guilty because you did, in fact, engage in the charges against you?"

"Yes."

"Mr. Peters I hereby sentence you to one year in the county jail, and 1080 hours of Community Service to be determined on day by day basis by the County Sheriff. Court adjourned. Dr. Cabot, will you remain for a moment?"

Doctor moaned and whispered to the Sheriff. "Now what have you gotten me into?"

The DA walked up to Doctor and the Sheriff and put his hand on the Sheriff's shoulder with a happy smile on his face. "What do you think the Judge has in mind for our own personal Sherlock? Let's go with him and find out," he said tugging on the Sheriff's sleeve.

The sheriff said, "Yeah, let's."

The Judge turned from hanging up his robe when the Doctor and his tag-along walked into his chambers. "Why the entourage, Doctor, am I so intimidating that you need a defense team?" the Judge joked.

"Your Honor, I have been shanghaied so many times recently that I do not require an engraved invitation to see another one in the offing."

"Evidence of your intuitive skills in play, and that is exactly why we have invited you here."

"The emphasis on the 'we' is ominous, Judge," noted Dr. Cabot. "Just what has this inter-legal conclave conjured up to disrupt my efforts to practice medicine in your County effectively?"

"Humor aside, Doctor, we were quite impressed with your intuitive skills in deciphering the puzzle initiated by the drowning at Bluestone. But more importantly you triggered an awareness of the diversity of a more sophisticated crime element in our County; indeed, in our State. We have been wearing blinders regarding the view of crime, but this recent event points to a multifaceted new-wave of activities that function outside of intentions such as the new black lung legislation. The laws are there, but unethical methods are circumventing their intent. You might say that thwarting the reception of a benefit created by industrial malfeasance cannot be equated to the manufacture and distribution of an illegal drug but, you would be wrong. In each, a beneficial law has been broken, resulting in the suffering of some citizens for the profit of others. Ordinary police departments do not possess the expertise to investigate such crimes. You have demonstrated that you have those skills and we are, therefore, opening up an opportunity for you to continue in your role as a deputy Sheriff or some other designee of official law officer where your authority goes beyond county lines…"

"Judge," interrupted Cabot. "Your confidence in me immensely honors me but, truly, the legalities, foundations, and nuances of the task you are suggesting for me. I..."

"We are well ahead of you on that concern. You will function as a team member so that you will not work in a vacuum. Just as you collect data as a physician and submit it to laboratories and specialists, you will also collect data related to your skill set and submit it to those who support you. One, for example, is Captain Blake, Commander of the Governor's Taskforce on Organized Crime."

"I know him," said Dr. Cabot.

"There will be others like him. He has suggested that you attend the Department of Justice's upcoming training session on criminal investigation to be held in Washington followed up by a shorter session at Quantico. The State will pay your expenses. The Health Department will help by providing residents for filling your practice while you are away."

"You have presented me with far more than I can assimilate off-handed. Right now, the entire scenario is so convoluted it will require careful consideration. Even though you say the Health Department will provide supplemental medical assistance, I cannot give up my practice for several reasons, the most limiting being my agreement with Dr. Fields' estate. I have not yet met my obligation under that contract, and I intend to stay on if for no other reason than my extensive involvement in black lung. I will not surrender that to anyone, much less a neophyte wet-behind-the-ears doctor. Furthermore. I have promised my new bride to be that I will not postpone our wedding still another time."

Sheriff Hare broke in excitedly, "Hey, why don't you use the training trips for a honeymoon? Ah bet Jenn would love that."

"If you were just married would you want to sit in a hotel room while your mate was involved in training?" asked the DA. "Heck, I know I wouldn't."

"Just a thought," said the Sheriff apologetically.

"I think we are through here today. Doctor, take the time to mull it over, discuss it with your new bride, and we can discuss it further later. Let's all go home."

Chapter

Seventy-Three

David approached Jenn with the new offer with extreme trepidation. Jenn was a direct approach person; she was leery of subterfuge or contrived scenes. So, the direct approach it was, with one exception: He went to the company store and acquired a pint of her favorite ice-cream. He invited her to the library after supper after that he presented her with a heaping bowl. She willing accepted it, put a spoonful in her mouth and asked him, somewhat muted by ice cream, "Alright, what have you done now?"

He feigned wounded and piteously pleaded, "Now why would you assume ill of my offering you your favorite sweet-stuff?"

"Cause I can see through you like a winda glass."

"Then you only see the purest of heart with intentions free of deceit or ruse."

"Okay. Get on with it. Ah'm listenin' with breathless anticipation," Jenn whispered.

"Now this is serious. I have been asked to take on the role of a special investigator for medico-legal crime in the

State. I would not give up my practice, particularly my black-lung research that Dr. Fields initiated. Judge Shaffer, the Sheriff, and the DA approached me after the Peters trial. They had previously discussed the nature of my unique acuity in the differentiation of factual evidence and decided that this skill would be most helpful in the new-wave crime armada, particularly those medically and legally entwined."

"Hey, it's me you are a'talkin' to. Talk plain English."

"Yes, my dear hillbilly articulator. What I am elucidating to you is employment that has a fluid job description that allows for a position..."

"Whoa, whoa, whoa...What did I just ask you to do?" Jenn implored.

"Alright! The position is brand new, anywhere, and I would make it up as I go along. Simple enough for you?"

"More like it. Go on."

"Fraud and crime are moving into our every-day lives in many ways. Here, in our own surrounding counties, we see a conspiracy amongst certain practitioners, legal, medical, etc., and coal companies, for example, to defraud workers out of legal entitlements. Legal channels are being used to funnel prescription drugs, i.e., opioids, for nonmedical purposes, through criminal brokers. Funds appropriated for education are siphoned off for non-essential administrator salaries and expensive travel. One we just recently stopped, albeit temporarily, is the manufacture of Meth here in our locality. The data needed to prepare indictments on these perpetrators are generally above the skill levels of the average sheriff's department. Therefore, being instituted is an experimental position that I would fill it on a trial basis. The decision to employ me in that role is because of my involvement in the Peters' case and my testimony in the black lung case—in which you held the key, pun intended. I will reduce my time at the Clinic to black lung only and hire two new residents to handle the routine activities."

"Sounds good," Jenn said with doubt in her voice. "But, you just turned—our house if I am permitted to call it that—into a small hotel with all of the many chores. Is that goin' to be my responsibility? For sure Annie can't do it. And the Clinic; who's goin'a run it? Me? Back up here and consider reality."

"I have given considerable thought to just those concerns. You are right that Annie cannot manage such additional responsibilities. She should retire, but she would vehemently rebel, so we promote her to the equivalent of 'chef' and hire two additional persons to assist her, as needed, and to do all of the housekeeping. I think Jim would gladly comeback as maintenance 'chief'. We hire a nurse to accomplish the tasks you have been managing in the Clinic and, as for you, you will be the General Manager of the whole operation. That way, you can 'manage by delegation' after we are married. Then you will be free to travel."

"My goodness you have been a busy little bee, haven't you? But Ah think you've forgotten one tiny-tiny detail; who's gonna' pay for all of this? Is our outgo more than our in go the way it is, and you're talkin' about hirin' a whole mess of new people? Dream on my love."

"That too has been solved. Firstly, I queried the bank about the status of the Trust Fund, and it is in excellent condition having been collecting interest at six percent compounded daily for over 20 years. Therefore, according to the trustee, I am allowed to spend the interest at any time irrespective of my ten-year obligation, so long as it relates to the welfare and care of our patient population. That changes if and when I fulfill my obligation at which time I become a co-trustee and principal manager of the account. In reality, I now function as a co-trustee with the interest reserves and can spend it as I chose. we have far more than we can spend available for black lung research including the continuation of a paycheck for me while so engaged."

"Wonder how much money is in the Trust now? did he say?"

"No, but if there were one half million in the original trust fund, it would be worth about a million and a half now, so we have plenty to do everything we anticipate as necessary. Also, The State will supply the residents. Our obligation is their room and board thus demanding only additional space and food service. One more thing, Since the Federal Government is involved in most of the regulations that I would be dealing with, I should take advantage of a two-week administrative indoctrination course at the Justice Department in Washington DC. However, that is not a requirement since my work will be for the State. My thinking is that we could get married now, go on a honeymoon and then possibly you go along for the training. It would give us a great opportunity to see all of the sites in the Capitol."

"That would work. Let's get busy gettin' married," Jenn bubbled.

Without their noticing, Annie had appeared at the entry of the library. She was crying as she said, "David, Ah thank Lonnie is dyin'. Will yew check on him?"

Jenn reached the door first with Doctor close behind. "David, get your bag. I'll go on!" By the time Dr. Cabot reached the cottage out-back, Jenn was at Lonnie's side checking his pulse.

"Annie was right," she said to David as he arrived.

"Pardon?"

"Annie was right. He was dyin'."

Dr. Cabot confirmed Jenn's observation and turned to find Annie. He opened his arms to her, and for the first time in their acquaintance, she hugged him. He held on to her, and she said into his chest, "He wa're a gud man. He di'nt do nobody no harm. They kil't him same's they put a gun'ta his head. Really though, he's been daid fer a long, long time. When ya'can't breathe yew mights'well be daid an' he ain't been able to breath fer mosta' his grod'up life and they's way too many jus' like him still servin' devil coal."

"My dear Annie, for Lonnie we were tardy in our actions. But that ends right this instant. Jenn, are you ready to go to work?"

Jenn could not speak. She just nodded her head in the affirmative.

Seventy -Four

Weddings transpose reality into a fairyland of frills, fluff, and flowers for women and, dragons and dungeons for men. Women charge forward with great passion while men cower in bewilderment. The mansion was in absolute chaos. The wedding day had been cast-in-stone by Annie and Mrs. Cabot, and nothing short of a volcano eruption of a local mountain would stop it this time. The ceremony was in at the Bluewell Baptist Church, childhood Church-home of Jenn and all of her brother and sisters, lovingly hand-built by their father, board by board, during the 'Great Depression.'

The church was as bland as the interior of a building could be. Yet, every conjunction met with a crispness hard to achieve by the most accomplished craftsman. All surfaces were of stained wood including the floors and gabled ceilings. The windows were straight cathedral, well proportioned. A simple embellishment-free box-like pulpit stood centered on a single-step ten-foot platform that extended the full width of the front of the 'nave.' Double doors entered directly into a single aisle down the center into the interior, dead-ending at the pulpit with straight-backed wooden benches lining each side. Annie and Mom had taken a very practical approach to the decorating of such a simple building: live trees and shrubs, as tall as eight feet and in full bloom, right out of the local hills. The effect was a wooded grotto requiring no other enhancement.

All was ready. Mrs. Cabot had 'companioned' Annie in the selection of a dress for this most proper of proper occasions from Annie's favorite catalog, Montgomery Ward. She chose navy-blue cotton woven dotted swiss coat-dress with white lace trim and single seam pocket. Accessories included a white cloche hat and low heel white pumps.

The Boston Knob community was there en masse wearing their Sunday-go-to-meeting best. A sea of artificial flowers flowed wildly on top of the heads of the women. The men were their nondescript usual in 1920's vintage well-worn, hand-me-down wool suits and hair slicked down with great care. The first four rows of both sides were reserved for the bride's family with all of the living brothers and sisters and their spouses present as were most of the nieces and nephews. Cars, pickup trucks and even a couple of horse-drawn buggies lined the old Route 52 in front of the church. The Delph School playground was filled as was Frankie's, the Sunny South Market and a short stretch of new US 52 on both sides.

From behind a pair of large rhododendron came the mournful sound of a Dobro playing Pachelbel's Canon. The Bride, escorted by her father, entered the wide-open double door. There was no entourage of attendants. They met the preacher at the 'alter.' The bride was simply attired, but yet quite stunning, in a white woven two-piece, knee-length suit with short-sleeves, slim-line skirt, over-blouse with harmonizing trim and a white dickie. Accessories included a white pill-box hat with large veil and high heel white pumps. She carried a wedding spray of locally-grown small white carnations. The groom was handsome in a grey two-button suit jacket and straight slacks. He wore a single white carnation in his lapel. They met, turned to face the preacher, and were wed.

The party moved like a herd of Wildebeest from the church to the La Saluda where tubs of iced RC Cola and Nehi Fruit drinks waited to wash down hamburgers, hot dogs, barbeque sandwiches and a wide variety of chips, and of course, wedding cake. The dance floor was open, and a band played an assortment of music suited to the heterogeneity of the crowd. David and Jenn broke the ice by dancing the first dance to Sentimental Journey, after which they said their farewells and departed for the airport to venues undisclosed. Given no problems, they would return in about six weeks, ready to embrace a new lifestyle, in a completely remodeled home and workplace, with a renewed mission devoted to the long-standing plight of the perpetually down-trodden people of Appalachia.